P9-DMT-943

Jessica Fletcher Presents...

MORE MURDER, THEY WROTE

14 All-New Stories From Today's Most Popular Mystery Authors

Featuring:

Jo Bannister · K. K. Beck · Joyce Christmas

Margaret Coel · Eileen Dreyer

Kathy Lynn Emerson · Kate Gallison · Sue Henry

J. A. Jance · Stefanie Matteson · Sharan Newman

Laura Joh Rowland · Janice Steinberg

Kathy Hogan Trocheck

From Berkley Boulevard Books

Jessica Fletcher—the beloved heroine of television's *Murder, She Wrote*—is famous for *writing* mysteries as brilliantly as she *solves* them. Now, in this delightful anthology series, America's favorite storytelling sleuth creates a literary showcase for *her* favorite storytellers.

Jessica Fletcher presents . . .

MURDER, THEY WROTE
Edited by Martin H. Greenberg and Elizabeth Foxwell

Nancy Pickard's delicious serving of "The Potluck Supper Murders" is just one of the many treats in this feast of fatal surprises, featuring acclaimed mystery writers Jane Dentinger, Kate Kingsbury, Jean Hager, and others.

MURDER, THEY WROTE II
Edited by Elizabeth Foxwell and Martin H. Greenberg

Anne Perry turns up the gaslight and exposes the shadows of Victorian intrigue, in this glowing collection of mystery and mayhem, featuring Margaret Maron, Susan Dunlap, Gillian Roberts, and others.

MORE MURDER, THEY WROTE
Edited by Elizabeth Foxwell and Martin H. Greenberg

This all-new treasury of mystery gems—hand-selected by Jessica Fletcher—highlights the dazzling talents of J. A. Jance, Sharan Newman, Sue Henry, Margaret Coel, and many others.

MORE MURDER, THEY WROTE

EDITED BY

Elizabeth Foxwell AND
Martin H. Greenberg

BERKLEY BOULEVARD BOOKS, NEW YORK

This is a work of fiction. Names, characters, places and incidents are either the product of the authors' imaginations or are used fictitiously, and any resemblance to actual persons, living or dead, business establishments, events or locales is entirely coincidental.

MORE MURDER, THEY WROTE

A Berkley Boulevard Book / published by arrangement with Universal Studios Publishing Rights, a division of Universal Studios Licensing, Inc.

PRINTING HISTORY
Berkley Boulevard edition / October 1999

The Penguin Putnam Inc. World Wide Web site address is
http://www.penguinputnam.com

ISBN: 0-425-16990-1

BERKLEY BOULEVARD
Berkley Boulevard Books are published by The Berkley Publishing Group, a division of Penguin Putnam Inc., 375 Hudson Street, New York, New York 10014.
BERKLEY BOULEVARD and its logo are trademarks belonging to Penguin Putnam Inc.

PRINTED IN THE UNITED STATES OF AMERICA

10 9 8 7 6 5 4 3 2 1

Contents

Introduction

Dear Reader,

Hello, and welcome to the third collection of mystery fiction by some of today's leading female mystery authors. With the success of *Murder, They Wrote* and *Murder, They Wrote II,* it seemed only logical that another showcase volume of top fiction by top mystery talent was in order. And while it seems like my life and career are more hectic than ever, I still managed to find a few minutes to see what the other women mystery writers were up to.

One of the things I love most about doing these books is reading about the different settings and time periods that crime authors invent. This collection is no different, I can assure you. From gritty, modern-day murder in New England to a crime of passion that happens against a backdrop of seventeenth-century Japan, there's something here to satisfy every type of mystery lover. Visit a lush tropical island with an almost-bride in Bora Bora, experience the glittering thrills of Hollywood in the 1920s, or track down a thief in Renaissance England. Whatever your taste in crime, I guarantee you won't be disappointed.

Of course, we've assembled a fine cast of female detectives as well. From a coffee shop waitress who takes up sleuthing to save her job to a Native American who relies on otherworldly insight to trap a murderer, these women are strong, positive forces in their worlds, especially considering that social conventions have tended to look down on the "weaker" sex throughout much of history. Regardless, these women detectives uphold their ideals and manage to solve the crime while not bowing to the expectations of society.

I even noticed, once again, that two of our fictional detectives also happen to be female authors. This only goes to show how imaginative a writer's mind can be. Despite the suspenseful occurrences in both stories, let me assure you that a writer's life is by no means that exciting. Of course, given my adventures, it wouldn't be surprising if many of you out there didn't believe me. But honestly, I much prefer solving imaginary crimes than real ones.

I wish to extend my thanks to our gracious and stellar cast of authors for participating in this group effort. Our participants include J. A. Jance, Sue Henry, and K. K. Beck, and many others who either use female detectives as their series characters or write about them in short fiction. It is gratifying to see that the female detective is alive and well, and in more incarnations than ever, in mystery fiction today.

Unfortunately, I am once again unable to make an appearance in a case (and believe me, in several instances, I wish I could have), but I have jotted down a few notes about each story. I hope you enjoy them as much as I did.

—Jessica Fletcher

*There comes a time in everyone's life where one has to de-
cide where one's loyalties lie: to oneself, or to one's place of
employment. Although I've never had to practice office pol-
itics, thank goodness, I do know that I would certainly
hate to match wits with the secretary in this story.*

The Fall Guy

Jo Bannister

Miss Agnes Armitage liked working on Saturday
mornings. As Mr. Ingram's secretary she had of
course a full set of keys, and it gave her positive pleasure to let herself in at about ten o'clock and have the
entire building, normally so busy, to herself for three
hours.

The late start was an indulgence. On weekdays she
habitually began work at eight-thirty in order to have
the chief executive's office up and running before the
rest of the staff arrived at nine. When she started work
thirty-five years ago most offices opened at eight
o'clock and everyone worked Saturday mornings, and
she still looked back to those days with a certain fond-
ness. When people had to be in at eight, no one was

late. Now that they were allowed to start at nine, they wandered in at any time up to quarter past; and they wore unsuitable clothes and studs in their noses, and came back from lunch smelling of lager and chips.

Miss Armitage couldn't imagine why Mr. Ingram put up with it. But then, he was not a man who led by example. Pleasant enough but no backbone. People who knew him were always surprised at how efficiently he ran Apex Imports. They called him a bit of a dark horse. Miss Armitage smiled into her Tippex and kept her peace. People who knew *her* knew that the secret of an efficient operation is not the man behind the big desk but the secretary behind the man behind the desk.

Mr. Ingram knew it too. He called Miss Armitage his secret weapon. He knew that he would not have been able to run a business as complex as this one without her assistance. His predecessor, Mr. Summers, had not appreciated that fact. He had called her Agnes to her face and the Gorgon behind her back, and talked about replacing her with a twenty-five-year-old blonde who could learn shorthand at night-school. Mr. Summers hadn't lasted very long at all.

Hanging her coat on the bentwood rack, Miss Armitage collected the post from the mat and sorted it into two piles. Everybody else's could wait until Monday, but she would go through Mr. Ingram's post and deal with anything urgent herself. Mr. Ingram would endorse any decisions she took. Mr. Ingram knew which side his bread was buttered.

After that she would make some phone calls. As

secretary to the chief executive she had some duties which were more easily performed when the office wasn't full of people. If she knew she needed a long, candid chat with one of their overseas representatives, Saturday morning made sense on grounds of both discretion and economy. Miss Armitage never shouted; but sometimes it was necessary to speak severely, and she preferred not doing it with third parties hovering outside her door, ears akimbo.

Also, when the office was in full swing, interruptions were inevitable. Everyone at Apex Imports knew that if things needed sorting, Miss Armitage was the person to sort them.

This morning she had a couple such phone calls to make, and she had the numbers in front of her and was logging on to the computer in order to have any information she might need immediately to hand, when all hell broke loose in Mr. Ingram's office next door. Someone was in there; and unless the chief executive had broken a habit of four years, it was not Mr. Ingram.

One of Miss Armitage's neatly manicured, slightly plump hands flew to her mouth, the other to the notepad in front of her, ready to shield the information it contained. But even as she did so her quick brain was separating the general cacophony into the elements that made it up, and then she didn't feel as threatened by the intrusion as she might have done.

Much of the noise was the result of a bookcase falling over—the bookcase that stood against the internal wall and thus approximately beneath the skylight. Some of it was produced by an object heavier than the

heaviest book, weightier even than the collected Department of Trade & Industry guidelines, bouncing off
Mr Ingram's desk and onto the floor; and some of it—
and this was the reassuring part—by the mingled
groans and obscenities of someone who had clearly
had even more of a shock than Miss Armitage.

It never occurred to her to flee the office and call the
police from O'Leary's papershop up the road. But for
the groans, which were of a satisfyingly heartfelt nature, she might have barricaded herself in here and
telephoned for help. But even a lady of a certain age,
finding herself alone in a building with a strange man,
could hardly stay scared at an intruder who'd fallen off
a bookcase and hurt himself enough to whimper.

Arming herself with the first thing that came to
hand—it was, in fact, a small fire extinguisher—Miss
Armitage opened the connecting door an inch and
peeped through.

It occurred to her, just too late, that there might be
more than one intruder and only one of them hurt. But
luck was on her side. There was only one; and he was
hurt; and he hadn't been that impressive before. Of
course, forcing an entry through a skylight is an option
available only to thin burglars.

He was thin, of around medium height, and he might
have been twenty-four years old. Under a baseball cap
advertising a well-known brand of dog food was a mop
of fairish hair that would have been none the worse
(thought Miss Armitage) for a cut and a good wash.
His narrow face was scratched and twisted in pain, and
his eyes when they flared at her were startlingly blue

and also afraid. He'd propped himself against the side of Mr. Ingram's desk but made no attempt to rise further. His left elbow was clamped against his ribs as if one or both were damaged, and his left foot was stuck out in front of him at an odd angle. He was breathing hard through clenched teeth. At least for the moment he'd stopped swearing.

"Stay right where you are," said Miss Armitage, sternly and a little shakily; and also quite unnecessarily. If the young man had been capable of moving he would have done it before now.

"My ankle's broken," whined the intruder.

"Well, let that be a lesson to you," said Miss Armitage severely. And then, because she didn't like to leave room for misunderstandings: "I take it you're a burglar?"

The man on the floor didn't know whether to laugh or cry. "No, in fact I'm the after-sales director for the Acme Skylight Company. There's been a problem with the catches on these"—he gestured above his head, using his right hand—"I wanted to be sure yours was OK. As you see, it wasn't. I think we owe you a replacement."

Miss Armitage went on regarding him levelly for half a minute. Then she said, "That isn't actually true, is it?"

He shut his eyes and leaned his head back against the desk. "Not actually, no."

"Then I was right first time?"

"Yeah."

"You're a burglar."

"Yes."

"So I suppose I'd better call the police."

"I suppose you better had."

She reached across him to Mr Ingram's telephone. Then, mid-dial, she paused. "What's your name?"

He blinked. "What?"

"Your name," she said again, patiently. "Oh come on, it's too late to be coy. You'll have to tell the police when they get here. I'd like to have something to call you in the meantime."

He thought about it for a moment, could see no reason to refuse. "Charlie."

"Charlie." She nodded an acknowledgement, her choirboy bob of iron-gray hair nodding an instant later. He supposed she was in her mid-fifties: a stout woman whose idea of dressing down for the weekend was a pale pink twin-set instead of a suit. "I'm Miss Armitage." She frowned. "You're looking awfully peaky, Charlie. You're not going to faint, are you? Perhaps I should get you a glass of water." She put the phone down and bustled out, returning a minute later with a tall glass rattling with ice. She kept a small fridge because Mr. Ingram was partial to a Scotch on the rocks at the end of a trying day.

He drank the water. Then he sucked on an ice cube, staring lugubriously at his foot.

"You're a bit new at this, aren't you?" ventured Miss Armitage.

He sniffed defensively. "You're not exactly seeing me at my best."

She smiled. "Perhaps your ankle isn't broken. It

could just be a sprain. I did a First Aid course once: do you want me to put a pressure bandage on it? It would feel better, and it wouldn't swell as much."

He watched doubtfully, but she really did seem to know what she was doing. She carefully took off his sneaker and his sock, and her plump fingers worked their way up and down his thin bones without hurting him as much as he'd expected.

"Sprain," she said decisively. She wrapped the bandage in a professional figure of eight, testing the tension at intervals. "There. Try standing on it."

Eyes down, Charlie mumbled something.

"What? Speak up."

He glared at her. "I said, my side hurts too!"

"Oh, for pity's sake!" Without asking permission, she unbuttoned his shirt and ran her fingers over his prominent ribs like somebody playing a xylophone. "Take a deep breath. No, deeper than that."

He did as she said, and flinched. "It hurts," he said accusingly.

"Of course it hurts; you're going to have a bruise the size of a football. But I don't think you've broken anything. Did you feel a creaking when you breathed in?"

He thought for a moment. "No."

"No crepitation then," she said, as if that settled the matter. "Come on, get up. There's nothing that won't heal in a few days."

He took the hand she offered and carefully, with a certain amount of hissing and grunting, levered himself up until he could sit on the desk.

"There," said Miss Armitage. "Isn't that more comfy?"

"I suppose." He sounded less than enthusiastic. "Are you going to call the cops now?"

"I suppose I'd better." Miss Armitage smiled impishly. "Even with your ankle strapped, I don't think you can make a run for it."

"Ha bloody ha," gritted Charlie.

Hand on the phone once more, she paused and leaned towards him, her brows knitting. "Haven't I seen you somewhere before?"

The young man looked away quickly. "Shouldn't think so."

"Yes, I have," Miss Armitage said with certainty. "I never forget a face. You were here two months ago. You were looking for a job."

He cleared his throat. "Could have been."

"You didn't get it, though. A problem with your references."

"That's right," he retorted tartly, "I forged them. I wanted a job, I hadn't the right experience, I lied and I got found out. All right? I was no good at that either."

Miss Armitage had set the phone down again. "You don't have a lot of luck, do you?" she said softly.

"I thought the place would be empty on a Saturday."

"Officially it is. It's just that I've usually got work I need some peace and quiet to catch up on."

He chuckled at that. Now the shock was passing a little colour had returned to his cheeks. "I must have scared you as much as you scared me."

"At least as much." Miss Armitage regarded him

with regret. "Oh, Charlie. Do I really have to hand you over to the police?"

He watched her carefully. "You could let me go. But a law-abiding citizen like yourself might have a problem with that."

"Letting a thief go scot-free? Yes, indeed," she said acerbically.

"Oh, don't worry." Charlie vented a weary sigh. "I'm not scared of going to jail. They have all sorts these days. Television, and snooker tables. And gyms. If I put in a bit of work on the climbing machines, maybe next time I do this I won't fall."

Miss Armitage smiled obediently, but she was thinking of something else. "No, you're really not, are you? Afraid of going to prison." Her troubled eyes cleared suddenly to a diamond-sharp appreciation. "There's no chance of you going to prison, is there? You're not a thief—you're a policeman!"

He didn't admit it, but she saw at once that she was right. "Then—whatever are you doing here? Investigating us? *Why?*"

She was too astute; in his present state he couldn't fence with her any longer. Besides, soon she would call the police and then an operation which had depended on utter secrecy would be a matter of common knowledge.

Detective Constable Charlie Wood rolled his eyes in despair. "Miss Armitage, how long have you worked for Apex Imports?"

"Since it started," she said crisply. "Nearly ten years."

"Ten years. And you had no idea it's being used as a front for drug-running?"

She stared at him as if he'd suggested oral intercourse to pass the time. "Drugs?" Then she said it again, in case she'd taken him up wrong. *"Drugs?"*

"Don't sound so surprised," Charlie said reproachfully. "Any company with extensive overseas connections has the potential. You must know how attractive a set-up like yours would be to a drugs cartel."

"I—suppose—" But Miss Armitage looked as if the thought had never crossed her mind; as if her idea of a premium consignment was pre–price hike Brazilian coffee. "But—we wouldn't get involved in something like that!"

"You already did. You've been importing drugs on a regular basis for years. You don't have to believe me, it'll all come out in court, but Apex Imports have been muling drugs alongside their legitimate business for at least the last four years—which is how long Mr. Ingram has been your boss, yes?"

She couldn't deny it and gave a fractional nod.

"That doesn't make him guilty," conceded Charlie, "but he's been our prime suspect for some time. No one at Apex is in a better position than the chief executive to make this work. My job is to find the evidence. There'll be a set of books somewhere that aren't for auditing but do show exactly how much money has been made from what source." He looked around. "They're probably in here. This seems like a very select operation; he may be the only one involved.

Maybe everyone else at Apex really does think you're here to import cocoa and video recorders."

Miss Armitage was left breathless. Her hand, spread on her pink angora bosom, rose and fell like a duck in a lock. She had lowered herself on the other end of Mr. Ingram's desk, the telephone forgotten. The first thing she could think of to say was "You're not going to arrest me?"

Charlie chuckled, even though it hurt. "No, Miss Armitage, you're not a suspect. Unless you plan on spilling the beans to Mr. Ingram, of course. That could be considered aiding and abetting."

"No, no, no," she flustered. "I mean, Mr. Ingram is my superior, I have always given him my best service, but I never imagined he was involved in anything criminal! Oh no, I won't help him with that. And not because it might get me into trouble but because it would be wrong."

Detective Constable Wood was feeling better all the time. Fifteen minutes ago he thought he'd blown, single-handedly and with nothing closer to official approval than a nod and a wink, an operation that had engaged some thirty police officers for the last two years. He thought he was facing a career in traffic control, or perhaps schools liaison. Now, thanks to this old-fashioned, severe, palpably honest woman, he glimpsed the possibility of snatching success from the jaws of total bloody disaster.

"Listen, Miss Armitage," he said pressingly, "if you won't help him, will you help me? Those books are here somewhere. Nobody knows this office like you do. I know that until just now you didn't even know they existed, but I'd still put money on you to find them. What do you say?—will you help me?"

It was not an easy decision. Agnes Armitage considered herself a loyal, nay, a dedicated, member of the Apex Imports team. The idea of colluding with the police to show that Apex had been involved, possibly for its entire existence, in a trade as dirty as it was illegal was anathema to her. And yet . . . if she did nothing, Ingram could drag them all down with him. If she refused her help would the authorities accept, as this young policeman seemed prepared to, that the chief executive had been milking the company for his own benefit and that no one else here was involved? Apex could continue, the staff could retain their employment, if the blame could be fairly settled on just one pair of shoulders.

Or she could decline, and let one man bring down a company to which she had devoted ten years of her life.

Viewed in that light, it wasn't such a difficult choice after all.

But halfway through a nod of consent a certain incongruity struck Agnes Armitage. She looked up at the skylight, its catch dangling brokenly; she looked at the capsized bookcase and its scattered cargo. Her eyes narrowed on Charlie Wood's face.

"Just a moment," she said. "If you know what Mr. Ingram's been up to, why did you come here alone; and why did you break in through the skylight? There is, I believe, an instrument known as a search warrant available to the police in such circumstances."

A little flush raced up Charlie's scraped cheeks, which Miss Armitage could only attribute to the guilty conscience of someone caught in a deliberate lie. She waited for an answer.

"Well, all right," he mumbled at last. "Maybe we can't prove it yet. But we know, all right."

"That's easy to say," exclaimed Miss Armitage indignantly. "The essence of our legal system is that it's not enough for you to 'know,' you have to have proof. Vague suspicion is not enough!"

"It's more than that," snapped Charlie, piqued, "a damn sight more. We know how he does it. We know who his contacts are, how the shipments are arranged, how the distribution is handled. We know these offices are the end of the pipeline. We've suspected for some time, and you confirmed it, that the company itself is not involved—it's being used by an employee. You have as much reason to want him stopped as I have."

"Well," conceded Miss Armitage, "that's possible. I still don't see why you had to break in rather than going through proper channels."

"Because if we go through channels, and we don't get what we need first shot, we'll lose him. He must have paperwork, maybe computer disks, containing all the details of his little side-line, and it makes sense that they're here somewhere. Either here or his home. But if we guess wrong, turning up here with a search warrant will not only not gain us anything, it'll give him time to hide the records where we'll never find them, even if that means destroying them. And without the records we don't have a case."

"So you're here in order to . . . ?" Miss Armitage still wasn't sure why.

"To try and find his hidey-hole. A secret compartment in his desk; a space under the floor-boards; damn it, I'd settle for a loose brick in the privy wall right now! If we were sure this was where he kept his papers, we'd get our search warrant and strip the place to the foundations should it take a week to do it. But if we do that and still don't find them . . ." He left the sentence hanging in mid-air like a guillotine.

"We've worked hard on this for two years. I applied for a job here so I could look for proof; but I forgot to prime the guy I'd quoted as a reference and Ingram smelled a rat."

He raked thin fingers through the fairish hair and cast Miss Armitage a harrowed look. "Can you imagine what it's like, being the guy responsible for wasting sixty man-years of work? I've been getting hate e-mail. Somebody sealed my locker up with superglue.

"And I thought, maybe I could make amends. If I can just be sure that this is where we need to search, everything will maybe work out OK. So here I am." He looked tentatively at her. "What do you think? Is it going to work out OK?"

Miss Armitage was still considering. "Do your superiors know you're here?"

"Ah," said Charlie heavily. "Well, yes and no. Yes, they know; and no, they haven't been told officially, so they have deniability. If the shit hits the fan, the only one it sticks to is me."

Miss Armitage knew about deniability. She knew about people using other people to further their own interests. So she had a certain amount of sympathy for the young policeman who had got himself into trouble through inexperience and was trying to buy his way out at the possible cost of his career.

Clearly she could turn him away. He hadn't the authority to demand her help. He shouldn't even be here. She could show him the door—well, help him to the door—and the law would support her.

But if she did that she would only delay the inevitable. Perhaps the police lacked the proof they needed right now, but they weren't going to give up on two years' work because some young detective made a hash of perhaps his first undercover operation. They were going to keep looking, keep digging, and when they had what they needed they would return. And then they wouldn't just be interested in John Ingram. They would also be interested in his secretary, who'd had the chance to help them and had declined.

"All right, Charlie," she said quietly, "I believe you. And yes, I'll help you if I can. What is it you're looking for—paperwork? Ledgers, disks?"

"Any or all of the above." His eyes were glued on her face as if he was afraid she'd change her mind if he blinked. "Is he what you'd call computer literate?"

Miss Armitage saw a mental picture of her chief executive trying to master the Mario Brothers on his PC and shook her head. "Not that you'd notice."

"Then it's probably papers we're looking for. Ledgers, maybe some files. Do you know of anywhere in the office he could hide two or three ledgers and a couple of files without anyone knowing?"

"There's a wall safe. Behind the picture of his predecessor with the Prime Minister." During Mr. Summers' brief sojourn in this office, Apex had won an Imaginative Importing award. Having contributed almost nothing to it, Mr. Summers had been so inordinately proud of collecting it that he'd had himself framed and hung on the wall. After his departure, Mr. Ingram had thought it would be churlish to move it.

"Does anyone else have the combination?"

"Only Mr. Ingram."

"That sound promising," said Charlie. He watched her intently.

"Shall we have a look, then?"

Charlie's bruised face split in a grin. "You're a lady of many talents, Miss Armitage."

She smiled primly. "It's nice to be appreciated."

Inside the safe were two leather-bound ledgers and a slim file of paperwork. Charlie lifted them out reverently, spread them on the desk and tried to make sense of them.

But he wasn't an accountant, or even a secretary, and he couldn't be sure if he'd found the Holy Grail or just a nice brass bowl inscribed "A Present from Jerusalem" on the inside and "Made in Birmingham" underneath. His side was aching again. So was his head.

"I don't know," he confessed at last. "I thought I'd

be able to tell but I can't. I think this is it, but there are no—"

"What, invoices?" Miss Armitage's tone was gently mocking. "Receipts? Statements, bills of lading? Consignment notes saying 'Heroin, cocaine and assorted little white pills. Payment due on delivery: please do not ask for credit as a refusal often offends'?"

Charlie grinned wryly. "It would have been useful, wouldn't it? On the other hand . . ." He pushed the ledger towards her. "You're pretty familiar with this business, Miss Armitage. Take a look. Does that show about what you'd expect it to?"

Miss Armitage let her eye travel slowly down the page. The further she read, the higher her eyebrow climbed. "No," she said at last, surprised by her own calmness. "No, I can't say it does. At a rough estimate it shows our annual turnover at perhaps two million pounds more than I understood it to be."

A glow like Christmas kindled in Charlie's eyes. "This is it, isn't it?—the proof we need. Let's see him try to explain this! What about the file?" He pushed assorted letters and documents, and brief hand-written notes, across the desk at her. "These people. Are they firms Apex have dealings with?"

She shook her head. "A few are but most aren't. There is no business on Apex Imports' books—that is to say, on our official books—to explain Mr. Ingram's involvement with these men."

"Look at the addresses," Charlie said softly.

Some were rather cursory, but his point was clear enough. Some of these extra-curricular correspondents lived in the Far East—Cambodia, Thailand, Laos. Others lived in South America.

"I'm satisfied," said Charlie Wood. His voice actually quavered with relief. "We'll get the search warrant today and find these things, officially, as soon as we can organize a team. We'll have your Mr. Ingram in custody by teatime." His blue eyes flickered. "At least, we will if . . ."

"If?" prompted Miss Armitage, stiff with anticipation.

"If nobody warns him."

"Meaning me."

Charlie shrugged apologetically. "Well, I'm not going to. But then, I haven't worked with the man for four years. I'm not going to start wondering if it's all been a horrible misunderstanding, if there isn't a perfectly reasonable explanation. I'm not going to sit on my own for a couple of hours, fretting, and finally pick up the phone and tell him what's happened."

"And neither am I," snapped Miss Armitage. "If Mr. Ingram has an innocent explanation for these things I'm sure he's quite capable of telling you. I hope he has. But if you're right, he'll have to manage without my help. People who traffic in drugs deal in human misery—they don't deserve any sympathy. If you're right, you're welcome to him. I couldn't go on working for a man like that."

Charlie Wood wanted desperately to believe her. He felt he had no choice. He couldn't lock her in the cloakroom until the search party arrived. He couldn't even stay with her to stiffen her resolve if it wavered.

He needed to tell his superiors what he'd discovered, and he needed to do it in person. Plus, he needed to see a doctor. He hoped Miss Armitage was right and he hadn't broken anything, but if she was wrong he could have a permanent limp through walking on a broken ankle or puncture a lung through ignoring a broken rib.

He had to leave here, and hope that Miss Armitage would keep her promise not to warn Ingram of the gathering storm. He thought he could trust her. It was only for a few hours. Surely he could trust her for a few hours.

"Listen," he said, standing up cautiously. "I have to get things moving. What I need you to do, if you can, is exactly what you planned to do when you came in this morning. If Ingram expects you to be here, I need you to be here in case he calls. Anything out of the ordinary could alert him. We're so close, I don't want to lose him now."

Miss Armitage nodded agreement. "That's all right, Charlie. You can count on me."

He smiled. It was going to happen. He was going to redeem himself. "I know. There is one more thing."

"Yes?"

"I've got a car outside but, er—you couldn't help me out to the street?"

After she'd seen him safely down the steps and across the yard Miss Armitage returned to her desk and sat down, a little stunned, going over in her mind everything that had happened. Ingram. The police thought John Ingram was a drug runner. They had traced the pipeline here, to Apex Imports. She supposed she was lucky they hadn't marked her down as a gangster's moll!

So one way or another, with the police or ahead of them, Mr. Ingram was going to be leaving Apex. She was going to get a new chief executive. Well, it wasn't the first time. Chief executives came and went, it was only necessary that the firm go on. She hadn't put ten years' work into making a success of it to see it collapse through one man's stupidity.

The only question now was what would be least damaging to Apex in the long term. If Mr Ingram ran, perhaps the police would follow. On the other hand, if they caught him they would close the file. It was hard to know what to do for the best.

She sat at her desk for half an hour, staring perplexedly at the phone, before she picked it up.

Ingram was with her inside ten minutes. She showed him into his own office as if he were a stranger.

"I was in there checking some invoices," she explained, her voice carefully expressionless, "and I noticed the picture was crooked. So I went to straighten it. And this is what I found." She moved the photograph of Mr. Summers with the Prime Minister, and the steel corner of the wall safe appeared.

Mr. Ingram stared at it in amazement. "And you had no idea it was here?"

Miss Armitage shook her head. "Mr. Summers must have installed it without saying anything. He was an odd man—maybe you've gathered that?"

Ingram nodded absently. "A few people have said

the same thing. Disappeared one day and was never seen again?"

"Um," agreed Miss Armitage noncommittally. "I thought you should know about this right away. I mean, there could be anything inside it."

Ingram lifted down the picture and tried the handle. But the safe was locked. "I don't see how we'll ever find out. Summers had the combination, and Summers is gone."

"Um," said Miss Armitage again.

Ingram turned and caught her looking pensive. "You know something, don't you?"

"Well—possibly. I was Mr. Summers' secretary as I am yours. I did things for him, kept things for him, remembered his appointments. . . . And once he asked me to make a note of a phone number for him, and then he never used it. He said it was just for emergencies; and it was an overseas number which accounted for all the extra digits; and I had no reason to disbelieve him. I added it to my list—and I think it's still there."

Mr. Ingram thought hard. "You mean, someone at the other end might know the combination to Mr. Summers' safe?"

A pleasant man, Miss Armitage had always felt, but not the brightest. "No, I think that number might *be* the combination to Mr. Summers' safe."

She produced her calling list, a little dog-eared with use, from the top right-hand drawer of her desk. The number she was looking for was filed under. *S*.

"*S* as in . . . ?"

"Summers," Miss Armitage said crisply.

She read out the numbers and Ingram turned the dial. When she said, "That's it," he tried the handle again and this time it turned. The safe opened.

"Good grief." Inside were ledgers and a slim file of papers. He went to open them.

Miss Armitage put a restraining hand on his arm. "Mr. Ingram, I'm not sure you should look at those."

"Whyever not?"

"I told you, Mr. Summers was an odd man. He installed this safe specifically to keep those papers where no one could see them. Whatever he did that for, it seems to have worked—they've caused no trouble; no one's come looking for them.

"If you look at them now, you may see something you feel you have to act on. It would be like opening Pandora's Box. If you want my advice, you'll put those away, just as they are, unread, and shut the safe, and put the picture back, and we'll go back to not knowing there's anything there. It's gone undiscovered for four years; now we know not to move the picture it could be longer still. I suggest we don't know there's a safe there, we don't know the combination, we never opened it and we have no idea what it might contain. If anybody asks, we never met here today. We know nothing."

John Ingram thought for a long minute, then he gave a decisive nod of the head. "You're right, Miss Armitage." He did as she said, closing the safe, replacing the picture. He smiled gratefully. "Whatever would I do without you to look after me?"

When the police arrived, in the middle of the afternoon, he played his part for all he was worth. Picture?—no, he'd never moved the picture. Safe behind it?—good heavens! His predecessor must have put it there. No, sorry, no idea how to get inside or what might be in there. And the reason for this search is . . . ?

The young detective with long hair and a limp seemed to be the team's safe expert. He waited until the Scenes of Crime Officer had dusted the steel door for prints—that gave Mr Ingram a bit of a jolt: had he remembered to wipe it when he'd finished?—then, wearing rubber surgical gloves, he had it open in a jiffy. Almost as if he'd known the combination.

SOCO moved in again, dusted round with his powder, then let them take out the books. One of the older officers took over. "Oh yes, this is what we're looking for, all right."

"Mr. Summers," said Mr. Ingram unsteadily. "My predecessor. Mr. Summers installed the safe; Mr. Summers must have left the books there."

"Then Mr. Summers must have nipped back at regular intervals to keep them up to date," said the Senior Investigating Officer, dead-pan, "because the last entry is less than a week old." He waited, an eyebrow cocked quizzically, but Mr. Ingram had no explanation.

He never did come up with an explanation that made sense. The safe he said he'd never seen had his fingerprints all over it; he claimed not to know the combination but his prints were on the inside too; and the ledgers and files accorded faithfully with information the police had gathered from people further down the pipeline. The case was unanswerable. Mr. Ingram, wild-eyed and babbling, was taken from the premises of Apex Imports and set on his way to Pentonville.

By the time he appeared at the Central Criminal Court he had changed his story so often it was hard to be sure what his defence might be on any given day. An embarrassed-looking counsel rose to blame everything on the defendant's secretary. An appreciative chuckle went round the court. Miss Armitage had already given evidence: the very idea of her as a co-conspirator was risible. John Ingram went to prison for twelve years. Miss Armitage went back to Apex Imports to draw up an advertisement for a new chief executive.

Honesty was the first requirement, of course; and reliability; and a track record in business management. But an in-depth knowledge of importing was not an essential since the successful candidate would receive expert guidance and support from a thoroughly experienced personal assistant.

Thinking about recent events, Miss Armitage found she'd lost the thread of what she was writing, and she looked at the computer screen to see how far she'd got. A strange expression stole across her face and she started giggling. Quickly she hit the delete button and began again.

"Senior position unexpectedly vacant," she'd written. "Long-established and successful import company finds itself in immediate need of a new fall-guy. . . ."

*I really don't know what is more fantastic about Holly-
wood, the subtle air of complete unreality that envelops it,
or the people who think they're living relatively ordinary
lives there. The suspects in our next story are a group of
characters who would be at home in any 1920s movie,
which is particularly apt, considering when this particular murder takes place.*

Hollywood Homicide

K. K. Beck

"Come on, Iris, you're a swell typist. And I've got it
all arranged. The landlady, Bessie LeBeau, has a
place for you to stay. I've even got your train tickets."

"But Jack," I said, "I only have a week before
classes start again. I can't just go gallivanting off to
Hollywood." Jack was calling from Los Angeles,
which lent a sense of urgency to the proceedings. I had
rushed to the parlor of the women's residence hall in a
panic, wondering who could be calling long distance
and if all was well at home in Portland.

Jack is not a college man, and doesn't seem to understand that there are rules. "Stanford University is

acting *in loco parentis*," I explained. "Coeds aren't allowed to smoke. Or run off on mad adventures." I looked nervously over at our housemother to see if she was listening, but she seemed preoccupied with sewing on a button for one of the more helpless girls.

"Get your aunt to wire them, say she needs you at home. I'll do it, if you want."

It was very difficult to say no to Jack Clancy, the newspaperman who had played such an important part in my adventures. While it was perhaps not quite proper to act as a spy for his newspaper, *The San Francisco Globe,* the chance to have anything to do with another mystery interested me strangely.

But was it a mystery?

I had read all about the death of Blanche Talbot, the promising young movie actress. Her body had been found at the bottom of a swimming pool in the Moorish Court Apartments in Hollywood, where she lived. She had apparently taken a night swim alone, dived into the pool at the shallow end, knocked herself out and drowned. The papers had said her death appeared to be accidental.

I pointed this out to Jack.

"You can't always believe what you read in the papers," he said, an interesting admission from a newspaperman, "or what the DA's office says either. I have good reason to believe Blanche Talbot was the victim of a brutal crime. This wholesome farm girl, whose matchless beauty proved to be her undoing, thrusting her as it did into the hotbed of sin that is Hollywood today, was a human sacrifice on the altar of youth and beauty and her killing must not go unavenged."

"You always have too many clauses in those leads of yours," I said.

"That's what Rewrite is for."

"Come on, Jack. Of course it would be more interesting if she'd been murdered, but what makes you think she was?"

"First of all, I got it from a source in the coroner's office that the head wound seems a little too spectacular for the kind of bump she would have got. The skin was broken in a way that seems more as if she was struck with a sharp object."

"Was there water in her lungs?"

"Yes, a little. It's my belief she was knocked out, then thrown into the pool, where she drowned. But that's not all. I just made a little trip up to Castroville and talked to some of her childhood pals. Get this. Little Blanche was terrified of the water. Even since she fell into an irrigation ditch when she was a tot of three. Wouldn't go near the stuff."

"But she was wearing a bathing suit," I protested. "I read all about it. The newspapers said it was scarlet wool with white stripes across the bodice."

"Of *course* she was wearing a bathing suit," said Jack impatiently. "She was a professional bathing beauty. I've been down snooping around at the Moorish Court Apartments, where the tragic beauty lived and died. She spent a lot of time lounging around the pool half dressed, drinking cocktails. It's that kind of place."

"Well then, I won't have to pack much, will I?" I said.

"I'm not suggesting you join the revels with too much enthusiasm," said Jack. "In fact, you'll probably do a better job if you act quiet and mousy."

"I would much prefer to act abandoned and wild," I said, hoping to annoy Jack.

"Don't be silly," he said patronizingly. "You're supposed to be a respectable young lady there to type a manuscript for this writer who lives there. I fixed the whole thing up for you. This Baxter Carlson fellow didn't have much to say about Blanche's last days, but he did mention he needed a typist, so I said I had just the girl for the job."

"You mean *the* Baxter Carlson? The Baxter Carlson who write *Young, Wild and Doomed*?" Like a lot of people my age, I had read this novel of college life which had been banned in Boston but praised for its ruthlessly honest picture of modern youth casting off conventional morality while suffering intellectual despair.

"That's right. Now that there's this craze for talking pictures, he's making some dough writing photoplays, but he's also working on another novel and he needs someone to type it while he's at the studio. Kind of a tortured soul, I gather."

I was terribly excited at the idea of meeting Baxter Carlson. I'd seen his photograph in a magazine, and he looked awfully sensitive, with a high forehead, a soulful expression, and sad, pale eyes.

I was intrigued by poor Blanche Talbot, too. I had

seen her last picture, *Dancing Debutantes,* about a society girl who wins a Charleston contest at a disreputable roadhouse and falls in love with a handsome rum runner, and she was sensational. I had also read how the studios predicted a great future for her, how she had been discovered in Castroville, California, when she won the Miss Artichoke crown, and how Elinor Glyn had proclaimed that she had "it" in spades. On campus, the boys had voted her "the girl we'd most like to be stranded on a desert isle with."

"Well," I said to Jack, "I suppose I could go down there for a little while. At least until the semester starts. But I can't think I can learn anything. Just because the poor thing fell in that ditch doesn't mean she didn't go in the water later. I almost drowned in Lake Oswego when I was five, but I still learned how to swim."

"There's more," said Jack darkly. "I got a tip that her studio is trying to hush something up. It's possible they put the fix in somehow. The word is, some goons from Corinthian Pictures were at the scene before the cops were. I can't be three places at once, so while I cover that angle and follow another big story I've got down there, I want you to make friends with all those Moorish Court people and find out what they think happened."

The next day, I took a train down to Los Angeles and arrived in the afternoon at the Moorish Court Apartments on Santa Monica Boulevard near Fairfax Street. Jack said he'd pick me up for dinner at seven, by which time he was sure I'd have plenty of copy for him. I wasn't so confident.

I wore a plain navy blue dress with a white collar and cuffs and a simple black straw hat, from which I had removed a bunch of bright yellow silk poppies too gay to adorn the millinery of a quiet office girl. Carrying my portable Underwood and my suitcase, I wandered into the central courtyard under palm trees and past beds of bright flowers.

The apartments were a collection of Spanish-style bungalows arranged around a swimming pool. Also arranged around the pool was a trio of laughing people sprawling on garden furniture. They turned to look at me. A young man in a one-piece bathing suit with hair slicked from a perfect center parting wielded a cocktail shaker. A dark woman of about thirty-five, in scarlet silk pajamas, heavily rouged, her eyes outlined with smudges of kohl, her hair in a smooth Colleen Moore bob, eyed me over a cigarette holder. I recognized Baxter Carlson in a white linen lounge suit looking blasé and smoking a pipe.

I immediately felt dowdy and thought I might have overdone the simplicity of my ensemble, so it didn't take much acting to mumble shyly, "Mr. Baxter? I'm Iris Cooper."

"Oh. The typist," he said, giving me a searching look from top to toe which seemed rather insolent. Although perhaps novelists, who made their living as observers, did get into the habit of staring. "Have a drink."

"Well, all right," I said, although it was barely past

lunchtime. I set down my typewriter and suitcase and sat gingerly on a lawn chair.

The young man with the cocktail shaker poured me something from it and handed it to me. "I'm Adrian Fleming," he said pleasantly. "And this is Alice Chester. You've probably read her stuff in *Movie Mirages*."

I accepted the drink and thanked him. Feeling over-dressed, I removed my hat and pushed the waves of my hair back into place.

"Oh, my dear," said Adrian, "you mustn't sit in the sun without your hat. Redheads should stay out of the sun entirely. It's devastating for the complexion."

"That's what my aunt Hermione tells me," I replied, taking a sip of what seemed to be a lethal potion.

"Adrian's a studio makeup artist," said Alice Chester. "You should listen to him if you want to be a movie actress, as I'm sure you do."

"It had never occurred to me," I said, annoyed.

"How very original. You must be the only pretty girl in Hollywood who doesn't."

"Miss Cooper will probably succumb to the lure of fame," sighed Baxter. "The producers will whisper sweet promises into her shell-like ears. We all become corrupted here. I just hope she finishes my manuscript first."

"I'm sure you will find that I do a very good, professional job," I replied, setting down my half-finished drink. Frankly, the cocktail was so strong that I feared if I drank the whole thing and rose too quickly, I would fall into the pool. "I will start immediately, if you wish."

"Oh, please do!" said Alice Chester. "The world has waited so long for Baxter's next novel it's almost forgotten him."

"Pay no attention to her," said Baxter. "Alice is the poor man's Dorothy Parker. All of the malice but none of the wit."

"And Baxter is the poor man's Scott Fitzgerald," said Alice in return. "The aristocratic good looks, but none of the talent."

"Come on, kids, knock it off," said Adrian. To me he said, "Come with me, Miss Cooper. I'll take you to Bessie. She's expecting you."

"Goodness," I said to Adrian as soon as we were out of earshot, "they sure seem to have it in for each other."

"They have a past," said Adrian, arching a well-shaped eyebrow. "She followed him out here, and gave up a good job in New York to write for that gossip sheet just to be near him. It's officially over, and he chases young girls, while she still carries the torch and pretends to despise him. I don't know why he puts up with it."

"Perhaps he finds it flattering that she still cares," I said. Or perhaps he enjoys being despised, I thought to myself.

Adrian took me up to a big house overlooking the Moorish Court Apartments, and walked inside without knocking. The room was decorated in an opulent, gloomy style, with plenty of polished tiles, brass orna-

ments and potted palms. "Bessie, darling, she's here,"
he trilled out. A stout, middle-aged woman in a plumed
turban and what looked like an Oriental potentate's
robes appeared. There was a large tropical bird on her
shoulder, which nibbled in turn at the turban's feathers
and its own.

"Hello, my dear," she said. "I am so glad you are
here. Mr. Baxter needs your help. That book of his was
to have been sent back East months and months ago. I
can't let my boys and girls allow their careers to go
bust. They must learn to think of the future."

"You remember Bessie, don't you?" said Adrian.
"She was in *The Terrors of Tatania*. I spent my entire
childhood worried about her."

I nodded, but my attempt to feign familiarity with
The Terrors of Tatania were apparently unsuccessful,
because Miss LeBeau waved her hand, bracelets jan-
gling, and said, "Aw, she's too young to remember. It
was almost twenty years ago. They had me tied to rail-
road tracks and going over Niagara Falls in a barrel
every week. I was younger then, but not as young as I
said I was. Thinner too." She shook her finger at me in
a schoolmarmish way. "But I wasn't ever stupid. I
saved my money and bought this place. These dopey
kids I've got staying here aren't planning for their future. They'll get old too."

"Except for poor Blanche," said Adrian solemnly.

Miss LeBeau's eyes brimmed up with tears. "Ain't
it awful?" she said. "We still can't get over it."

"I read about the tragedy in the newspapers," I said.

Then added in a kind of naïve way, "Gosh, she sure was pretty. What was she really like, in real life?"

"That kid was going straight to the top, and she was doing it on the square. She told me, 'Bessie, I don't care if it means I can't be a star. I'm going to respect myself, and someday, when I meet the man who'll be the father of my children, I'll be glad I did.'" Bessie leaned over conspiratorially. "There's not many girls at Corinthian Pictures who've had the nerve to slap Fred Green across the kisser."

"Who's Fred Green?" I asked.

Adrian clicked his tongue. "Number two man at Corinthian Pictures. He was *crazy* about Blanche."

"I hope you don't mind my putting you up in her old bungalow," said Miss LeBeau. "You aren't superstitious or anything, are you?"

"Anyway, she died in the pool," added Adrian. I thought I detected a little ghoulish pleasure in his tone. "Not the actual bungalow."

"Oh, I don't mind at all," I said.

Draperies swirling, Bessie led me back down the paths to the courtyard once again, while the helpful Adrian went back to his cocktail shaker. Baxter Carlson and Alice Chester had now been joined by a quartet of very odd people, three of whom were sitting by the pool in formal evening dress at two o'clock in the afternoon! They were a stout couple in their fifties and a rather washed-out girl of my own age.

The gentleman wore a swallow-tailed coat and white tie, and there was a silk opera hat on the wicker table beside him. The lady wore a lavender blue evening gown that matched her marcelled hair, which was topped by a precarious-looking rhinestone tiara. The girl was dressed in a flouncy bright pink dress with a white satin sash around the hips and inserts of lace in the skirt. It was much too fussy and babyish for her. I couldn't help but think that she would have looked much better in something simple in a pale, clear shade that would have set off her delicate coloring better.

What was even more extraordinary, however, was that this overdressed trio was chatting quietly with someone whose dress was as shockingly underdone as theirs was overdone. He was a sinewy, nut-brown young man with a strange, fanatical light in his blue eyes. His fair hair curled around his shoulders, and he wore a long beard. He was dressed in nothing but a kind of leather loincloth and a pair of sandals with criss-crossed laces going up his muscular calves.

Miss LeBeau must have noticed my startled expression, because she whispered to me, "That's the Blessingtons from bungalow six. Mama, Papa and Baby Margaret. They're dress extras."

"Dress extras?" I repeated.

"The studios hire them and their clothes at the same time. For ballroom scenes and such. It pays better than regular extra work. They're a trio of old troupers who've seen better days. Baby was a kid star for a while. Did you ever see *The Happiest Orphan* or *Olive of the Ozarks*?"

"I don't think so. Who's the, um, gentleman with

them?" Perhaps he was an *undress* extra who appeared in biblical epics.

"Oh, that's David. Folks around here call him Nature Boy. Kind of a character. Sleeps up in a hollow log in the Hollywood Hills or something, and lives on nuts and berries and what he can sponge off of people. You'd be surprised some of the people he knows. Alice gets tips for her *Movie Mirages* work from him, so we put up with him. Claims to be an English lord." She rolled her eyes skeptically.

"I see," I said, fascinated.

She let me into Blanche's bungalow. Here, in refreshing contrast to the sun's glare, it was cool and dimly lit. There was a small living room with comfortable chairs arranged around a stucco fireplace with wrought-iron andirons, a cheerful, roughly woven Mexican hearthrug in bright colors, and a low, mission-style table with a matching desk and scarlet geraniums in blue pottery bowls. Beyond this room was a small kitchen in green and white tiles, and a bedroom with more vivid Mexican weaving as a bedspread. The window was covered by a mass of bougainvillea.

"There seems nothing of Blanche Talbot here at all," I said.

"The studio came and took it all away," said Bessie. She peered at me in a knowing way. "*Before* the police had a proper look, if you ask me. Fred Green is a powerful man in this town." Miss LeBeau lowered her voice and leaned toward me, the heavy scent of chypre enveloping us both. "I happen to know he'd written her a couple of mash notes. Pretty hot stuff! I told her to hang on to them. They might come in handy some-day, I said. I bet he sent those studio gorillas around to find those notes!"

"Do you think they did find them?" I asked.

She shrugged. "Who knows? It doesn't matter now, I suppose. The thing is, Fred Green is the son-in-law of Julius Fisher."

"Who's Julius Fisher?"

"The head of Corinthian Pictures. And a real family man. If he ever found out that his son-in-law was mak-ing a mug of Mrs. Green—that's Julius's daughter Gertrude—Fred Green would be finished in this town."

Baxter Carlson now appeared in the open doorway with my suitcase in one hand and a cocktail glass in the other. "I've taken your typewriter to my bungalow," he said. "I'd like for you to work over there where the manuscript is." He set down the suitcase.

"Shall we begin right away?" I asked.

"No," he said, gazing thoughtfully at his glass. "It's still lunchtime for me. Why don't you have a swim first?"

"That would be wonderful," I said. After the train trip, it would be very refreshing, and I'd get my first crack at some of the people sitting around the pool.

For form's sake, I swam for a little while, and the water was lovely, but my chief interest was to get on with the business at hand, engaging the others in con-versation and pumping them for details about Blanche

Talbot. Adrian made it easy by introducing me all around.

The Blessingtons and Nature Boy were still there, and Adrian, Baxter Carlson, and Alice Chester were smoking and playing cards.

I had already decided that the washed-out Blessington girl, now changed from her evening clothes and wearing a drab, housedress sort of a garment, would be a good person to start with. She looked as if she would welcome the society of someone her own age, and after my swim I collapsed in the empty chair next to hers. She was reading a book called *Rambles in the Forest with Our Woodland Friends* with a border of squirrels and acorns on the binding, and looked up from it to smile shyly at me. Her mother was on the other side of her, still decked out in a costume suitable for a ball at the Winter Palace before the Bolshevik Revolution, and fiercely knitting what appeared to be a sock.

"Gosh, that felt good," I said. "Really, Miss Blessington, you are lucky to live here in a place with a swimming pool!"

"Oh, please call me Margaret," she said in a whispery voice. "Yes, I suppose it's pleasant, although a mountain stream dashing over the pebbles as it courses to the sea strikes me as much more exciting."

"I love to swim," I burbled on. Then lowering my voice to a dramatic whisper, I said, "But I understand Blanche Talbot never swam."

"She paddled around a little," said Margaret. "But I don't believe she knew how to swim."

"Did you know her well?" I asked breathlessly.

Margaret shrugged. "She was only interested in show business. We didn't have much in common."

"But I thought you and your family had been in show business for many years," I said.

Margaret's face took on a slightly bitter look. "That's right, I was born in a trunk, but it doesn't mean I have to *like* show business. I'd give anything to get away from it." She turned to me. "I envy you, because you have a real profession and independence."

"Well, surely you could learn to type," I said. "It isn't difficult at all."

"Actually, what I would like to do is start a nature camp for children," said Margaret, sighing. "David and I talk about it all the time."

"David?"

She gestured over at Nature Boy, who seemed to be resting his eyes while Mr. Blessington, still in white tie, droned at him, "The critics compared Mrs. Blessington to Mrs. Patrick Campbell, but of course, that was many years ago. Now our hopes are pinned on Margaret." In the bright afternoon light, his black suit had a decidedly greenish tinge. Up close I also noticed that Nature Boy, despite his very eccentric appearance and state of near nakedness, did look *clean,* which was a blessing.

"Yes," continued Margaret to me, "David has so many ideas about the proper education of children—out in the country, with flowers and animals as their textbooks, and the fields and bosky dells as their classrooms. And proper nutrition." She sighed. "If only we had the money to start it, I know it would be a success."

I wasn't quite sure many people would want to turn over their children to Margaret and Nature Boy for any length of time, but I didn't say so. "I guess Blanche Talbot grew up in the country," I said, trying to wrench the conversation back to her. "What a sad thing her death was!"

Margaret's mother now turned to join our conversation. Up close, I could see that she was a real battle-ax of a woman, with a pugnacious jaw and a dominating look in her eye. "On the surface, it was a terrible tragedy that Talbot girl died when she did," she announced. "I had just about arranged for Margaret to be her stand-in on her next picture, where I'm sure she would have caught the eye of the producers, and been offered a real part."

Margaret glowered, and I could see that underneath her quiet demeanor she had some of her mother's belligerent quality.

Mrs. Blessington leaned around her daughter to catch my eye, her tiara listing, and said, "But really it's for the best. Actually, Margaret is perfect for the role Blanche was to play. I've been able to arrange for a screen test now that Blanche is, er, unavailable." She dropped her voice down to a whisper and said, as if Margaret weren't there, "Margaret had a great career as a child. Now she's coming out of that awkward age it's time for her to step into ingenue roles, and I will move heaven and earth to see she gets her chance to become the star she deserves to be."

"Oh, Mother! Honestly!" said Margaret with exasperation. Mrs. Blessington ignored this outburst, which led me to believe it was a regular occurrence, like a tic. "Have you met David?" the older woman asked me now. Lowering her voice, she added, "He's really a titled Englishman. Traveling incognito, you know." She grew quite pink and happy at the thought. Whether Nature Boy actually had a title, it was clear Mrs. Blessington was thrilled to believe so. I doubted very much she would have tolerated the man otherwise.

Mr. Blessington had apparently stopped talking, and Nature Boy began to hold forth. His accent was English, all right. Perhaps he was an English sailor who had jumped ship and gone native here. "Blackstrap molasses, that's the ticket!" he proclaimed. "This precious food contains all the nutrients and goodness for a completely healthy life. I was talking about this just recently with my dear friend Vera Nadi, and convinced her to give it a go. A week on the stuff and she felt a new woman."

"Vera Nadi, the famous movie star?" I interrupted, acting impressed. I had actually met the legendary screen vamp on a transatlantic crossing, but I didn't say so.

"A wonderful woman," said Nature Boy. "Very receptive to some of my ideas about healthy, wholesome living. A forward-thinking, open-minded sort of woman. In fact, she's invited me to spend some time in her guest house up at Villa Vera."

I supposed it would make a nice change from the

hollow log Bessie LeBeau had described. A hollow log sounded not only damp, but as if it would harbor a great many insects.

"But I turned her down, of course," he went on. "My little dwelling beneath a canopy of moon and stars, sheltered by the stately oaks, furnished with the salvaged castoffs of a wasteful and profligate world, is enough for me."

Margaret beamed at him over her book, and he returned her gaze with a rather yearning one of his own, while an oblivious Mrs. Blessington peered at her work, counting stitches and looking for one that had dropped.

It was some time later, after I had dressed and approached Baxter Carlson's bungalow to begin work, that I heard Alice Chester's angry voice coming from within. "Don't pretend, Baxter! You know you were just as besotted as everyone else was with that little tease! You even bought that innocent farm girl act. I saw the way you looked at her with your greedy, depraved eyes. Plus, she was about to become rich!"

"Please, Alice," he said, his voice trembling. "The poor child is *dead*!"

I began to back away, but wasn't fast enough to avoid a collision with Alice, who was flouncing out the front door. "Men are beasts," she snapped at me, elbowing me aside. "I need a drink!"

It seemed to me she had already had plenty. I gingerly approached the front door again.

Baxter Carlson was collapsed against the mantel,

one trembling hand on his forehead as he stared downward with a look of pure tragedy.

I cleared my throat and prepared to back out again, but he snapped into an upright position and said, "You must forgive us, Miss Hooper. We're all a little shaken by what happened to poor Blanche. Life is so . . ." He trailed off.

"It's very understandable," I said. "Actually, my name is Cooper."

"Yes. Cooper. Of course."

"Would you like me to begin work immediately?" I asked briskly. "Where is the manuscript?"

"It's all over the place," he said helplessly, looking around. This place was furnished exactly as mine was, but it was untidy and less cheerful. Drawn curtains and the absence of the gay hearthrug and bright flowers gave it a more austere look. It was cluttered with books, papers, and old gin bottles, and smelled of stale cigarette smoke. I resolved to give the place a thorough airing out as soon as I could.

"Well, the first thing is to put it all together," I said decisively. I turned to the desk and spotted a stack of pages. "Is this part of it?"

"Yes," he said, and began bustling around collecting loose sheets. Apparently, he had already typed up a draft, which was covered with corrections and annotations. Despite the general disorder, the manuscript itself seemed neat and clear, and the pages were all numbered.

Alice Chester burst back through the front door, carrying a cocktail glass. "I'm sorry I was cross, Baxter," she said. "Let's make up, shall we? Come over to the pool. Adrian, Nature Boy, and I need a fourth for bridge."

He left, rather like a younger brother being shepherded around by a big sister, and I set about gathering pages, many of which, I couldn't help but notice, bore the rings of highball glasses on them. After a sweep of the place and a lot of shuffling, I realized they all seemed to be there, although I was surprised to find other odds and ends interleaved, all of which I shamelessly read.

There was a letter from a publisher, which said that the manuscript was very late and threatened to cancel the contract, and another from an agent, which pleaded with the author to finish the work and send it; a bill from a bootlegger; a laundry list; and a telegram, signed "FATHER," which spared no expense and read "CANNOT JUSTIFY SENDING YOU MONEY UNLESS SURE YOU CAN LEAD RESPECTABLE LIFE STOP WHAT HAPPENED TO ALL MONEY YOU MADE STOP SUGGEST YOU ABANDON LITERARY FOOLISHNESS STOP MOTHER WORRIED STOP I ON OTHER HAND DISGUSTED STOP CAN GET YOU GOOD JOB IN BANK HERE IN MUNCIE STOP."

The most startling finds, however, were two notes in a mad scrawl on thick, creamy notepaper with the letterhead "Corinthian Pictures."

"Dear Blanche," read the first one, "I am mad with desire. How can you be so cruel? My marriage is an empty vessel. Do I not deserve a little happiness? Your eyes are windows to a soul that is a pool of purity and goodness in which I long to bathe! I ask for a few crumbs of happiness. Is that so much? I am not like other men. My capacity for love is so deep. Your own boy, Freddie."

The second one was along similarly desperate lines, but ended with an invitation for Blanche to come to Palm Springs for the weekend and the assurance that no one need ever know. It included an ominous post-script: "I am desperate! If I can't have you then no one must!"

I stacked all these papers, put them on the mantel-piece, and sat down at the desk and began to type the manuscript. Presently, I abandoned typing and read ahead. The novel was about a sensitive young East-erner who comes to Hollywood and finds everyone there very vulgar, except for a young actress named Madge Mayhew, who senses the young man's superi-ority and tearfully reveals to him that she was drugged and presumably taken advantage of by an evil studio chief at a wild Hollywood party.

The description of Madge was so much like Blanche Talbot I could only think she had been the inspiration for the character. Baxter described her as "a creature from another, better world, angelic, with the large blue eyes of a wise child, and fair, tousled curls like the petals of some huge alpine wildflower."

This struck me as silly. Aunt Hermione had once taken me to a lecture on alpine gardens at her Flower Club, and none of the species we learned about there looked like tousled curls. In fact, they were mostly quite small and not at all showy. But then, Baxter Carlson seemed to me to be a man unlikely to know about gardens or other domestic matters.

My suspicions about the origins of the character were confirmed in a scene where Madge declares her love for the hero and collapses in tears on his manly chest, telling him how intelligent and perspicacious he is. Here, Carlson had typed her name in as Blanche, then crossed it out and penciled in "Madge." Alice Chester was right. Baxter had fallen for Blanche Talbot in a big way.

There was a rustle at the door and I hastily began typing again.

Baxter Carlson wandered in, clearly in a better mood. "How's everything going, Miss Hooper?" The sounds of laughter and splashing came from the courtyard.

"I've found all the pages as far as I can tell and have made a good start. There were these, um, other papers too. Maybe some of them are important." I handed him the stack, watching him carefully.

"God!" he said.

I cleared my throat. I had noted both how easily he had been led around by Alice Chester and the bullying tone his father took with him and had decided he was easily bossed. "I'm afraid I couldn't help but notice those," I said firmly. "Perhaps, considering their nature, the police should see them. That PS could be construed as a threat."

"But Blanche's death was an accident!" he exclaimed. "Surely you don't think this fiend could have harmed her!"

"I don't know much about it," I said, "but those letters could be important. How did you come to get them?"

In his agitated state, he didn't seem to notice that my question was impertinent. "Poor Blanche gave them to me for safekeeping. She was young and innocent. She came to me asking for advice. Said I was like a big brother to her." I sensed a little bitterness at this last. "I told her I'd hang on to them. She knew they could ruin Fred Green and that he'd do anything to get them back."

"I think we should give them to the police," I said.

"But the scandal!" He gazed down at the telegram from his father. "My family would hate to see my name in the papers connected with some Hollywood scandal. They're horrible, bourgeois little people. And the studio—my work there—I feel I'm just about to be taken seriously there. If Fred Green found out, this would be the end for me!"

"I can say I found them underneath the sofa cushions in my bungalow or something," I said. Of course I had no real intention of lying to the police.

"I must think about all this," he muttered, staring back down again at Fred Green's indiscreet pleas.

As he stood there, weaving a little from side to side, three thoughts occurred to me. The first was that Fred Green, who had clearly made a complete fool of himself over Blanche Talbot, might have been crazy enough to come and confront her, perhaps killing her in a struggle, because he was spurned. Second, if Blanche had intended to blackmail Fred Green—and why else would she keep the letters?—he might have killed her or had her killed to ensure her silence and get his letters back and save himself from the wrath of his father-in-law and professional ruin. Third, Baxter Carlson was clearly at the end of his financial rope. He might be tempted, if he managed to steel his nerves, to parlay those letters into some money or a well-paying job from either Fred Green or his father-in-law.

I cleared my throat. "It might be dangerous to possess those letters," I said.

"You're right," he said, dropping them hastily on the table. "Yes, you should take them to the police. Would you do that for me? Keep my name out of it?"

"Of course," I said. "I have an idea. That Mr. Clancy who recommended me to you seems the kind of person who could handle this discreetly. I'll call him and ask him to get them to the right people."

"Gosh, that's wonderful, Miss Hooper!" he said, and suddenly his melancholy face blossomed into a happy, smiling one. "You're a swell kid." He lurched toward me. "I could kiss you!"

As he lurched, I made an instinctive evasive maneuver and practically fell into the fireplace. "Ouch!" I said, as the wrought-iron andiron poked me in the calf.

He looked horrified as I inspected my silk stocking. There was a hole in it, and when I turned my ankle and looked over my shoulder for a better view, the hole predictably took off in a spectacular run parallel to the seam.

When I looked back up at Baxter Carlson, his happiness had vanished, and he looked like a nerve case once again, apparently horrified at what he had done and clutching his forehead in a dramatic way. Before this volatile man changed his mind, I snatched up the notes and fled.

Outside, it was dusk, and the evening air was cool and heavy with flowery scents, in contrast to Baxter Carlson's oppressive bungalow. As far as I could tell, the man needed a complete rest cure on top of a Swiss mountain, drinking nothing but buttermilk and building up his nerves.

I was pleased with my progress so far. I could hardly wait to tell Jack about the notes, which fit in with his own inquiries. I also wanted to tell him that Baxter Carlson had apparently been in love with Blanche and Alice Chester was extremely jealous, and that Mrs. Blessington seemed to be pleased that Blanche was dead, thinking it would benefit her daughter.

On my way back to the bungalow to change my stocking, I saw a strange figure crouched in the shrubbery. I let out an instinctive gasp, and then realized I was looking at Nature Boy, and that he was stirring around inside a big galvanized garbage can.

Thinking he might be embarrassed to be discovered going through the garbage, I fell back a little, and tried to compose myself, but he looked up and saw me. "Oh! Hullo!" he said cheerfully. "Amazing what one finds in these things. People throw out the most useful things. Why, just last week I found a perfectly good—"

"Hearthrug!" I said suddenly.

"Well, yes, actually," he said. "How did you know?"

I stared at him for a moment. How did I know? Then it all came to me. "Where is it now?" I asked.

"At home," he replied.

"Where is that, exactly?"

"In Griffith Park."

Just then, Jack came up the path, and looked startled to see me chatting with a half-naked man.

"Jack, this is David," I said urgently. "He has something out at Griffith Park that I think might be of interest to the *Globe*."

"I've worked with the press before," said David. "For a consideration, of course. No one can live entirely off the land."

It seemed we had been on the trail for half an hour. Crickets chirped as Jack and I followed Nature Boy past stands of oaks and tangles of manzanita. Finally, we reached his lair. It wasn't a hollow log at all. Actually, it was kind of a wooden lean-to in a grove of trees, and not unattractive. In this balmy climate, living outdoors suddenly seemed less eccentric than I had thought. There was a lovely view of Los Angeles by night, the lights twinkling.

David lit a lamp and set it on a nearby stump, where it cast a rosy glow over everything. Inside his shelter was a camp bed, a collection of pillows, an old steamer trunk and, underfoot, a rug that looked identical to the one in my bungalow.

"It was perfectly good. Just some stains on the back," David explained, handing it to me. "I'll make us some tea, shall I?" Presently, he was squatting next to a small fire outside the little hut.

"The rooms were identical," I said. "But his hearthrug wasn't there." Jack and I turned it over. There were stains on it all right, rusty brown stains that certainly looked like blood to me. The police would find out soon enough. If it had come from Baxter's bungalow, he'd have a hard time explaining why he'd thrown it away.

"It was that look in his eye when I fell back against the andiron," I said. "He had been very cheerful, and all of a sudden, he looked horrified, as if it were all coming back to him. I really believe it was an accident. It's clear from his manuscript that he was mad about her. She was confiding in him, showing him those letters. He dramatized the whole thing in his novel, making those mash notes into something much more horrible, and having the girl throw herself at the hero.

"In reality, I think he threw himself at her, maybe drunkenly and clumsily. He lunged. She slipped on the hearthrug, and hit her head on that pointed andiron. He panicked, thought she was dead, and threw her unconscious body in the pool. Then the hearthrug with her bloodstains on it went into the garbage. Very stupid, really."

"But why not just say there'd been an accident?"

"That's what poor Fatty Arbuckle said, and neither the police nor that first jury believed him," I replied. "Anyway, even if it was accepted as an accident, it's conceivable Fred Green at Corinthian Pictures, the number two man, would hold it against Baxter for causing the death of the woman he was so fascinated by. I imagine his career in Hollywood would be over. And Baxter's parents were thinking of giving him some money if he managed to avoid scandal. A dead actress in a bathing suit in a bachelor's living room surrounded by empty gin bottles might be considered more than a little risqué in the quiet circles in which the elder Carlsons apparently moved."

"If this is true, it's the greatest story around here since Sister Aimee's kidnapping," said Jack excitedly. "A lust-crazed man's struggle with innocent beauty ends in disaster. East Coast aesthete cold-blooded killer. Lovely breathes last in literary lion's den."

Nature Boy came toward us with some steaming cups on a tray. He looked rather like a half-naked butler. "This all sounds rather important," he said mildly. "I did wonder why Baxter Carlson was throwing it out."

"Are you sure that's who threw it out?" I asked.

"Yes. I saw him. I was taking a little nap nearby, in the branches of a pleasant tree. I often do when I'm visiting Margaret."

I was suddenly overwhelmed by the tragedy of it all. "Oh, it's all so sad," I said to Jack. "Poor Blanche. And poor Baxter, too. He's so weak and ruined by drink, his nerves are shot. Your stories never have happy endings!"

"Don't get soft on me," said Jack, setting his tea down on the steamer trunk and taking out his notebook. "Wild man of Hollywood Hills finds blood-stained clue. Cops scooped by modern caveman. Now, before you tell me in your own words how you came across that bloodstained hearthrug cast aside by a cruel and heartless killer, tell me your name, and how it's spelled."

"Oh, I'd prefer not to," said David dreamily. "I belong to no family. I belong to the hills, the wind, the sky, the earth."

I glanced down at the trunk where the teacup sat. Over the lock was a monogram above some kind of a crest, and on the top there was a glued-on label that read very clearly "David Penworthy, The Manor, Little Threadington, Hants."

"Your name wouldn't be David Penworthy, would it?" I asked.

"David Penworthy!" said Jack. "That's the other big story I've been working on. A lot of people have been looking for you. You're famous—David Penworthy, the Vanished Viscount!"

"I'm not a viscount," said David a little petulantly. "I'm just an honorable. My elder brother is a viscount."

"I'm sorry to tell you," said Jack solemnly, "that your brother died in a tragic hunting accident."

"Then I suppose I am a vanished viscount," said David thoughtfully.

"Actually"—Jack cleared his throat—"as of the latest dispatches, you are a missing marquess. Your father was also injured in the accident, but he lingered a little longer." Perhaps because David Penworthy seemed to be bearing up so well, in fact he seemed completely unmarked by grief or shock, Jack explained, "Their horses collided and they both fell off and broke their necks."

"Father and Harry broke their necks?" said David, now beaming. "Really? But this is fabulous! We can run our children's nature school in Threadington Manor! Mummy can move into the dower house and Margaret and I can live in the old grotto behind the gazebo. And Margaret can be a real marchioness, with real jewels, not that shabby old paste her mother wears!"

And so it came to be that when Jack's stories ran, side by side, there was one tragic headline, "Blood Found on Andiron. Carlson Confesses: 'I Killed the Thing I Loved,'" next to a happier one, "Real-life Tarzan Weds His Jane; American Girl Finds Hollywood Ending with Rich, Titled Englishman."

Sometimes I'm not very proud to call myself a woman, especially after reading this virulent tale of poison pens and malicious gossip. While a certain amount of investigation is necessary to solve a crime, there's certainly no good reason to go around spreading rumors and half-truths to everyone one meets. It's a pity the socialites in this story didn't learn that lesson sooner.

Social Death

Joyce Christmas

"But what does she *do* with herself all day?" people would ask about Poppy Dill. Then they would add, "Besides write this garbage?" They'd ask that question after Poppy's "Social Scene" gossip column contained a juicy item about a scandalous affair, a pending divorce, a tragically underattended charity ball.

Yet those same people would save any laudatory item about themselves, and send Poppy a thank-you note for being mentioned.

"I'll tell you what she does." Leonora Collier had just asked the question herself in the comfortable surroundings of her East Side Manhattan townhouse (only $5.5 million, an absolute *steal*). "She sits in that apartment of hers like a spider in her web and goes through her files, reliving old scandals and finding deliciously cruel new things to say. She has no shame."

"It can't take much time to write four hundred words three times a week," Leonora's best chum Meredith Berks said. "It's not like she has to go out and look for items. Those pets of hers go around and feed her all the gossip she needs."

"She certainly never goes out," Leonora said. "She just sits there in her boudoir and broods about who to savage in her column."

Leonora's had recently been a boldfaced name in "Social Scene," linked with another boldfaced name belonging to someone who was male and married. Everybody had suspected for ages about her and Tom, even his wife, but now that it had been trumpeted in print, there was no avoiding the unpleasantness.

"I shall never forgive her. She made me sound like a tramp. She got her information from someone." Leonora narrowed her eyes and gazed at blond, innocent Meredith. She didn't like to think her so-called friend, in whom she had confided a bit too much about Tom, had shared details with Poppy, but Meredith could be bitchy, and was given to fits of bad temper that readily turned into rages.

"Maybe Poppy meant slut, hussy, baggage," Meredith said with a look of innocence. Leonora let that pass. Meredith would be on the receiving end of Poppy's poisonous pen soon enough. Everyone was, eventually. "You probably haven't been nice enough to her," Meredith said, unaware that she was under suspicion. "Believe me, it pays. I drop by to see her every few weeks, with some little treat—those Godiva truffles she likes or a little nosegay of roses. She's never written an unkind word about me. Ever."

But she will, Leonora thought. "Merry, darling, you're so *good*, so . . ."

"Ordinary? Scandal-free? William and I are very happy. He doesn't fool around, and I behave well. Always." A slight frown creased her brow, as though she was recalling some reprehensible action better left unconfessed.

Leonora knew what she said about William wasn't strictly true. Her own husband, Ed, had dropped hints about William's extramarital activities, and there had been that truly boring reception when the tedium of meeting society arrivistes had been relieved by a harmless flirtation with William in the library. She'd put a stop to that at once. Meredith was her best friend. Finally she said, "Never is a long time, but Poppy is a poster child for long time."

Poppy Dill was certainly old, nearly eighty, but still in good health, possibly because for years now she never emerged to face the rigors of New York society or the rough streets of Manhattan, where even the Upper East Side held certain dangers. Someone from the newspaper used to fetch the copy for her column, although nowadays the tabloid required her to put aside her old typewriter and compose on a computer so her copy could be sent electronically. Poppy hated that, as she hated most changes.

"I hate these damned computers!" Poppy screeched to her empty apartment, where she lived in solitary splendor. There was no Mister Poppy, although it was rumored that she had once married very well, possibly a titled gentleman seeking an escape from the coming of World War II.

Poppy rapped the computer—not gently—with an aged fist, and went in search of a cup of tea. The gauzy baby-blue peignoir she habitually wore floated out behind her. She paused to glance at herself in the hall mirror. She did not like what she saw.

The ornate gold frame showed little nests of dust in the curlicues. There were fingerprints on the glass. She looked at the pale strip of hallway carpeting, and frowned at the dark flecks of New York grit that regularly insinuated their way into an apartment even when the windows were tightly closed. The walls of the shower needed a good scrubbing, and the kitchen floor could use a mopping.

It was so hard to get good help nowadays. Her cleaning lady, Elvira, had vanished a month before for a holiday on her native Caribbean island, and had never reappeared. That's what came of giving her too much money for some information she'd gotten from a friend. Elvira was willing to share both news she picked up at other clients' places and anything she learned from others who labored in the gilded purlieus of the wealthy: tales of abused wives, drug-addicted sons, promiscuous daughters, all the more interesting to her readers because the stories were about the rich, the famous, the people who had everything.

The latest tale (and evidence) that Elvira had provided was worth the money. It would cause a sensation when Poppy wrote up her piece on mischief behind the scenes at charity events. Committee ladies were definitely not saints.

Poppy occasionally suffered twinges of conscience for buying her gossip from the likes of Ellie and others, but not enough to make her stop doing it. And now Ellie was gone. It was time to find a replacement. Poppy couldn't keep up the apartment alone. She hated to admit that she was getting old. When Ellie left, Poppy had arranged for a man to pick up and return her laundry and dry cleaning, and she ordered her groceries to be delivered, but a distinguished journalist like Poppy should have someone to handle such things for her.

In her bedroom with a cup of tea, Poppy glared at the computer, and picked up her white telephone. It too needed cleaning.

She telephoned her friend, Lady Margaret Priam, a recent arrival in New York, who had mastered life in the city. Surely the daughter of the late Earl of Brayfield could recommend a cleaning lady. Young people nowadays seemed to know how to run things, even if, like Margaret, they had grown up with servants to do the running.

"Margaret dear, it's Poppy. How *are* you? I haven't seen you for ages."

"It has been a long time," Margaret said. "We were

promised your presence at that fund-raiser where Fergie put in an appearance. I was disappointed when you didn't come. It was a lovely affair."

"I wrote it up for the column," Poppy said, "but I couldn't come. The Duchess of York isn't quite . . ." Poppy stopped. It took more than a Sarah Ferguson to get Poppy Dill out of her apartment. Princess Margaret or Prince Charles, perhaps, the Queen certainly, and Diana if she were still alive. Poppy moved for few others. "I need a favor, Margaret."

It was easy to imagine Margaret sitting up ready to oblige. It paid to be on Poppy's good side, even if Margaret had never done anything that would warrant a negative item in "Social Scene."

"My Elvira has disappeared. I need to replace her."

"I see," Margaret said, and tried to remember of whom they were speaking.

"My cleaning lady. You must remember her from your visits. A rather large lady from Trinidad. This place is a mess, and since I spend so much time here . . ."

Every waking and sleeping moment, Margaret thought to herself, and said, "Ah, you need a recommendation. My lady has only the one day a week to give me, as she's fully engaged every other day. Poppy, there are agencies you can call for this sort of thing."

"I'd rather have someone known to someone one trusts," Poppy said firmly. "I'm certain some friend of Elvira's works for Leonora Collier and the Berkses. Meredith sent her around here once." She didn't have to explain that she couldn't ask a favor of Leonora directly. Margaret read Poppy's column regularly, and understood that Leonora might harbor some hostility toward Poppy.

"I will ask," Margaret said, and later that afternoon, during a committee meeting to organize an event for a very worthy cause, Margaret did ask Leonora Collier and Meredith Berks and others for leads on a cleaning lady for Poppy Dill.

A few were reluctant to share their "treasures" with Poppy. The rumor was common in their circles that for a price, the help shared with Poppy private news they'd picked up. Margaret diplomatically persuaded Meredith and Leonora to put their shared cleaning lady at Poppy's disposal. They agreed that their Deirdra might satisfy.

"I don't imagine Poppy is very messy," Leonora said. "Would she mind a West Indian? Deirdra is from Saint Lucia."

"Deirdra told me that Poppy's other woman was from the Caribbean too," Meredith said. "An old friend of Dierdra's."

"Deirdra's very clean, honest, and intelligent," Leonora said. "Good with flowers too." She spoke as though flowers could be as difficult to control as a yappy Pekingese.

"Poppy knows her," Meredith said. "I send her around to her often with little gifts."

"I'd have saved myself a lot of problems if I'd done that," Leonora said, still enraged by Poppy's item about her and Tom. Suddenly she wondered uneasily if

Deirdra had found—and read—the passionate notes Tom had been sending her. They were safely hidden (she hoped) in a box on a shelf of her closet where Ed never ventured, but if the cleaning lady found them, and told . . . someone . . . No, it was impossible to think that sweet, round-faced Deirdra would dare to repeat the contents to someone like her friend Elvira, who might then (horrors!) tell Poppy, who would proceed to report it in print to every slatternly housewife in Queens, the maître d's of all the best restaurants, and the smirking shopgirls who attended her at Bendel's and Bergdorf's.

In fact, it was also hard to understand why Poppy, a woman who was well known for never revealing the truth about that sensational affair of the lingonberries (involving Madame Ambassador and a back staircase at the Ambassador's residence in a cold Scandinavian capital), would bother to chip away at the serenity of Leonora Collier's life. The press had certainly gotten out of hand.

When she returned home after the meeting, Leonora hurried to her closet and found her letters from Tom as she had left them. Almost. One or two seemed to be missing. Perhaps it was time to destroy them and fire Deirdra.

Margaret went home to telephone Poppy to fix a time for an interview with Deirdra.

"Ah, I know her," Poppy said. "Meredith sends her here with bribes, and she did know my Elvira."

"Why would Meredith be bribing you?" Margaret

didn't care, but you never knew when such information would be useful.

Surprisingly, Poppy decided to confide in Margaret. "I think Meredith suspects that I have an account book from the time she was treasurer of that dinner and ball for those poor souls with that vile disease. The party where Lilian Prunty got drunk on champagne and fell down the grand staircase just as the Senator arrived. It doesn't take much champagne to make Lilian's knees give out.

"Little Meredith didn't keep a very sound accounting of funds. Quite a sum went missing. I suppose she has more expenses than her husband is willing to pay for. All too common."

Margaret didn't ask how Poppy had acquired the damaging account book. Poppy had her ways.

A week later, Deirdra appeared at Meredith Berks's apartment for her scheduled cleaning day.

"Did you interview with Miss Dill?" Meredith asked. She yearned for a full-time housekeeper instead of daily help a few times a month. Someone in a nice uniform to answer the door and serve drinks to her friends. William refused to consider the expense. Meredith would never forgive the stock market for behaving so badly and spoiling her comforts.

"Oooo-eee, I did, and such a place! All shiny curtains and big old lamps with dangles like a Christmas tree. Is goin' to take hours to polish them up good. I goin' one day every two weeks," Deirdra said. "Gave me a key and everyt'ing. Good money. I tole her I got chil'ren to look out for and if they's ailing or something, I got to be with them. And my other ladies come first if they need me. Is not goin' to be any big t'ing to clean she place. Don't touch the wardrobe in the bedroom, she say, private t'ings behind the door, is always lock." Deirdra smiled, satisfied that she had an easy job ahead. Elvira had hinted that there was extra pay for telling the old lady tales about the rich folks she worked for if anything happened to fall off the bushes.

"She's always there," Meredith said. "I saw her at a party only once. They gave her an award. Probably for being unkind to someone. She's been unkind to Mrs. Collier, and I'm probably next." Meredith was sure that nobody could be aware of her appropriation of a few dollars from the charity treasury. She was going to pay it back before there was an audit. She'd needed the money to pay for a visit to that spa in Arizona. She had to get herself in shape. She didn't want William straying.

"Why, Miz Berks, I don't imagine anybody could find a reason to be unkind to you."

"Thank you, Deirdra. But people say she knows lots of secrets, and is just waiting for the right moment to tell them. And maybe you could tell me who visits her, and what you overhear."

Deirdra shrugged her agreement. There was no understanding the ways of these New York folks.

So it was that on the next Wednesday, Deirdra appeared at Poppy's door, with her coverall and working shoes in a bag. She changed from her nice orange blouse and dark skirt, tied up her hair in a kerchief, and started to scrub the kitchen. After the kitchen, she descended to the basement and set a load of laundry to wash. She ran the vacuum across the drawing room carpet and dusted the picture and mirror frames. She polished the tables at either end of the sofa and mopped the wooden floors around the edge of the carpet. All the while, Poppy kept to her room, tapping out sentences on the computer keyboard.

When Deirdra knocked on Poppy's door to straighten the bedroom, she heard a cross "Come in." Deirdra found herself in a dim place, scented with ladylike perfume. The windows were covered with satiny pink drapes, and she could scarcely believe her eyes when she saw the white marble statue of a naked lady on a little bookcase, an indecent object for a white-haired old lady to own. The screen of the computer glowed from where it sat in the corner of the bedroom on a white vanity table skirted in pink ruffles.

"Ma'am?" Deirdra didn't see Poppy. "Where you at?"

"I'm in here." Poppy's voice was muffled. She stepped out of the big walk-in closet with a handful of papers and a black leather notebook. Deirdra recognized the notebook at once and wondered if trouble was coming. "I was looking through my files," Poppy said.

"The private t'ings," Deirdra said. Would she be accused of stealing the notebook and giving it to Elvira? But the old lady didn't look angry. A closet stuffed with secret things was the kind of whim expected of eccentric rich folks. Didn't Miz Collier keep a box of racy letters hidden in her closet from some man who wasn't her husband?

"You must never touch the files in that closet," Poppy said. "Even if I forget to lock it."

Deirdra's expression said, Why would I want to touch such a thing? What she said was, "No, ma'am, I surely won't touch a thing." And she wouldn't. She'd reformed.

Poppy settled into her chair in front of the computer. "Just dust a bit in here, make the bed, and see that this telephone is cleaned up a bit. Then that will be all for today." Poppy opened a drawer in the vanity and took out a roll of currency, peeled off three twenties and a ten, and handed the money to Deirdra. "I think this is what we agreed to. I'll see you two weeks from today."

"Ma'am, two weeks from today, I have a t'ing at school for the chil'ren." Poppy frowned, and Deirdra went on, "But I could come on the Sunday after, unless you entertaining or goin' to church."

"I doubt it," Poppy said. "Let me see." She leafed through an appointment book empty of appointments. "Sunday will be acceptable." One day was pretty much like another to Poppy, although she did like autumn.

That was when the New York social season got started. The endless phone calls urging her to attend this party or that one. The socially busy days and nights, as the right people drifted back to New York from their summers in the Hamptons or Europe. She had plenty of copy for her column, and so many people did drop in to share the latest gossip. She always made sure to have extra tea, sugar, milk, and lemon on hand for those visits, as well as vodka, limes, and tonic for visitors who preferred to gossip over strong drink. And everyone would bring her lovely chocolates from Teuscher or Godiva.

"Sit down, Deirdra," Poppy said suddenly. Deirdra almost dropped the telephone she was carefully wiping clean, but she sat, upright and attentive.

"I don't know if you understand what I do," Poppy said. Deirdra shook her head. What did rich old ladies do except sit around all day and do nothing? Deirdra couldn't imagine.

"I write for a newspaper. News about the kind of ladies you work for, who raise money for sick people, encourage people to give money to museums, find ways to get money to help people who are less fortunate than we are."

Deirdra didn't think of herself as more or less fortunate than many others. Her life wasn't bad. She had a good husband, two children, and she earned a few dollars doing house cleaning. In any case, the ladies she cleaned for were more interested in filling their wardrobes with new dresses and shoes and making sure their hair was just so. She never saw a one of them going out of her way to help a sick person.

But who was she to deny what Poppy stated to be a fact? Poppy's pay was good. In fact, her friend Elvira said she made out well by doing a few extra things for her. Elvira had managed her trip home to the islands because of money Miz Dill had given her for that little black book full of numbers Deirdra had found tossed in a wastebasket at Miz Berks's apartment.

She felt a clutch of panic again as she saw the very same book on the vanity next to the computer. Deirdra hoped this conversation would lead her to doing something extra and earning more, rather than a lecture about taking away Miz Berks's property. It had been discarded, but would she be believed?

Poppy was still going on. "The people who read the newspaper are interested in what people in society do, so I need information about them. What they're doing, who they are seeing. I need the help of people like you."

Deirdra knew where this was going. She wanted her to be a spy. Elvira had said that Miz Dill paid well for stories about the foolishness of these rich folks. When Deirdra had told Elvira about Miz Collier's letters from the man who wasn't her husband, the very next time they talked, Elvira said how valuable that information had been. Now there was that account book staring at her. Elvira had given her twenty dollars for it, but Elvira surely received a lot more from Miz Dill.

By rights, all the money should have come to Deirdra. She had removed the notebook from the trash, while Elvira had done nothing. Then Elvira said Miz Berks had stolen a lot of money, so she deserved what was coming to her. Deirdra felt better.

"I understand," Deirdra said.

"I'm interested to hear anything you learn about Mrs. Berks or Mrs. Collier, or any of the ladies who visit them," Poppy said. "Anything at all." She handed Deirdra another twenty. It was not her custom to pay for information in advance, but it couldn't hurt just this once, a goodwill gesture. "That will be all."

Deirdra finished her chores and went home to Brooklyn, a place that Poppy couldn't imagine in her wildest nightmares.

"She's entirely acceptable," Poppy told Margaret in a late evening phone call. "I can't thank you enough."

"It was Meredith and Leonora who recommended her," Margaret said. "You should be thanking them."

"I don't speak to either any longer," Poppy said. "Leonora was quite rude after I hinted at that little affair between her and Tom. I couldn't see the harm. It was the talk of every circle. Then Meredith, being such a great chum of Leonora's, said some extremely harsh things about me in public, which of course got back to me. I'm afraid I will have to even the score with Meredith. She must know that I am aware of her financial fiddling with the charity."

"Poppy, vindictiveness doesn't become you," Margaret said. "Doesn't what you do ever bother you?"

"I am a professional," Poppy said, defensively. "Just doing my job." Margaret searched her memory for gossip about herself that Poppy might report if she should seriously irritate the old woman. Her conscience was remarkably clear for someone who swam with the sharks of New York society. "No offense intended," Margaret said. She wondered if she should warn Meredith of the impending exposure of her misdeeds. "I'll come by in a few days," Margaret said, "for a good old gossip. I'm busy until Sunday next. I'll call before I come."

Margaret was plagued by uneasiness about Meredith. She wasn't a special friend, and if she had done something dishonest, she had her own conscience to deal with. Still. . . .

Finally, nearly a week and a half later, when nothing had appeared about Meredith in Poppy's column, Margaret telephoned her. "I know nothing of the matter personally," Margaret said when she reached Meredith, "but Poppy Dill has hinted that she knows of a situation involving you and some charity funds."

Meredith was silent. Finally she said, "I don't know what you are talking about. But please, Margaret, don't share this with anyone else. Poppy has been out to get me since I said some things about her at a rather well-attended dinner party. After she wrote about Leonora and Tom. What a vile person she is."

Meredith could see all manner of trouble if Poppy printed the information about her and the charity funds. She'd never be asked to chair a committee again; no one would speak to her or invite her out. Worst of all, it would be damaging to her husband and, by extension, to her charge accounts. It meant social death. All because of a few dollars. Several hundred, actually. That spa was very expensive. "I suppose," she said slowly, "that Deirdra must have found my account book and passed it on to Elvira, who gave it to Poppy. I misplaced it and searched for that book everywhere, but it was gone. Poppy probably paid her a lot for it, people say she does that, so Elvira decided she'd better disappear for a while."

"I said I know nothing about the matter," Margaret said. "I just thought you ought to be aware."

"I shall certainly find a way to pay back the money while there's still time," Meredith said. "I've been so foolish."

Margaret's conscience was clear now. She'd given the warning, and it was out of her hands.

Deirdra wept when Meredith Berks confronted her over the matter of the account book. She confessed that she had given the book to her friend Elvira, but she'd found it in the trash as though it had been thrown away. She had no idea that taking it was wrong. She swore she would never do such a thing again. Then she wept some more when Meredith, in a fury, fired her.

"Can we get it back?" Meredith asked coldly. She was not moved by tears, especially when her own reputation, her position in society, was at stake.

"I goin' to Miz Dill on Sunday, but she keep the book with her private t'ings in the wardrobe, always locked up, and she never leave she bedroom. No way I can get it."

"You must try," Meredith said. "If you return it, you can have your job back." Deirdra wasn't sure she cared. A big supermarket over on Lexington was advertising for check-out clerks. Good pay and benefits. It might be time to change her line of work.

On Sunday Deirdra was late setting out for Poppy Dill's. She was determined to retrieve the account book, even if she had to whack the old lady over the head, not that she cared so much about her job, or the troubles of these wicked rich people, but Deirdra had a conscience too, and it was troubling her.

Poppy waited impatiently for her cleaning lady to arrive, but as the hours drifted by without Deirdra, Poppy became irritated. She was expecting Lady Margaret that afternoon, and she wanted the apartment to look its best.

By noon, she was grumbling to herself about the unreliability of domestic help, and by one she was in a fury. Then the intercom buzzed. It couldn't be Margaret yet. Poppy tottered to answer the doorman's ring. She'd been feeling her age lately. The stress of keeping up with all the gossip was trying. It wasn't fun anymore, and she was beginning to have doubts about the value of the service she provided.

"Miss Dill, there's a young lady here who says she works for you," the doorman said. "A Miss Deirdra."

Of course George wouldn't know Deirdra. He only worked on weekends.

"She doesn't have to be announced. She cleans for me, and I've given her a key." Poppy was more irritated now. She heard rustles and clanks as George handed over the receiver to Deirdra.

"Miz Dill, you got to come down here and help me."

"I certainly will do no such thing. I expected you here three hours ago. There's work to be done."

"It's Miz Berks. She after me for takin' her account book and givin' it to Elvira for you. You got to talk to her, give her back the book. I'm afraid of her. She made me promise to stay down here where she could see me."

Poppy said, "I don't go out."

"Please." It was a wail of desperation. Poppy remained unmoved.

The doorman took the phone again. "The young lady seems to be in some distress, Miss Dill. Shall I have one of the men escort her up to your place?"

"That won't be necessary, George. I can mange to come down to the lobby." Maybe it was time to relinquish the power she fancied she had and make amends for trashing a few lives. She could give up the column and write the book she'd dreamed of. The truth behind the lingonberry affair. "Just sit her in one of the chairs. It will take me a few minutes to get ready."

Poppy felt a thrill of nervousness as she contemplated the act of emerging from her safe haven and descending to street level. Since she went out so seldom, it took thought to decide on a costume. Her rumpled peignoir was not appropriate, even if she threw a coat on over it. So she got out the dark blue dress with the white collar that she wore when she had to visit her lawyer or doctor. Low-heeled shoes and matching handbag. Her fluffy white hair needed only a run-through with a comb and she was ready. She checked to see that she had her keys and opened the door. Her hand was trembling, and her breathing ragged. Someone had told her that fear of going out was some sort of disease. She thought that nonsense. She simply did not care for elevators, large numbers of people, and fresh air.

The elevator ride down from the twelfth floor was painful, but at least she was alone until the fifth floor, when a woman with a frisky dog got on, and insisted on chatting, even though they had never been introduced.

"Lovely day," the woman said. Poppy ignored her. "A perfect day for the street fair."

Poppy looked at her and raised an eyebrow.

"It's all up and down Second Avenue, put on by one of the neighborhood associations. Such fun, things to buy, food to eat, masses of people." Poppy cringed inwardly. "Don't you just love New York? I always buy little Christmas gifts at the last street fair of the season."

Happily, the elevator soon came to a stop on the ground floor. The woman and her dog sprinted away to join the "masses of people" that Poppy hoped she would never lay eyes on. Poppy stepped out of the elevator hesitantly. George was at the glass doors observing the street, but she didn't see Deirdra in any of the lobby armchairs.

"Where's the girl, George?"

Startled, George turned, then told her, "She was just here with another lady. They said something about taking a look at the street fair up on the corner, but I didn't see them leave. Maybe they went upstairs to your apartment after all. Must have gotten into an elevator as you were coming down."

How tiresome, Poppy thought. "What did the other lady look like?"

"Kind of short, light hair. Good looking."

It sounded like Meredith, all right. She was blond and not very tall. And, of course, all these women worked very hard at appearing good looking, spending fortunes to achieve it.

Much as she longed to be back in her apartment, Poppy felt she had to confront Meredith.

"I'll just stroll up the street," Poppy said. "If the ladies come back, have them wait for me. I'll only be gone a few minutes."

It was a warm autumn day, and the sun was shining. Half a block up the street, on Second Avenue, Poppy could see a stream of people moving steadily southward, while another stream moved north. There were booths set up on either side of the avenue, and she could smell onions, sausage, peppers cooking. She walked toward the festival, willing her heart to stop pounding. There was nothing to be afraid of, only a bunch of grubby New Yorkers bent on wasting their money on useless things.

She could see people with plates, eating as they walked, people with cans of beer and soda. People with dogs and children. All of her favorite things. But she didn't see Deirdra or Meredith. She merged with the good-humored crowd, and started walking south. Ahead of her a wave of humanity undulated along the avenue as far as the eye could see. She wasn't tempted to pause at any of the booths selling T-shirts, jewelry, and useless knickknacks. She could not believe there was such a great demand for refrigerator magnets shaped like food items.

Even walking a block tired Poppy, but she looked around with a lively curiosity not many of her acquaintances would have believed. She stopped abruptly and almost caused a pileup of baby carriages, bicycles, and homeless men collecting empty soda cans for their five-cent redemption value.

Why would Meredith be after Deirdra for the account book, anyway? So she had found out that Deirdra was involved in getting it to Poppy—what good would it do her now to harass the girl? The damage had been done, and retrieving the book would not erase what Poppy knew.

People swirled around her. They were beginning to cause Poppy a certain anxiety. She paused under an awning that shaded a booth selling Philippine food, but refused when a round-faced woman with sleek dark hair tried to entice her to buy bits of roasted meat on a skewer. She moved on to the next booth, and refrained from trying the egg rolls and noodles.

She moved along past a jungle of potted plants, ignoring the Oriental rugs laid out on the street, the Somali handbag vendors, the sellers of T-shirts with rude sayings intended to be clever.

She found a dollar in her handbag and purchased a plastic cup of lemonade that wasn't very lemony or cold but was welcome on this hot afternoon. All the while she scanned the crowds for a familiar face. Deirdra wouldn't have gone far from Poppy's building if she wanted protection from Meredith. Poppy retreated from the busy street to a patch of shade on the sidewalk and thought. It came to her. Meredith's threat had merely been a pretense to get Poppy out of her apartment. Meredith wanted her account book, and she knew it was in Poppy's possession, so the place to find it was Poppy's apartment. Deirdra had a key. That was where they were.

Poppy had not walked quickly for sixty years, indeed, not since that time in Nice when she'd run toward the Hotel Negresco to elude an amorous Frenchman who had taken a sudden liking to her. Thank goodness Willy Maugham had been relaxing in a chaise out front and she'd been able to knock aside the youth paying court to him and beg his protection. Willy was always a gentleman.

Today, alas, there was no major twentieth-century author to rescue her. She just had two aged legs to get her back to her building and see if those women were there. Or worse, if Meredith was savaging Deirdra for her part in bringing disgrace upon her, for causing her quiet social death.

Lady Margaret was no Willy Maugham, perhaps, but she was nonetheless just then striding along the street, dodging dogs and wheelchairs and kids with balloons. She caught sight of Poppy, who did not see her. It was definitely alarming to anyone who knew Poppy to see her both out in public and moving fast. Margaret needed to know why, and stepped up her pace.

Poppy reached her building well before Margaret, and George assured her that neither the cleaning lady nor any other woman had departed since she left. The elevator moved upward like molasses. At last the elevator door glided open, and Poppy peered down the hall. The door of her apartment was ajar. She approached it cautiously but hesitated before entering.

She must be alert, since she heard sounds from inside. Great loud crashes, as though someone was trying to break down the closet door.

Poppy bravely entered the apartment and headed toward her bedroom. Before she could open the door, she heard a crash, and a moan. Then a wild—indeed, insane—laugh. The door was flung open and Poppy found herself face-to-face with Meredith. She was clutching her black account book to her chest and brandishing that lovely little marble statue of Venus an admirer had given Poppy. Over Meredith's shoulder, Poppy could see her closet door hanging on its hinges and Deirdra's body sprawled on the floor.

"Meredith, what have you done?" Poppy staggered out into the hall.

"You old witch, get out of my way." Meredith was reduced to bad movie dialogue. She tried to shove Poppy aside, but Poppy stood her ground even as Meredith raised the statue to hit her.

Margaret emerged from the elevator and stared at the scene in disbelief. Then she quickly took out her cell phone and summoned help.

"It's all for nothing, Meredith," Poppy said. "I know what's in the account book, and even if you try to harm me, the story is written and I've sent it to the newspaper."

Deirdra moaned. Meredith hadn't murdered her with a blow from Venus after all.

"I may try to harm you just to get even," Meredith screamed. "You're a wicked old woman, and you encouraged others to steal my property!" She shoved

Poppy, who caught herself before she fell. "Why did you come back so soon?"

"I knew Deirdra had a key to my apartment, I knew I had something you wanted. I didn't see Deirdra at the street fair, yet she was desperate to see me, so I deduced that you had lured me away so you could retrieve the book."

"Since you never leave your apartment, I thought I could come up here with her and kill you both for what you've done to me. But you did leave, so there was just Deirdra to finish off."

"Poppy hasn't done anything yet," Margaret said.

"You can have your book back," Poppy said wearily. "The story won't be printed. I did wrong and you are doing wrong now. Trust me to do the right thing. All you have to do is repay the money you took."

"You tell everybody's secrets and now you expect me to trust you."

"Remember the lingonberry affair," Poppy said. "No one has ever heard that story, not even Lady Margaret. You know you can trust me."

"Yes," Margaret said, "you can. Ah, here are the authorities to look into the . . . the accident."

The policemen didn't quite believe that a marble statue could have fallen off a shelf on its own and injured the cleaning lady, but they were sufficiently impressed to meet the columnist their wives read faithfully that they accepted her story.

Deirdra did not, however, but in spite of resulting rumors of an assault charge, Meredith did not die a nasty social death, but acquired a certain glamor, and struck fear into the members of committees she went on to chair.

Poppy, true to her word, never told the whole story. Everybody ended up trusting Poppy Dill.

While I've never put much stock in any of my dreams fore-telling the future, I'm also a bit more pragmatic than many. I believe in using the five senses I know, rather than relying on a mysterious sixth, if there even is such a thing. The heroine of our next story, however, does well to listen to her subconscious warnings, and catches a killer as a result.

The Man in Her Dream

Margaret Coel

Vicky Holden awoke with a start. Her heart thumped at her ribs like a bird flailing against a cage. The tangle of sheets and blankets was damp with her own perspiration. A wedge of moonlight fell through the window and illuminated a corner of the bedroom. The rest was dark. Red numbers on the nightstand clock glowed into the blackness: 4:23.

From far away came the drone of a truck lumbering along the highway north of Lander. It passed, leaving an empty quiet. Vicky kicked the damp bedclothes aside and forced herself to take deep breaths, willing her heartbeat to slow. It was just a dream.

A dream about a man she didn't know, had never seen before. He had brown hair combed straight back and a long, narrow face. The wide nostrils flared above tightly drawn lips; the dark eyes bored into her with a malevolence that left her stunned and immobilized. It was the man's eyes, she realized, that had tripped her heart into an erratic spin.

The man came walking toward her, kicking up clouds of dust with each step. The dust rose around his boots, licked at his blue jeans and brown corduroy jacket, swirled about his head and shoulders. Still he moved forward, in and out of the dust, eyes fixed on her. She tried to run, but the earth shifted beneath her feet. She couldn't move.

After a while Vicky felt her heartbeat subside to a normal rhythm. She wondered if she had received a vision, then pushed away the idea. In the Arapaho Way, only men received visions. When the warriors went into the wilderness to fast and pray, the forces of nature might reveal themselves and share their power: the strength of the buffalo, the determination of the bear, the cunning of the coyote. Women received dreams. And yet, some evil force had been revealed to her. Its power was mighty. It frightened her.

First chance she got, Vicky decided, she would drive onto the Wind River Reservation north of town and ask Grandmother Ninni to interpret her dream. Just as no man could interpret his own vision, no woman could discern the meaning of her own dream.

•   •   •

The phone on the nightstand jangled into the early morning quiet, and Vicky realized she had been hearing the noise in the distance for some time. She must have dozed off, despite the fact that every time she had closed her eyes, she had seen the man walking toward her and felt the evil force in his eyes. She shook herself awake and picked up the receiver.

"That you, Vicky?" A man's voice, someone she must know, but she had no idea who it might be.

She took a deep breath and said, "This is Vicky Holden."

"Derrel Running Bull here. I been tryin' to get a hold of you for thirty minutes or more."

Vicky swung out of bed, muscles tense, senses alert. A call from Derrel Running Bull meant one thing: Richard was in trouble again. Three times in the last four years, Derrel had called about his son. Richard had stolen a car. Richard had beaten up a man in a bar. Richard had been arrested on drug possession. Vicky had managed to keep Richard out of jail on the first two incidents, but he'd done time on the possession charge.

"What's going on?" she asked.

"Police got Richard locked up over in county jail." The words came like a burst of gunshot. "You gotta get him out, Vicky. He just got done with prison, and he can't be locked up no more. No tellin' what he might do. . . ." Derrel's voice trailed off. She heard a muffled sound, a choked sob.

"Tell me what happened," she said gently.

There was a half second of silence on the line. Then:

"Somebody shot Clifford Willow. Police say Richard done it, 'cause it happened over at the construction site where he's been workin'."

Vicky knew the site—a two-block apartment complex on the west side of town. A Los Angeles developer by the name of Stephen Jeffries had moved to Lander, bought a number of vacant lots, and seemed intent on covering every one of them with buildings. Not everybody liked the idea, but no one could deny that the man had created dozens of much-needed jobs.

"Police jumped to conclusions, all of 'em wrong," Derrel was saying. "Arapaho gets hisself shot. Another Arapaho must've done it. But ever since Richard got outta prison, he seen Willow was leadin' him down a bad road. He got off them drugs and started a new life. Been goin' to work every day, learnin' how to be a carpenter. No way he shot that no-good Indian. He don't even own a gun."

A picture had begun to form in Vicky's mind. Clifford Willow had sought out Richard at the construction site and they got into an argument over—who knew what? Richard had a violent temper. He whipped out a gun that his father didn't know about and shot the man. But if that were true . . . The picture shifted, like pieces of glass in a kaleidoscope. Why would Richard shoot him at the construction site, where he might come under suspicion? Richard Running Bull might be a hothead, but he wasn't stupid. And he didn't want to go back to prison.

"You gotta get Richard outta jail," Derrel said, his voice tense with fear and hope.

"I'll go see him," Vicky said before hanging up the phone. First she intended to find out what evidence the police had against him.

The skeleton of the apartment complex rose into the steel-gray sky like an ancient ruin on the plains. Workers in blue jeans, plaid shirts and hard hats darted among the posts and half walls, shouts mingling with banging hammers and screeching saws. Vicky peered through the Bronco's windshield, trying to spot Detective Bob Eberhart. The desk sergeant at the Lander Police Headquarters had said she'd find him at the construction site.

She slowed past the pickups along the curb, past the silver trailer that looked dull under a trace of morning dew. Black letters above the door spelled OFFICE. On she drove down the second block. Sounds faded and pickups gave way to three black-and-white police cars at the curb. Yellow tape enclosed a section at the end of the block. She parked behind the last police car and made her way across the hard-churned dirt, the loose nails and scrap wood strewn about. Beyond the tape two policemen in dark blue uniforms guided metal detectors over the ground, shoulders stooped to the task.

She spotted Eberhart and another uniformed officer in the shadow of a framed alcove. The detective was a slight man in dark slacks and a tweed sport coat that hung loosely from thin shoulders. As she stepped across the tape, he glanced up and started toward her. "Don't think your legal magic's gonna get Running Bull out of this mess," he said.

"What do you have?" Vicky ignored the comment.

"Your client called Clifford Willow and arranged to meet him here"—he glanced at the alcove—"at six-thirty last evening. He was looking to buy some cocaine, which Willow was looking to sell. We've been watching Willow. Had a tap on his phone. I had a car over here at six-thirty sharp, but Willow had already been shot. A couple workmen flagged down the police car. Said they saw Richard Running Bull leaning over a body. We picked him up just as he was getting in his truck."

Vicky felt her stomach muscles clench. Despite what his father had said, Richard was still using drugs. And the police had a phone tap. Witnesses. "What about the weapon?" She braced herself for the answer.

"Expect we'll find it soon enough." Eberhart nodded toward the policemen with metal detectors. "Richard shot Willow over by that pile of boards." Another nod. "Soon's he realized somebody saw him, he made a beeline for the truck." The detective raised one hand and traced the direction of Richard's supposed flight. "He stashed the gun right here somewhere. Dropped it in a hole, stuck it under some lumber. Might take a few hours, but we'll find it. Expect we'll find a bag o' coke in the same place."

"Wait a minute," Vicky said. "Are you saying you didn't find the gun or any drugs on Richard?"

The detective nodded. "Correct."

"No drugs on Clifford Willow?"

"We wouldn't still be lookin' for 'em, now would we?"

"What if Richard didn't make the buy?" Vicky said, marshaling her thoughts. "What if Willow was already dead when Richard got here, and somebody else had taken the cocaine?"

"Nice theory." Eberhart was shaking his head. "I'm willing to bet this badge here"—he patted the pocket of the tweed sport coat—"soon's we locate the gun, we'll find a baggie of coke. Richard ditched them fast. He would've come back for them later."

Suddenly the officer snapped to attention and stepped out of the alcove. "Mr. Jeffries," he called.

Vicky glanced around. A tall man in blue jeans and brown corduroy jacket was striding toward them, boots kicking up clouds of dust. The long, narrow face, the brown hair flattened along the top of his head, the flashing, evil eyes: the man in her dream. Vicky felt her mouth go dry, her breath form a hard rock in her chest. She staggered backward, struggling to find purchase in the chunks of dirt and scraps of wood, steeling herself against the force of evil drawing closer.

"How much longer you gonna keep this area shut down?" The man's voice boomed. "I got fifty men on the payroll sitting on their asses. I'm losin' a lot of money here."

"Sorry, Mr. Jeffries." There was a hint of deference in the officer's tone. "We're still looking for evidence."

Jeffries snorted, then raised a fleshy hand and began patting his nose. He sniffed several times. "What the hell more you need? You got the guy that shot that Indian. I can't afford to pay a bunch of men for not workin'.'" He was stomping back and forth now, punching both fists into the air.

Eberhart took a couple of steps forward and put out one hand in a gesture of peace. As soon as they found the gun, he began—cajoling, assuring—they would release the area.

Vicky stared at the man. The hair and eyes, the dust billowing around—she had seen it all in her dream. With a certainty that froze her in place, she knew that Stephen Jeffries had killed Clifford Willow.

"You got everything fixed?"

Richard Running Bull rose from behind the metal table in the visiting room at the Fremont County jail. He was half a head taller than she was, with a thick chest and muscles that rippled beneath his blue denim shirt. His black hair was parted in the middle and caught in two braids that hung down the front of the shirt. He was about thirty, she knew, but he stared at her out of the solemn eyes of a man twice his age.

"Hello to you, too," Vicky said. She knew he expected her to walk in with a ticket for his release, but it wasn't going to be that easy. The metal door slammed behind her, a low thud that reverberated through the windowless room.

Richard's expression slid from expectation to panic. "I been locked up all night. You gotta get me outta here." He crashed one fist down onto the table. The peaks of his knuckles showed white through his dark skin.

"Sit down, Richard." Vicky nodded toward the chair

he had just vacated. She sat across from him and extracted a pen and legal pad from her briefcase. "Let's start at the beginning."

The Indian dropped slowly onto his chair, shoulders hunched, head forward, as if he were about to launch himself out of the room. "They got it all wrong," he said. "I just knocked off work yesterday when these two clowns in uniforms showed up and slapped on the cuffs. Said I shot some Indian named Clifford Willow. Hell"—both hands flew into the air—"I don't know any Clifford Willow."

Vicky locked eyes a long moment with the man. He was lying. An innocent man did not lie. Last night's dream had overcome her ability to think rationally. She shoveled the pad and pen back into the briefcase, rose from the chair and started for the door.

In an instant, Richard Running Bull was around the table, blocking her way. "Where the hell you going?"

Vicky stepped past him, and he grabbed her arm. "I said, where you think you're going?"

"Take your hand off me." Vicky wheeled toward him. They both knew the guard was just outside the door.

Richard let his hand drop. "You've got to help me," he pleaded.

"I can't help somebody who lies to me. I want the truth from my client. I want you to tell me about the call you made to Clifford Willow, about the drug buy you set up for yesterday."

The Indian flinched, as if she'd slapped him. A look

of resignation came into his eyes. He turned and sank onto the chair. "All right," he said.

Vicky resumed her own seat. She retrieved the notepad and pen as he began explaining. He used to hang around with Willow, a long time ago. He gave a little shrug, as if it weren't important. The two of them—well, the truth was, they did drugs together. A little marijuana. Some coke. No dealin'. That was Clifford's bag, not his. Just usin' once in a while, when he got stressed out, when he needed to party a little.

"What happened yesterday?" On the pad, Vicky wrote: Willow sold drugs.

The man drew in a long breath. His eyes traveled to a corner of the small room before resting again on hers. "I've been real stressed out lately. The boss, Jeffries, wants more work done every day. Walks around the site shoutin' and yellin', 'Speed up, speed up. I'm not payin' you guys to sit on your asses.' Fact is, he hasn't paid anybody for two weeks. Says his money's all tied up. Says he'll pay us next week. Only reason I been staying around is to get what's owed me."

Vicky wrote down: Jeffries—money problems. She said, "So you called Willow."

Richard stared at her a moment, as if weighing his options. "Yeah, I called him. I been clean three months now, and where's it gettin' me? Workin' for a crazy man and not gettin' paid. Willow was supposed to meet me over by the alcove after work, but he didn't show. I waited five, ten minutes. I was headin' for my truck when I seen him over by a pile of boards. Jeez, there was blood everywhere. I got outta there fast. I was just about to get in my truck when the cops showed up."

He leaned toward her; the black braids drooped along the table. "I swear I didn't shoot him. I don't even own a gun."

Vicky was quiet a moment. Then: "Did Willow know Jeffries?"

Richard blinked and leaned back in his chair. "Yeah, I seen 'em together a couple of times at the site."

Vicky put her things back into the briefcase and got to her feet. She began explaining: He'd had the misfortune to be arrested Friday evening. The initial court appearance wouldn't be until Monday.

Richard had started to get up. He sank back against the chair and put one fist to his mouth. She knew that he knew he would spend the weekend in jail.

She said, "I'll do what I can." A hollow promise, she realized, given that he had set up the drug buy. But he didn't kill Willow. The trouble was, she had no idea how to prove it.

Vicky drove north on the reservation. The foothills of the Wind River Mountains raced by outside her window, a blur of pine trees and scrub brush. Beyond the passenger window, the plains ran brown and humpbacked into the horizon. Every mile or so a small frame house appeared on the landscape, as if it had dropped from the sky. Slowing the Bronco, Vicky swung into a dirt driveway and stopped in front of a white bi-level.

Everything seemed familiar. The dirt yard with a

truck parked at the edge, the sheets and towels flapping on the clothesline, the hollow rap on the front door and the footsteps hurrying inside, the feel of Grandmother Ninni's arms gathering her in.

Vicky sat across from the old woman at a small table wedged under the kitchen window. Pale daylight slanted over the table as she sipped at the mug of tea and told about her dream: a man she had never seen before coming toward her through clouds of dust. The evil in his eyes. She kept coming back to the overwhelming sense of evil. "He's a murderer," she said. "But there's no evidence, and Richard Running Bull is going to be charged with the murder."

The old woman ran one finger around the rim of her mug, as if she were testing the ridge of a tanned hide to which she meant to sew a beaded design. She said, "You must pay attention to what the Earth is telling you about this evil man, granddaughter."

Vicky waited as Grandmother Ninni took a sip from her mug. Then she went on, her voice so quiet that Vicky had to lean forward to catch the words. "The Earth is angry. It erupts in clouds of dust. You must ask yourself what has made the Earth angry."

Vicky gasped. In her mind's eye, as if in a dream, she saw Stephen Jeffries at the site, sniffing and pawing at his nose, striding up and down, shouting, punching the air. A man on cocaine. He'd been getting his supply from Willow—Richard said he'd seen the two men together at the site. He had taken the coke, then shot the man. And he had hidden the gun in the earth. Stephen Jeffries had defiled the sacred earth.

• • •

Vicky clamped down on the gas pedal. The speedometer needle jumped at eighty as she sped south, diving in and out of the black shadows that drifted down the foothills. She slowed at the outskirts of Lander and threaded her way around the trucks and 4x4s on Main Street. A sharp right, then another right, and she was parking in front of the stone building that housed the Lander Police Department.

She found Eberhart in a small office halfway down the corridor, hunched over a desk piled high with papers. "What do you know about Stephen Jeffries?" she said, dropping onto a metal chair.

The detective pushed back in his chair and shot her a puzzled look. "Jeffries," he said. The pencil in his hand beat out an impatient rhythm on the edge of the desk: tap, tap-tap. "Newcomer to these parts. Brought a lot of jobs to the area."

"He was high on cocaine this morning."

Eberhart gave a burst of laughter and flipped the pencil across the desk. "The man's always like that."

"Always shouting and stomping around. Always impatient."

"You'd be impatient if we shut down part of your operation."

"He's a man with a drug problem, Bob. And a money problem. He hasn't paid his workers in two weeks. My bet is, the money's gone to cocaine."

"As soon as we find the weapon—"

"It's not where you think it is," Vicky interrupted. "Jeffries hid it."

Eberhart raised one hand in protest, but she hurried on: "He saw Willow at the site. He followed him, probably figuring he had drugs on him. They had some kind of argument, and Jeffries shot him. He ran off before Richard showed up."

A look of comprehension crept into the detective's eyes, and Vicky wondered how much he already knew. She said, "Jeffries bought drugs from Willow in the past, didn't he? You were tapping Willow's phone."

Eberhart blew out a long breath. "There's nothing to connect him and Jeffries, but . . ." He hesitated. "There was one call from a pay phone a couple nights ago. Some guy begging Willow for cocaine. Willow told him no more until he'd paid what he owed him."

Silence fell over the small office like a dense cloud. After a moment, Vicky said, "I know how to find the gun."

The street was deserted when Vicky parked in front of the silver trailer. A thin light glowed through the front windows. Beyond the trailer, the construction site was quiet, the framed walls and piles of lumber elongating into dark shadows. It was almost six. Jeffries could have left. She could be too late.

As she hurried up the wooden planks that formed the sidewalk, a voice broke through the dead quiet: "I don't want any more excuses." He was still here! She took a deep breath and knocked at the door.

It swung open. Jeffries threw her a glance before turning back to the desk and shouting into the phone clasped at his ear: "You get the framing finished up

next week, you hear me? You'll get your money then."
He slammed down the phone and, sniffing a couple of
times, allowed his gaze to travel over her. "Didn't I see
you out on the site this morning?"

"I'm Vicky Holden." She forced herself to enter.
The trailer was filled with evil, a presence as real as the
large, brown-haired man behind the desk. She could
hear her own heart beating. "I represent Richard Running Bull," she managed.

The man's eyes bored into her. "What can I do for
you, Madame Attorney?"

"Richard needs this job. You'll take him back, won't
you?"

"Take him back?" Jeffries let out a long whistle.
"That's gonna be kinda hard, with him locked up in
prison the rest of his life."

Vicky forced a smile. "I see you haven't heard."

"Heard what?" A wary look came into those eyes.

"The police found the murder weapon today. It
wasn't near the alcove where they'd expected to find
it, and Richard didn't have time to hide it anywhere
else. He'll be released soon and . . ." She allowed the
information to float between them. "No doubt the police will arrest the real killer."

The man was quiet. Vicky watched for the slightest
twitch of a muscle, the flick of an eyelid. There was
nothing. She said, "What about the job?"

"Why not?" Jeffries pinched the tip of his nose between two fingers. "He gets himself out of jail, he's
got a job."

Vicky thanked him and backed out the door, pulling

it shut behind her. She could feel his eyes on her through the window as she stepped along the planks and slid into the Bronco. She drove a half block and parked behind a Dumpster. There were no police cars about, no sign of anyone, yet Eberhart had said he'd send some officers. For a sickening moment, she wondered if the detective had only pretended to believe her theory.

She let herself out of the Bronco and started across the construction site, picking her way by the light filtering from the street lamps, past the half walls and the piles of boards, until she had a clear view of the trailer. The front door opened. Jeffries stepped into the doorway, a dark figure backlit by the dim glow inside. He cast his eyes about, making sure the way was clear. Then he stepped out and started toward her. Vicky felt her heart turn over. She pulled back into the shadows and held her breath as he passed. He was so close she could have reached out and touched him.

She watched him head across the site, boots kicking at the wood scraps and bent nails, at the earth, and the dust rising, rising. And then he was lost in a forest of posts and shadows. She hesitated a moment, half expecting a police car to pull up to the curb. Then she started after him, trying not to stumble over the loose boards.

She spotted him leaning over a large wooden box. Metal clanked against metal as he pulled out a shovel. He took several steps to the right—counting the steps, she thought—then veered left a few more steps before he rammed the shovel into the earth and tossed some dirt to the side. Dust rose around him and hung in the faint light.

Suddenly Jeffries jerked about and squinted into the dust. Vicky stood still, praying that the shadows would hide her. Satisfied, he tossed the shovel aside, fell onto his knees, and began pawing at the earth with both hands.

Still no sign of the police. Where were the police? Vicky moved behind a post, her eyes still on the man. In another second he would have the gun. He would dispose of it somewhere, and no one would ever find it.

Jeffries was on his feet. In his hand was a small, dark object. He swung around and started toward her. She had the sickening realization that she'd waited too long, that she was trapped. There was nowhere to run.

The man was coming closer. He saw her now. The brown eyes bored into her with a look of pure malevolence. Slowly he raised his arm and pointed the small object at her. She was frozen in place, her breath stopped in her throat, just as in her dream. The earth shuddered beneath her feet. And then she heard the crunch of footsteps approaching from the side.

"Drop the gun, Jeffries." Eberhart's voice reverberated off the framed walls. Jeffries swung around, then let the gun fall to the earth. In a moment, the detective and two officers were surrounding him, clamping on handcuffs, reading him his rights. "You're under arrest for the murder of Clifford Willow," the detective said.

Vicky stepped from behind the post. "I thought you'd never get here," she said to the detective.

"Bitch," Jeffries hissed. In the glare he shot at her, Vicky felt the force of the man's evil, but she no longer felt afraid. The dust had settled, the air was clear. She could see beyond the shadows to the light glowing over the street. The earth was strong beneath her feet.

The inhabitants of Cabot Cove often remind me of the small, close-knit villages in the British Isles, where friendships are lifelong, and neighbors will pitch in to help out when needed. But woe to those who think they can just wander in and change centuries of tradition in one fell swoop. As the unfortunate business owner discovers in this next story, these types of villages also have their own way of dealing with outsiders.

The Most Beautiful Place on Earth

Eileen Dreyer

It didn't do a body any good at all to live in the most beautiful place on earth. Not that the old man would have put it that way. If the old man were wont to express an opinion, he did it in the age-old ways of a Kerryman. A twist of the head, a wink of the eye, a click of the tongue. Maybe if he were really moved, he'd spit. Just once. Right there at his feet. Or he'd carry up his pipes and join the session at the Islandman of an afternoon, where the music swept the room faster than a west wind and truths not told in words would curl and lift with the smoke beneath the low, dark ceilings.

But say it out loud? No. He'd just stand here in his doorway and watch the water, the velvet expanse of headland that lifted like a woman's bare shoulder from the sea. The thick rock walls and paint-spattered sheep. The sad-eyed, whitewashed houses that lay tucked into folds of land where the wind couldn't worry at them on an endless winter night. He'd stand there as he'd done nearly every evening of his life, as his father had done and his father before him, smoking and watching as the evening settled and the world went on in peace.

The old man had been born here, no more than fifteen feet behind him. He'd worked here alongside his father and brother, scratching a living from the land, a bonus from the sea, a whimsy from the wind. He'd outlived them all, even his Mary and the children she'd borne him. He understood this land in ways no man could explain, where the old ways held it was enough to have the land and its people who banded together to solve a problem free of asking, accepted thanks in the coin of a pint, and celebrated their success afterward with songs and stories and bawdy friendship.

It was enough. It had been, anyway, until the buses had begun to come. Big buses, the bedamned behemoths, with exhaust belching out the back and querulous voices drifting from the windows. Tourists with cameras and trash cluttering up his yard and following him around his farm with demands for just one more picture. They'd harried his animals and twice run over his bicycle where it lay near the barn and knocked over carefully laid fences without so much as asking his pardon.

He hated those great foul beasts, the buses. He'd even begun to hate the people who followed them around the headlands. Not all of them. Not most of them. But enough of them. The ignorant ones and the arrogant ones and the selfish ones. And more than any of them, he hated the ones who condescended in their fancy blue jeans and overpriced tourist sweatshirts that said "Ireland" on them, as if they needed reminding just what island it was they were littering all over, who treated the old men who watched them go by as if missing teeth and a shovel in the hand made a person simple.

But he'd been dealing with that lot all right, really he had. He'd been shooing them off with Irish imprecations they'd thought quaint and the bushy end of his broom if it needed it. And, after all that, by the time he stood out in his doorway at the end of the day, they'd gone and left him be with his pipe and his silence and his perfect peace.

And then Murphy had gone and died.

The old man took a look over at Murphy's old house, a good solid Irish type of house with two grand stories and seven windows in the front, a house he'd always been welcome in. He looked at it, all right. And then he spat. Once. Right at his feet.

Murphy had died, and his family had sold his house to one of those people who'd stopped by on the bus. One who decided to stay. And that witch of a woman, coming over to the west coast of Ireland all the way from California, had created the abomination. Out of Murphy's house.

The old man spat again.

Bears. Bright pink bears. Painted all over two stories' worth of whitewashed walls. Ugly, ten-foot nightmares with maniacal grins and lumpy heads. Right there where he and Murphy had spent summers whitewashing over a couple pints of ale and a song or two.

He'd offered his help to paint them out. He'd offered the whitewash himself. Hell, he'd offered real paint, because she was a stranger, and a body didn't just walk up to a stranger and tell her she was daft as hell for desecrating the most perfect place on earth.

She had looked down at him when he made the offers as if he hadn't a thought in his head. She told him she *wanted* the bears up there; she didn't care what anybody else thought. It was her house, and her bears, and he could just live with it. He could live with the bears and the parking lot she'd poured over the remains of the old monastic enclosure and the bad circus music she thought would attract people to her house. The kind of people, he was finding, who thought old men had no rights.

The old man looked over, just one more time, the sight of those grinning bears stoking up his indignation. He'd be dead before he just "lived with it." He thought to spit again, but it wasn't enough. It wasn't the old way, and it wasn't his way. Reaching behind him into the house, he grabbed his cap and set it on his head. He had business to attend to, and he had to do it at the pub. Maybe he'd spit there.

•   •   •

What was the point of having money if you couldn't live in the most beautiful place on earth? Mary Thelma Ware, who swore her family was probably from Cork some time back, even though she couldn't exactly prove it, stood at her front door for just a moment watching her neighbor stomp off up the road.

Old coot. Who the hell did he think he was, God? Martha friggin' Stewart, telling her she couldn't have her cute bears here where she could bring in the bus traffic to eat quick-bake scones and Lipton tea at the new shop she was opening? And like calliope music really offended his damn cows or something. What kind of idiot did he think she was? He didn't like what she was doing to his precious peninsula, he could just move. God knows she had. Seven times. And that was just in the last five years.

This time, though, she was staying put. If the locals couldn't figure out what a fat tourist dollar this place could bring in, well, she could. And she didn't need the locals with their smiling, carefully polite dissension to show her the better way, either. Yeah, yeah, they had their old ways and centuries of tradition here. They had neolithic tombs and stone circles and those cute little stone huts where monks used to live back around Christ or something. So what? The monks had been dead fifteen hundred years. They weren't going to miss a rock or two. They sure as hell weren't going to use any of those rooms she'd turned into parking spaces, were they?

Mary Thelma Ware (ancestors definitely from Cork County—or maybe Dublin) squinted out toward the western sea, where the water foamed gently against the lip of the Great Blasket Island. She had to get out there today. She'd left her good Icelandic sweater out there yesterday when she'd gone to gather material from those old empty houses—another one of those protected places everybody crabbed at her about—and now she was afraid she wasn't going to find it when she went back.

They'd do that, too, purely for spite. Sneak off with a three-hundred-dollar sweater and hide it from her as if they didn't have a perfectly good idea how much it was worth. They'd sure hurried her to the ferry, as if the fate of the western world rested on five people in an oversized tugboat making schedule for some piss-ant little dock in the middle of nowhere. And they sure as hell hadn't helped her look for it once she'd realized it was missing. Which meant they were probably going to sneak out today and steal it, just to pay her back in their close-mouthed, close-minded way.

Like she was going to be any more upset than any of the other times they'd tried to convince her to behave. She didn't have to behave, damn it. That was why she had money.

Only one thing to do. Swinging her oversized carpetbag purse over her plump, pink-and-sequin–sweatshirted shoulder, Mary Thelma pulled out her car keys. The old man next door had said that the Dunquin ferry wasn't in service today. Well, somehow, she was going to get to the Blaskets. She guessed she'd just have to ask at the bar down the road.

•   •   •

"No," the girl behind the bar said as she carefully pulled a pint for a customer. "I haven't heard there's any difference. Joe? You heard if the ferry's back in?"

From his place at a battered square handkerchief of a table, a ruddy, bushy-browed local shook his well-endowed red head. "Ah, no, lass," he said. "That engine's somethin' desperate. Might take days."

Perched at the counter, his flat cap laid on the counter before him like an offering, the old man paid attention only to the pint the barmaid was handing him. She got a twist of his head. A wink of the eye. She smiled back as if he'd kissed her.

"I have to get to that island today," Mary Thelma insisted to the girl, as if Joe hadn't even spoken. As if the old man weren't even in the room, or the other handful of people—a couple of old men playing chess and a young, backpack-ladened couple trying to read topographical maps by the yellowing light that filtered in through handblown windows.

"You'll not be doin' that today, I'm thinkin'," Joe said. "Sure an' the sheep won't steal the thing. They've sweaters of their own, don't they now?"

The girl behind the bar, bright-eyed and blond, stacked glasses and giggled. The old man clicked his tongue. Mary Thelma flushed to the noticeable roots of her rather brassy blond hair. "There are squatters over there."

"Just the weaver and the lad from the north sellin' tea," the girl protested. "They're nice."

"Besides," Joe said, "the ferry's not goin'. Unless you can fly?"

"There was that fancy camera went lost last week," one of the locals piped up. "Weaver said a rabbit ate it."

Joe nodded in commiseration. "Them rabbits are fierce large now, aren't they?"

Mary Thelma held her temper. "I think you're all doing it on purpose," she snapped. "You've been trying to inconvenience me from the minute I showed up. You probably think this is delightful."

The girl stiffened with insult. "No, now really—"

"And you know it!" Mary Thelma insisted, a pudgy finger directed at the girl's startled face. "And you know damn well I don't need that damn ferry. Every one of you people rows some kind of boat out there. You want me to pay for the trip? Well, I'll pay for it. And if I don't pay somebody here, I'm sure I can pay somebody down the road."

"Not on a day like today," Joe demurred with a shake of his carroty head. "Most of the lads are up burning off the fields."

Mary Thelma glared at the young barmaid, as if this were all her fault. "And I suppose you don't know anybody either, huh?"

"You want to go so bad," the girl snapped back, "Mr. O'Connell has a curragh he takes over to fish. But then, the way you treat him, I wouldn't be surprised if he told you to swim."

Mary Thelma's first reaction was to blanch, hands clenched at her considerable sides. Even before her fingers loosened, however, she'd turned to consider the old man from next door.

"You really row out there?" she asked, her voice leveling magnificently.

"Happens I do," the old man said without looking her way.

There was silence then, even the couple in the corner forgetting their soda and sightseeing to follow the drama.

"I'll pay you," she said. "A lot."

The old man looked her way. The other people in the bar couldn't help but notice how thin the old man was, how his hair, let loose from beneath his flat cap, lifted in little tufts over the high dome of his forehead. How watery his blue eyes were in the cool dimness of an afternoon pub.

"I'll not take your money," he said and went back to his beer.

Mary Thelma ground her teeth. "I'll turn down my music."

There was another pause, tight and elastic, and then the old man made a show of finishing his pint. "I'm goin'," he said, setting the glass on the bar with a thunk. "You can come or not. Though, you'll need to follow my orders. A curragh isn't a toy boat, and that, by God, isn't a bathtub out there."

Mary Thelma swung her great bag over her shoulder once more. "I'll be waiting."

She didn't follow his orders. At least that was what the old man said when they fished him out of the water two hours later. They brought him back to the pub where they wrapped him in blankets and warmed him with tea and whisky and waited as the bright new Garda officer gently asked him how the tragedy had transpired.

"The daft thing wouldn't listen," he said fretfully. "I told her the curragh is a delicate thing. That she couldn't just be standing up in the middle of the ocean like it was a swimmin' pool. I had enough just handling the boat, didn't I then?"

The audience nodded as if at a recital. The young couple had gone with the light, but the neighbors had come, drawn to the smell of tragedy and drama, the flicker of blue lights and a shrouded figure rolled up from Dunquin harbor.

"She insisted you row her out, Mr. O'Connell?" the policeman asked, his young eyes only seeming to focus on the palsy of the old man's hand, the liver spots on his high, domed head. It was the lad's first posting from Dublin, after all, and he didn't really know curraghs or currents yet.

The old man gave his head a twist. "Daft," he said again. "Told her the ferry'd be back tomorrow. Wanted that sweater."

Another round of nods, contemplative sipping at half-full glasses. Communal bemusement, commiseration. The Garda officer sketched a few more notes, reclaimed his hat from the bar and climbed to his feet.

"Come on back after, then," said Joe, who owned the pub. "You'll have a pint on us, sure."

The officer nodded, set his hat and patted the old man, and then he left to follow the wagon across the mountains. Left behind, the neighbors sipped and thought and pulled out their smokes.

As the weather went bad for them, it wasn't yet until another two days before they got the chance to gather again. They came with ladders and buckets and brushes and beer, with smiles and stories and the shared memories of all who lived on the peninsula. And together they buried the bears.

"What happens now then, girl?" the old man asked the young blond girl from the pub as the two of them perched twenty feet above the ground on rickety ladders.

Taking a moment, the girl considered the land where it dipped and swept to the sea. She listened to the music of laughter and song and bawdy camaraderie that surrounded her. And, for the first time since she could remember, she smiled with a sense of homecoming.

"Well," she said, slathering good, thick white paint over a big, brown bear eye, "now that my mother's dead, I guess the house is all mine. I hope you don't mind if I stay. This is the most beautiful place on earth."

The old man looked at the bright-eyed young girl and smiled. "You're very welcome here, lass. You're very welcome indeed." And then, with a wink, he patted her on the arm. "But then, now that we fixed the ferry you might want to go over and get that grand little sweater you hid from the old girl, shouldn't you?"

In all my travels, England ranks as one of my favorite places to explore. I find the sense of history almost palpable in the Tower of London. Reading this next story made Renaissance England come alive, as a lady of a country estate takes up her maidservant's cause to uncover a thief in the manor.

lady Appleton and the london Man

Kathy Lynn Emerson

❧

"Folk hereabout call him the London Man." Jennet gestured toward the stranger at the far side of the gardens. "That is Master Baldwin."

Even as she wondered how her housekeeper could identify the fellow with such ease when this was his first visit to Leigh Abbey, Susanna Appleton had to smile at the sentiment behind the ekename. To country-dwellers who'd never traveled farther from their homes than Dover or Canterbury, London was as foreign a place as France or Spain. Wealthy city merchants like Master Baldwin aroused their darkest suspicions, especially when they purchased rural estates from the impoverished heirs of local gentry. Bald-

111

win might now own a goodly parcel of land in Kent, but he was an outsider and would remain so.

"We will wait for him here," Susanna said, coming to a halt in the ornamental garden, a semicircular space planted with shrubs, flowers, and a few fruit trees.

Their visitor had not yet seen them, although 'twas plain one of the servants had told him where to look. The gardens on the south side of Leigh Abbey covered nearly an acre, far more extensive than the ones the monks had planted when the manor was, in truth, an abbey.

On this early August day in the year of our Lord fifteen hundred and sixty-two, Susanna had suggested a midmorning walk in pleasant surroundings in order to assure that Jennet, once her tiring maid, long her friend and companion, and now her housekeeper, did not wear herself out with work. Jennet would be delivered of her third child in a few months, several weeks before the second reached the one-year mark.

From a stone bench situated beneath an ancient oak planted on a little knoll, the two women had a splendid view. Susanna watched Baldwin pass through her herb garden and continue his advance between the long rows of parallel beds in the vegetable garden. He looked, she decided, like one of his own sturdy merchant ships under full sail.

Her new neighbor was stocky but not fat, with broad shoulders and surprisingly small feet. As he came closer, Susanna judged that he was a bit shorter than she was, but then she was tall for a woman, a legacy from her father. She'd also inherited his square jaw and his inquiring mind.

Baldwin appeared to be no more than thirty, though his brown hair had some white in it. He had regular features behind a fine beard, but at the moment, having spotted the two waiting women, they were much contorted by irritation.

She rose when he reached the base of the knoll, making her countenance stern as a schoolmaster's. Why should a man she'd never met be so wroth with her? He seemed to be glowering at Jennet, too.

"Who are you, sir? And what business brings you to my home?"

Taken aback by her challenging stance, Baldwin hesitated, but only for a moment. "Good day to you, madam." He doffed his plumed bonnet, then replaced it with enough force to tell her he could barely contain some powerful emotion. "I am Nicholas Baldwin, your neighbor."

Had he been a dragon, Susanna decided, he'd be breathing fire. She thought his scowling face and snapping eyes would look well on a carved wooden figurehead . . . if the piece graced the prow of a pirate vessel.

"And your business here, Master Baldwin?"

He glanced at Jennet, then quickly back to Susanna. "It might be best if your husband were present."

"Impossible," Susanna informed him. "Sir Robert left five days ago on the queen's business. I do not expect to see him again for many months."

Gentleman, courtier, and sometime intelligence gatherer for the Crown, Sir Robert Appleton was often away for long periods of time. In his absence, Susanna ran his estates. In truth, she managed them even when he was in England. Though it galled Robert to admit it, she was better at such things than he was.

Again Baldwin looked in Jennet's direction, but this time his gaze remained fixed upon her. "I came here seeking this woman, Lady Appleton. I believe your servant stole something that belongs to me. Something of great value."

Deluded as one fit for Bedlam, Susanna thought, until she remembered that Jennet had been able to identify Master Baldwin before he introduced himself. And the look now overspreading the housekeeper's face might indeed be guilt. Jennet's eyes were wide and her skin had lost all color. For a moment, Susanna feared the younger woman might faint.

She should have known better.

Servant she might be, but Jennet had never been backward about speaking her own mind. Hands on her ample hips, she recovered in a trice from her shock at Baldwin's claim and returned his irate stare with one of her own. Her position atop the knoll allowed her to look down her nose at him.

"I never stole anything!" she declared. "I am innocent as a newborn babe."

Had the accusation not been so serious, Susanna would have applauded the show of bravado. Unfortunately, the law was clear. Theft of goods worth more than a shilling was punishable by execution.

Baldwin looked unconvinced by the heartfelt protest. He shifted his attention to Susanna once more.

"I must have my property back, madam. If it is returned to me without further ado, I will not bring charges against anyone in this household. Indeed, I will say nothing more of the incident to anyone."

If the claim that Jennet was a thief had been outrageous, this promise of leniency seemed more so. Master Baldwin, Susanna concluded, had something to hide.

"You are blunt, Master Baldwin," she told him.

"I am truthful, Lady Appleton."

"Why do you suspect Jennet?"

"She was seen in my house a week past, lurking in places she had no business, creeping about in a furtive manner."

"I did but pay a visit to Master Baldwin's cook!"

Susanna motioned for Jennet to remain silent, fearing she might say too much. Jennet did have a habit of listening at keyholes, but that was a far cry from stealing.

"You delayed long in coming here," she said to her neighbor, and met his eyes, unblinking.

Baldwin looked away first. "I did not discover my loss until this morning, but no one else could have taken it. Of all others, including mine own servants, only your own good husband even knew I had this particular object in my possession."

Susanna did not like the sound of that, but for the moment she let it pass. "What object?" she asked. "What does Jennet stand accused of taking?"

"You have no need to know."

Susanna's eyebrows lifted. She had heard those

words too often from Robert and been obliged to accept them. She owed Baldwin no such obedience.

Under her steady glare, her neighbor's uneasiness grew until 'twas almost palpable. There, she sensed, lay a weakness she could use to her advantage.

"I see no constable at your heels," she said. "No justice of the peace."

"You cannot want me to take the matter to law. Think, madam, of the consequences."

Beside her, Susanna felt Jennet tremble, vibrating with a mixture of outrage and fear at this reminder of her danger. A convicted felon great with child might delay execution until she delivered, but afterward the sentence would duly be carried out.

"I will not permit such an injustice," Susanna declared. She slipped a comforting arm around the other woman's shoulders. Jennet might be adept at spinning tales and able to lie without a qualm when necessity demanded, but she was no thief.

Baldwin looked thoughtful. "All I have heard of you, madam, from the vicar and from my servants, indicates you are a practical woman. This matter is easily settled. Allow me to search here at Leigh Abbey for what I have lost. I am certain I can rely upon your common sense to tell you this is a happy solution."

Flattery did not sway her, but neither did Susanna have any logical reason not to allow Baldwin to scour the premises. In truth, she could think of one very good argument in favor of permitting him to search.

"I will make a bargain with you, Master Baldwin," she said. "You may go through the entire house and all the outbuildings, look in any place you think Jennet might have secreted this stolen item. But when you have done, and have found nothing, you must grant me a favor in return."

"What favor?"

"To be taken to the scene of the crime, where you will answer any question I pose about the theft."

Master Baldwin began to sputter a protest, but Susanna was spared the need to argue with him.

"Lady Appleton is the most skilled person in all England at reasoning out the truth of strange events," Jennet declared.

Baldwin did not look convinced, but he agreed to her proposal with a curt nod of assent. Likely he felt certain he'd find what he sought. Susanna was equally sure he would not.

"Shall we start with the stillroom?" She led him back through the gardens and up to the door of that separate building near the kitchen. "You may look, but not touch," she told him.

Baldwin hesitated in the doorway, taking in the sight of drying herbs surrounded by all manner of equipment for distillation and dozens of jars, pots, and other vessels, all labeled and dated. Apparently, he did not know of her reputation as an expert on herbal poisons. When, after a thorough examination of the rest of the stillroom, his gaze fell upon the black chest in the darkest corner of the room, he did no more than request that she lift the lid.

"The thing I seek is not here," Baldwin admitted

when he saw that it was full of papers, all the notes she had made over the course of many years of study.

In Susanna's company, Master Baldwin investigated every nook and cranny of Leigh Abbey, combing kitchen and bake house, snooping in the servants' quarters, and in the stables, too. He found nothing, and at length the only room left to be searched was the study.

"A pleasant chamber," he remarked, taking in the hearth with the marble chimneypiece, the east-facing window, and the small, carpet-draped table holding crystal flagons and Venetian glass goblets. Susanna did not offer him refreshment. She had no desire to encourage him to linger.

A second table was heavy-laden with leather-bound volumes, and the presence of so many books seemed to intrigue Baldwin. One by one he examined them with something bordering on reverence. Susanna did not think he was still looking for the missing object. Simple curiosity drove him now.

A copy of *Rariorum plantarum historia,* written in Latin by a French physician and botanist, told him she was literate in more than one language. Then he found *A Cautionary Herbal, being a compendium of plants harmful to the health.* This small volume, printed by Master John Day of London two years earlier, bore only the initials S.A. to identify its author, but Baldwin, having just seen the papers in her stillroom, guessed at the truth.

"You wrote this?" he asked.

She nodded. Remaining anonymous had been

Robert's idea, not hers. It had allowed him to claim credit for her work.

Without comment, Baldwin abandoned the books and prowled the small room, stirring the rushes with every step to release the scent of bay leaves strewn among them. He stopped in front of a large engraved map, mounted for hanging, which occupied a place of honor in the room.

Susanna felt herself tense. She forced herself to relax. "Mayhap you would care to look behind the *mappa mundi*?" she asked. "Doubtless there is a hidden panel in that wall."

"This, madam, may be a map of the world, but the term *mappa mundi* properly refers only to written descriptions."

"My husband calls it a *mappa mundi*."

"Sir Robert is a gentleman who dabbles in seafaring and exploration . . . in books and conversation." Baldwin's superior tone implied he himself was a participant in such things, and therefore an authority.

"Have you finished your search?" She heard the testiness in her voice and that annoyed her nearly as much as Baldwin's attitude.

"Aye, I have done what I set out to do."

"Good. I gave orders some time ago for my mare to be saddled."

A few minutes later, she was perched sideways on her horse, both feet resting on a velvet sling and supporting one knee in a hollow cut in the pommeled saddle, but there was a delay in setting out because Jennet

insisted upon coming along and she required the help
of two stout fellows to hoist her onto a pillion.

"You hate going anywhere on horseback," Susanna
reminded her. "Even when you are not great with
child."

"This journey is short," Jennet argued, grasping the
waist of the man in the saddle in front of her.

Plainly, she did not intend to be left behind, and Susanna had to admit that she had every right to accom-
pany them. There was little likelihood now that Jennet
would be arrested or tried, let alone convicted and ex-
ecuted, since Baldwin had found no proof of her guilt,
but neither had he rescinded his accusation. Jennet's
honor was at stake.

Baldwin's house was less than two miles distant if
one went by way of a footpath that ran through Leigh
Abbey's orchards and a small wood and led straight up
to his kitchen door. Master and servant alike had often
used this shortcut over the years. But by the road, the
distance was nearly double, and because there had
been rain during the night, the going was slow.

So was pulling information out of Master Baldwin.
He still refused to reveal the exact nature of the missing item.

"'Twas something meant to be presented to the
queen," he allowed after considerable badgering on
Susanna's part, "to be given to her once certain diplo-
matic goals have been met. I do but hold it in trust for
someone else."

With further encouragement, he was persuaded to
talk about his travels. A merchant adventurer, he'd

only lately returned from Persia where, to hear him tell it, he'd been the first Englishman to set foot in that far-off land, arriving there a full two years ahead of the merchants of the Muscovy Company. He'd been to the court of Tsar Ivan the Terrible, and that of Shah Tahmasp of Persia, and met someone called Abdullah Khan, King of Shirvan. In all, Master Baldwin had spent six and a half years out of England and come home a wealthy man.

When they at last arrived at his house, Baldwin escorted Susanna and Jennet into a private chamber on an upper floor. From Jennet's look of surprise, and by the way she peered with such curiosity into every corner, Susanna concluded that her housekeeper had not had an opportunity to explore this part of the premises on her earlier visit.

There were many charts and maps on the walls, and the London Man kept other treasures in chests and on tables. The display comprised an odd collection of objects, some of which Susanna could not identify.

"Navigational instruments I brought back from my travels," he said, noticing the direction of her gaze. "Your husband found them as fascinating as you seem to."

She was about to ask more about the occasion of Robert's visit when Jennet let out a shriek. Her face was bright red with embarrassment. "I did not think it was alive," she stammered, pointing toward a creature perched atop a silk-covered cushion on the window seat. "And then it opened one eye and stared at me."

"It" was a cat, larger than those Susanna was accustomed to. It had a pushed-in face and was covered with long, white fur.

"His name is Bala," Master Baldwin said of the odd-looking beast. "I brought him back from Persia, too."

Bala continued to stare at them with baleful eyes while Master Baldwin retrieved a small, ornately carved ivory box from a chest and handed it to Susanna. "The queen's gift was kept in this."

"Jewelry," she said. "Of what description?"

"What makes you think it was a jewel?"

"Simple enough. I watched you search Leigh Abbey, saw where and in what you looked. Together with the size of the box, I perceive the object you seek may be contained in a space no bigger than the palm of your hand. Add to that conclusion all you told us of your travels, and my deduction is reasonable. Everyone knows that traders carry valuable jewels to exchange for other goods. The first Muscovy merchants took pearls and sapphires and rubies with them, and travelers to the East regularly bring back jasper and chalcedony."

"It is not a jewel, as it happens, but I cannot fault your logic. You are a most . . . unusual woman."

"Unusual enough to prompt you to tell me what was stolen?"

Baldwin came very near a smile. " 'Twas a carved stone of great age and beauty. The like has never been seen in England before now."

"Why did you think Jennet took this ornament?"

"She was the only one with opportunity, unless you wish me to accuse your husband."

He smiled.

Susanna did not.

She'd known for years that her husband had . . . flaws. It was possible, though it seemed unlikely, that he had removed something he should not have from Master Baldwin's house.

"I discovered the stone missing this morning," Baldwin continued. "The last time I lifted the lid of this box before that, Sir Robert stood beside me."

For a moment, Susanna thought she heard something in Baldwin's voice, a hint that it had not been Jennet he'd first suspected, but Robert.

"You did not check to be certain it was still there as soon as he left? How careless of you, Master Baldwin." To avoid meeting his eyes, she crossed the room to the window seat to make a closer inspection of the odd-looking cat. The fur was passing soft to the touch.

Her mild sarcasm had Baldwin blustering. "I had been advised, by someone high in Her Majesty's government, that the head of the household at Leigh Abbey could be trusted."

"Whoever told you that, he's more likely to have meant Lady Appleton than Sir Robert," Jennet blurted.

Baldwin trained his intense gaze on the housekeeper. "You are a strange sort of servant," he told her.

Deciding he'd had enough of a stranger's attentions, the cat Bala abruptly rose and leapt down from his cushion. A moment later, he began to play with a lightweight wooden disk. A checker, Susanna realized. Part of a set.

"I have been looking for that," Baldwin muttered,

stooping to retrieve it. "This is yours," he told the cat, and tossed a square of canvas stuffed with pungent-scented catnip toward the center of the room.

Bala ignored the offering.

Susanna smiled. If Master Baldwin was the sort to make toys for a pet, there was hope he might yet learn to appreciate the advantages of individuality in servants and to value intelligence in women. The best way to convince him was to solve the mystery of his missing carving.

"What does your stolen stone look like?"

Still watching the cat, he answered her. "In color it is an intense apple green. No more than six barleycorns high, it has been wondrous well-carved and fashioned into a little figure of a horse."

Jennet would have no interest in such a thing, Susanna realized, but Robert was uncommon fond of horses. After a thoughtful silence, she began to muse aloud. What was most important at the moment was to clear her housekeeper of suspicion.

"Although I see no sign that anyone broke into this room," she said, "you must agree it is scarce secure. This window is an easy climb from the ground. The stone might have been taken at any time since you showed it to Robert. Tell me, was it in this chamber that he inspected the piece?"

"We took the box with us when we went down to the winter parlor near the kitchen, where my cook had set out a modest repast. It was there that your housekeeper was seen, Lady Appleton, though none of my servants thought to mention her presence to me until after I discovered the carving was missing and began to question them."

Master Baldwin led the way to the lower floor, with even Bala following after him, but the cat soon tired of their company and left the winter parlor by way of yet another open window.

"When is Jennet supposed to have had opportunity to steal the carving?" Susanna asked. "When was the box out of your possession?"

"I left it on that table when I bade Sir Robert farewell. I saw him off, through the front of the house, then returned here to collect the stone."

So, he had not looked again into the box. To clear Jennet, all Susanna had to do was accuse Robert.

Instead she asked for a few days to consider the problem, hinting that the local folk would confide in her, where to Master Baldwin they would plead ignorance, "You are a foreigner in their eyes."

"Aye," he agreed. "A London Man."

"Well, Jennet?" Lady Appleton asked when they were well on their way back to Leigh Abbey. They had sent the horses on ahead with the groom and taken the footpath. No one was in the wood to overhear what they might say to each other.

"I did not take the little horse."

"But you were at Master Baldwin's house the day Sir Robert visited him."

Reluctantly, Jennet nodded.

"And you were in the parlor."

"Aye. How could I not be curious when I heard Sir Robert's voice?"

"So you crept into the room and hid yourself so that you might listen to whatever he said to Master Baldwin."

Jennet did not try to deny it. Susanna knew her habits too well. "When they left the little box behind, I wanted to see what was in it. I dashed across the room and opened the lid to peep inside."

"And was the stone there?"

"Oh, aye, but I scarce had time to admire it before I heard Master Baldwin returning. I closed the lid again and hid myself in the alcove behind the wall hanging until Master Baldwin collected his box and carried it away. Then I left his house and came straight home."

So, the carving had still been in the box when Robert left.

"What do we do now, madam? I find it passing unpleasant to be thought a thief."

"Nor do I like having Master Baldwin think you one, Jennet."

And she did not like suspecting Robert, but she knew her husband well. Though she could not guess his motive, she accepted that it was within the realm of possibility that Robert had returned to Baldwin's house and stolen the stone from the upper chamber.

She would find the truth, she vowed. She was just not certain what she would do with it when she did.

Sir Robert Appleton had given his wife no reason to expect him to return to Leigh Abbey before he left the country on his latest mission for the Crown, but he was there when Susanna and Jennet reached home. Susanna found him in the study, just lifting down the *mappa mundi* to get at the wall behind it.

"I thought you were to set sail from London," she said as he removed a panel to reveal his accustomed hiding place for small valuables.

"I must cross the Narrow Seas to meet my ship off the coast of France." Leigh Abbey was on the road between London and Dover. To break the journey there was not suspicious in itself, but Susanna could not like this new development.

"You had best make haste," she advised, "before you are arrested."

The glance he shot at her over his shoulder conveyed annoyance. Theirs had been an arranged marriage, and although they managed as well as most couples, nowadays there was little love between them and less liking. "Have you some particular reason to think I will be?"

In clipped sentences, she told him of Master Baldwin's visit and his search of the house. She did not, however, mention that it had been Jennet he'd accused of theft.

A furrow appeared in Robert's high forehead, centered between an escaping lock of dark, wavy hair and equally dark brows. Something disturbed him in her report, but she was not certain that meant he had stolen the carving himself. Being accused was reason enough for worry.

"What was in that box was intended as a gift for the

queen," Robert said after a moment. "It was to have been given to Her Majesty after the men of the Muscovy Company, with whom Baldwin was associated in his youth, make the first official contact with the Shah. Baldwin's visit to Persia was not authorized."

Susanna waited, letting the silence lengthen until he was driven to fill it.

"The theft of that piece could thwart a political alliance between England and Persia."

"Who would want to do that?"

"You have no need to know."

"I have every need if blame falls on anyone at Leigh Abbey. What was your business with Master Baldwin? Why did he show you the carving?"

"I tell you, madam, that is none of your concern."

As Susanna watched, unable to subdue the anger his attitude provoked, Robert removed a number of oilskin-wrapped papers from the opening behind the panel and tucked them into the front of his dark green doublet. Then he reached in again for something smaller, which he likewise tucked away beneath the heavily embroidered velvet garment. She blinked. Had he just palmed the little horse?

She wished she'd had time to look behind the map before he returned. No woman wanted proof her husband was a thief, but not knowing one way or the other was far worse. Perhaps she had been too clever earlier, diverting Baldwin's attention from the map with her sarcastic suggestion that he might find a hiding place behind it. She had not suspected then that Baldwin might have his own doubts about Robert's honesty.

Now she realized that by accusing the servant rather than the master, he'd achieved the same end, a search of Leigh Abbey, with far less opposition.

When Sir Robert's hiding place was once more concealed, he approached his wife. "Farewell, my dear," he said, catching her to him for a rough parting kiss before she could evade him. "I have no time to deal with our new neighbor. You must take care of the matter as you see fit."

He knew she took seriously the vows she'd made when they wed. She had sworn to obey him. Echoes of his taunting laughter lingered in the room long after he'd gone.

Susanna did not follow after her husband to see him away on his journey. The days were long past when she'd felt obliged to offer the traditional stirrup cup and blessing.

Instead she stared at the map. In her mind, she saw Robert reaching into the wall that second time. To take something small out? Or to put something in?

Master Baldwin had said the carving was no more than six barleycorns high. She glanced down at her own hand. Strong and work-hardened, the nails blunt, the skin stained with the residue of various herbal preparations, it was large enough to conceal an object that size. A hand half as big could do so. It followed that Robert might easily have concealed the little horse from her just now.

Susanna knew the nature of professional intelligence gatherers, her husband in particular. They tended to complicate matters which otherwise would have been most simple. It would be just like him, she decided, to put back the carving while trying to make her believe he'd removed it. Her mind full of possibilities, she took a step closer to the map.

Early the next morning, Susanna once again followed the footpath, this time walking from Leigh Abbey to Master Baldwin's property alone. She paused to examine several likely places along the way, the last just at the point where the path came out of the wood and plunged steeply downhill toward the manor house.

Barely a quarter of an hour later, when Master Baldwin joined her in his winter parlor, she handed over the missing horse. His fingers curled tight around the apple-green stone, he waited for an explanation.

"You said, did you not, Master Baldwin, that you left the box containing that stone unattended when you escorted mine husband to the door?"

"Aye, I did."

"And the box was not locked?"

"No. I did not turn the key until I returned. You know already that I did not look inside."

"And Bala, I perceive, is a very clever cat."

"Bala?" He blinked at her in surprise.

"The cat took your little carved stone."

"Bala?" he repeated, thunderstruck.

"I found that carving along the footpath that runs between this house and Leigh Abbey," she explained. "It is small and lightweight. Easy enough for a cat to carry off in its mouth. When Bala tired of it, he must have dropped it there, where it could not be easily seen for the ruts and twigs and leaves."

"I did not search along any path," Baldwin admitted. "I did not realize there was one connecting our two properties until yesterday."

As she'd expected, Susanna thought.

Baldwin abruptly crossed the room to where the large white feline slept atop a carpet-covered table. There was no question in Susanna's mind that the cat could have done what she'd said he had. And she knew that he, in common with all cats, must roam far and wide in search of mice and other prey.

"This cat was well named," Baldwin muttered. "In the language of Persia, Bala means nuisance."

For a moment, Lady Appleton feared Master Baldwin might harm the animal. He picked Bala up and held him at arm's length, but all he did was give him a hard stare. Then, shaking his head, he cuddled the cat in his arms and turned to face his neighbor.

The show of affection wrenched at Susanna's heart. She was suddenly very tired of cleaning up after Robert, of allowing him to take the credit for her accomplishments, of letting him shift the blame for his less honorable actions to others. And she had never liked lying.

Did she dare tell Master Baldwin that the carving *had* been behind the map? That Robert had by stealth entered the upper room of this house and stolen the stone? When he'd believed his theft discovered, he'd shown no remorse, only left his wife, as always, to clean up after him, to "take care of the matter" as she thought best.

Words came out in a rush. "Bala did not—"

"Mean to cause so much trouble," Baldwin finished for her. "I am well aware of that. Perhaps you will allow me to send a small gift to your housekeeper, by way of apology?"

"She would appreciate that, but I—"

This time he held up a hand to stop her. "The end result is the same. Through your involvement, your desire to protect those close to you, I have the carving back. 'Tis best we say no more about it."

The look in his eyes brought to an abrupt end any need to confess. It was a curious mixture of triumph and compassion.

For that brief moment, Lady Appleton and the London Man shared a perfect understanding of the truth.

As much as I enjoy being an author, I'm even happier when someone comes up to me and says that my novels have inspired them to try their hand at writing. Although not easy, the craft is one of the most rewarding I know. Writing takes center stage in this story, as a guest teacher uncovers more than she bargained for in this story of plots within plots.

The Workshop

Kate Gallison

It was only a two-hour fiction workshop. There wasn't any way to know my students in depth. All I had were the fifteen manuscripts, and the faces of the twenty or so people gathered in that small classroom. Sometimes I didn't know who wrote what, since the conference didn't supply tags that year, and I have a marked inability to match faces with names.

If one story, one writer, was different from all the others, was somehow not right, I wasn't experienced enough as a teacher, or as a reader of other people's work, to pick up on the abnormality. I had never taught a workshop before. I was more interested in impressing these people with my competence as a teacher of writing than in analyzing them. The fact is, I have no academic credentials whatever; what I am is a self-taught, published writer of fiction, which is why Professor Byfield asked me to do the workshop.

But there they all were, paying good money to receive some sort of value from me, some help for their own writing.

And it was bad. I must tell you that I was horrified by most of the manuscripts Professor Byfield sent to me before the event. What could I tell them without giving offense? Professor Byfield had been so careful to impress upon me the importance of giving encouragement to everyone who enrolled. Yet many couldn't spell or parse sentences, let alone manipulate the ordinary tools of writing—foreshadowing, pacing, transitions, metaphor and what-have-you.

I was terrified. Later I came to understand that the level of emotional investment in their writing was different for each student. Some were not serious at all. For some, as it turned out, what they handed in was something hastily slapped together, or an old piece pulled out of a drawer as a sort of ticket to get into the workshop. For others, what I was looking at was their life's work.

But I didn't know that, sitting with this pile of papers on my kitchen table in the middle of the night. I knew only that I had to say something meaningful and helpful about every one of these efforts, having no idea what effect a severely negative comment might have on a writer.

And I wasn't thinking only of hurt feelings. My agent, for example, receives unsolicited manuscripts all the time, and among the slush one day she found one of those dysfunctional confessions, very badly written, a story of how cruelly its writer had been treated by her psychiatrist. As was her usual habit, having no office help, my agent popped the manuscript into an envelope and returned it with a polite, impersonal note declining to handle it and wishing the writer better luck elsewhere. She did not keep a record of the woman's name or address, which she regretted almost immediately, as soon as the abusive telephone calls began.

The nutcase continued to call, many times a day, leaving ugly messages on my agent's answering machine, curses and death threats. Just when my agent was ready to involve the police (caller ID wasn't available at the time, it was a number of years ago) the final call came.

"This is the end, you rotten bitch. I'm going to kill myself, and it's your fault." The caller hung up and never called again.

Probably she didn't kill herself. Probably she simply turned her attention elsewhere. Probably she's lying on yet another psychiatrist's couch complaining about her treatment at the hands of the person who might have been, with better judgment, her agent.

But maybe she did kill herself.

Thoughts of this sort went through my mind as I confronted the pile of manuscripts. What to say about them that wouldn't drive their writers over the edge, or

worse, send them to Professor Byfield demanding their
money back? I'm very bad with other people's work. I
have my own harsh methods of editing, the methods I
use on my own stuff. Cut, slash, throw out, redo completely. I had to stifle these impulses and work on a
gentler approach.

Okay. What is the intention of the work? Is it successful on its own terms? Why or why not? Working
from this angle, I went through them one by one, and
found to my relief that I was able to write something
encouraging about all fifteen of the papers, even the
one penciled in block letters on yellow legal paper.
You'll be happy to know that this was not a threatening work, but instead a clumsy piece by a sad woman
without access to a typewriter exploring her own reactions to her lover's death.

Hey, I believe in that too. Therapy through writing.
But you don't show it to people. You can't sleep
through grade school, sleep through high school, never
read a word afterwards, and suddenly decide at the age
of forty to express your soul to the public through the
written word, any more than you can suddenly decide
to pick up, say, the violin. Still, her work had a touching directness, and I was able to tell her that. It was
not, of course, publishable.

None of them were, although two or three showed
promise. One of these was a strangely elusive tale
about a boy and girl on their first date. Although the
writer's name was sexually ambiguous, the story was
told from the viewpoint of the girl.

The narrator describes herself as a young, single

professional, comfortably off but looking for something more, some excitement in her life. Her date shows up on a motorcycle, a loner in a leather jacket. She puts on a helmet and climbs on behind. Masterfully, he carries her away on what he says is to be an adventure. They go to the Devil's Teatable, where they sneak through a fence and gaze off the cliff at the distant scenery. She is both thrilled and frightened by him. In the end he takes her home and they part friends, both of them aware that they are not one another's type.

Parts of this story were very well done. I don't know how well you know the Devil's Teatable. It's a dangerous cliff on a privately owned piece of wild land along the Delaware River. The owners were forced to fence it off some years ago because of teenage drinking parties and other trespassers who sometimes met accidents and death. The writer described the Devil's Teatable at sunset—the misty world below, the light fading slowly from crimson to bruise-colored, the silence pierced by the evening call of a songbird, then the still air humid as breath. It was very immediate, very real. The writer had a certain gift.

The girl's fright, too, was lovingly described.

Strangely, I felt the hair rise on the back of my neck. Then, nothing; he drove her home, they parted. I couldn't understand the point of the story.

The title itself, *Close,* was resonant, but without graspable meaning. All overtones. Did he mean that the girl and the boy almost came close? Or was it something else that came close?

So I suggested that the writer try to be more clear.

It was an uncomfortable thing to write notes not knowing to whom I was addressing them. The writers might be what they seemed, or they could be men writing from the viewpoint of women, women writing from the viewpoint of men, old people pretending to be young, or young people imagining themselves old. Who were they really? Why were they doing this? Presumably all wanted to be writers, whatever that means—to write for money? to write for fame? To make art? Or to communicate with readers, perhaps with future generations of readers? What they wanted from their endeavors was not always apparent from reading what they wrote.

The morning of the workshop dawned at last, and I thought, *Now I will find out.*

They were all seated around the table when I came in, eagerly waiting for me, college boys and girls, grey-haired men and women, everyone beaming. I was charmed. My nervousness about doing this began to dissolve at once. These people were nothing like their work, not clumsy, not whining, not tentative or obscure, but friendly, attractive, and delightful. *They just don't know how to write very well,* I thought. *But I can help them.* The presentation I had prepared, I now saw, was probably too bullying and rigid. Nevertheless I went on with it, as kindly as I could, discussing a bit of each piece in relation to various literary techniques.

As I lectured I tried to guess who had written which story. One by one the faces came forward to me out of the group. The person who did the Devil's Teatable thing (Oh, what was that name? Ashley? Jesse? Lesley? Two syllables, I remember that much) could have been anybody, the intense woman at the other end of the table, the eager young boy at my elbow, or the woman with the florid complexion and dyed red hair.

Now, I must tell you that I'm very bad with names and faces. I know that everyone over a certain age claims to be bad with names, everyone except career politicians, who can get the name, the face, and sometimes the street address on a first meeting. But with me the problem of immediate forgetting is so serious as to make me think of it as a neurological disorder. It isn't that I don't care about other people. I can remember their life stories and things they tell me about themselves long after a single conversation. And I can remember their voices, the pitch and timbre and the way they phrase things. But I have no faces or names to attach these memories to until the third meeting. I believe it's an area of the brain. If you were to open my head up you would probably find it atrophied.

Anyway. Here I was, surrounded by avid students hanging on my words, each waiting for me to help him improve his own particular piece of writing, or to admire it. And even without name tags it was after all possible to identify the writers of most of the things I was reading to the class. The florid woman, for instance, blushed to her roots but said nothing as I read a paragraph from her romantic fantasy. I turned my attention to a page and a half of descriptive material about a person walking into a small town at midnight—evocative description but ultimately pointless.

The intense woman at the end of the table fixed her gaze on me like an eagle sizing up its prey. Her piece, clearly. She was a genius; I had neglected to recognize her genius; what she had come to the workshop for was to find out how to get published in *Atlantic Monthly*. Alas, this was a market I myself had never approached, and I was unable to help her. Maybe they liked stories without any point.

I talked a little bit about each work, and then the writer (if he or she wanted to own up) would say something, and after that anyone else with an opinion would voice it. We talked quite freely. I found the courage to ask them why they wanted to write fiction at all. That was when I found out how little it mattered to some, how much to others. Only a few raised their hands when I asked who was writing for the sake of art, among them the boy who had placed himself next to my chair.

The moment I began to read from the Devil's Teatable story I knew he was the one who wrote it. He seemed to be having, how can I say this, an inordinate amount of fun, a disproportionate amount of fun. I know it can be enormously amusing to have someone look favorably on your work, but for God's sake, it wasn't that good, and I wasn't praising it that highly. He grinned at me, holding my gaze, his face wearing the strangest expression.

When I told him how the point of the story had escaped me, his smile grew all the more broad. I couldn't imagine what was up with him.

Years have gone by since then. I didn't keep a copy

of his manuscript. I've tried and tried to remember his
name and his face; it's no good. I don't know what he
was called, except that his name had two syllables and
could have been used for a girl, and I'm not sure about
the color of his hair or the shape of his face or anything
useful. All I remember is his story, the way he twitched
in his seat to hear me discussing it, and his eyes. Blue,
I think they were. Or maybe hazel. At any rate they
were compelling. Arresting. Mocking.

I keep seeing those eyes, ever since the newspaper
reported the discovery of that poor girl's skeleton in
the woods by the Devil's Teatable. And that's why I
called you, officer. All at once I understood that his art
was not the art of writing at all. He had another art that
he was perfecting.

Once again a writer is at the heart of this story, as our detective's writer's block leads her to attempt to solve a murder in her apartment building. I don't know where these authors get the idea that mystery writers' lives are filled with such goings-on. I daresay that I've never had the problem our heroine is faced with when sitting down to the typewriter.

Murder She Wrote

Sue Henry

"It was a dark and stormy night," Marge entered, desperate to see words, almost any words, on her computer screen.

In a fit of pique she had just deleted three whole pages she had struggled over word by word and finally abandoned the day before—another abortive attempt in a week of trying to write the short story she had promised for an upcoming anthology. The deadline for its submission loomed only a few days away and still it stubbornly refused to come together in her mind or on the page. Every idea had gone nowhere, sputtered to an ignominious halt, or capriciously waltzed off in

some unexpected direction with no form or substance
that resembled a whodunit. Thoroughly frustrated, she
had even looked up words in her thesaurus, vainly hoping one of them would provide a gleam of inspiration;
thumbed fruitlessly through several mystery anthologies; finally given up and gone to a movie billed as
"best action film of the year," which provided her
nothing but nightmares of automatic weapons and
pools of blood.

Now she was again feeling the lack of an idea to get
her started. For a long minute she stared blankly at the
useless phrase she had just entered. A cool fall breeze
swept in through an open window, faintly scented with
dry leaves and a hint of wood smoke, making Marge
wish she were outside in the bright Saturday afternoon
sunshine, but, until her story was written, guilt and determination held her captive in her own apartment.

Abruptly, she stood up, crossed the room, and ran-
domly yanked a couple dozen paperbacks from her extensive collection of mystery authors. Dumping them
onto her desk, she grabbed one, opened it, and entered
its first line into her computer, deleting the *dark and
stormy night*.

"All I had to do to earn some dough was kill a guy."
How ironically fitting, she sniffed. Bruno Fischer
could have had her situation in mind.

Casting *The Fast Buck* aside on the desk, she picked
up another Fischer, *Run for Your Life.*

"Like everybody else, he wanted a handout."
I might as well be reading fortune cookies. She
sighed, but it was true; she was hoping that somewhere

down the line this story would expand her limited budget by a few dollars, if only she could somehow get beyond her infuriating block.

Vaguely, she was aware of angry voices coming from somewhere in the apartment building. As she reached to lay the book atop the first she had closed and put down, something heavy suddenly crashed against the other side of the wall before her desk, hard enough to jar a picture that hung on it and startle her into dropping the volume, which hit the floor with a thump. A female shriek drifted through the thin wall from the bedroom of the apartment next door, followed by the shout of an angry male, "Answer me, you bitch!"

Late Saturday afternoon, and her neighbors, Carole and Larry Ferguson, were at it again in another round of their bitter, ongoing battle that could explode at any hour, but frequently, and usually, kept Marge awake until after midnight, steaming in annoyance at their lack of consideration.

Familiar irritation renewed, she retrieved the fallen book, muttering to herself in exasperation. Then, determined to ignore the intrusion, she opened another mystery and entered its first line.

"It was one of those jobs you take on when things are very lean."

"Thanks a lot, Bill," she told him, placing Pronzini's *Undercurrent* on the growing reject pile. "You're preaching to the choir."

"Something unpleasant was going to happen, something incredibly and overwhelmingly unpleasant,"

Craig Rice informed her from the first page of *Knocked for a Loop*.

"Something already has," she responded, discarding the book and reaching for the next without bothering to enter the line.

She could still hear furious voices from the apartment next door, but the couple had apparently moved to another room, for the sound of their exchange had decreased and she could no longer distinguish their every word.

Frowning, she listened closely for a moment, concerned in spite of herself. Less than a week earlier she had passed the young woman on her way into the building, dark glasses not quite concealing a black eye above a bruised cheekbone. With a helpless shiver of disapproval, Marge returned to her search for literary motivation. There was little she could do about the Fergusons, short of calling the police, and they had already twice come pounding on that door in the past month in response to some other tenant's complaint.

The first line of the next book gave her a chuckle, considering her position as eavesdropper.

"From the broom closet, Consuela could hear the two American ladies arguing in Room 404."

She closed it and laughed again at the title, *The Listening Walls* by Margaret Millar.

The next opening line was advice from Charles Willeford from *Cockfighter:* "First, I closed the windows and bolted the flimsy aluminum door."

"Good idea, Charles."

Rising from the desk, she crossed the room and

eliminated the distant sound of the quarrel by closing both the window and the sliding door that led to what her landlord euphemistically called a balcony. The neighbors had obviously left their sliding door open, not caring that their fights disturbed others and were the subject of gossip.

Heading back to her desk, she noticed a basket of soiled clothing that she had sorted that morning and left by the door, ready to wash. Might as well take it down to the laundry room in the basement and accomplish something worthwhile before resuming her search for a murderous theme. Collecting her house key and a box of detergent, and balancing the basket on one hip, Marge let herself out her front door into an unusually dark hallway. The overhead light was burned out again.

Damn. How long will it take the landlord to replace it this time? she wondered. Tucking the detergent box into the basket, she awkwardly shifted her load, blindly felt for the dead bolt, and finally succeeded in securing the door.

Halfway to the stairs at the far end of the hall, she reached Joel Allen's apartment, number twenty-three, directly across from the Fergusons', heard loud classical music from behind his door, and wondered if he had also been disturbed by the altercation between his nearest neighbors. Joel was a cheerful sort, inclined to be helpful and friendly to other tenants. She had even seen him comforting Carole on the stairs, the morning after one particularly stormy Ferguson combat. But she couldn't blame him for turning up the volume of his beloved music system in an attempt to shut out the repetitious conflict across the hall. As she passed between the two doors, her ear caught the sharp smash and tinkle of breaking glass from behind number twenty-two.

"You bastard. That was my grandmother's," Carole's tearful voice shrilled.

"To hell with you, slut. And to hell with your family, too," the hoarse male voice responded.

"No. Not again. Please don't. . . ."

"I'll kill you. . . ."

Whatever happened next within the apartment generated the unmistakable crashes and thuds of a physical struggle so intense they brought Marge to a halt, staring in distress at the shiny brass knob, dead bolt, and number on the door. Familiar with the layout of the apartment, which was the reverse of her own, she could hear that they were wrestling in the kitchen. More glass shattered against something. Metal cooking utensils and pans clattered to the floor, and what could have been one of the two combatants fell against the wall with a thud. Wordless grunts and cries resounded, along with the sounds of flesh hitting flesh—punches or slaps.

The fight sounded more violent than any Marge had overheard to date. Carole was evidently defending herself more vigorously than usual, for it was noisier and more things were being thrown and broken than in past battles. Seriously troubled, Marge involuntarily put out a hand toward the knob, but resisted, having no desire to join the fracas and uncertain what she would do if she found the door unlocked.

As she hesitated, some other glass item shattered against the wall. As she took two steps backward, the door flew open and Carole came flying out and ran headlong into Marge, hard enough to make her drop the laundry basket.

"Oof, Marge," she yelled, raced on by, and disappeared down the stairs, leaving the apartment door wide open.

Expecting Larry Ferguson to follow in enraged pursuit of his wife, Marge moved closer to the wall, but he did not appear. There was nothing but silence from within the apartment.

Leaving the scattered clothing and spilled detergent where they had fallen, she stepped cautiously to the open door.

"Larry?"

There was no answer and what she saw made her catch her breath. Larry Ferguson lay sprawled on the floor, a widening circle of red slowly spreading around his torso, clearly the result of a butcher knife that protruded from his unmoving chest.

For a minute she could do nothing but stare, appalled. Then she turned and dashed back to her apartment to call the authorities, once again frustrated at the lack of light as she fumbled for the lock. Somewhere behind her in the hall she heard a door close quietly and was glad there was at least one other concerned tenant to back up the story she would soon have to relate.

•   •   •

It was late that evening before Marge was able to return to her desk and the attempt to write her short story.

The police had come and gone, taking Carole Ferguson with them in handcuffs. Found sobbing in the parking lot, she had tried to convince the officers not to arrest her, protesting loudly that the stabbing hadn't been her fault. Their examination of the scene, removal of the body, and questioning of those tenants who had been near enough to hear the struggle that had ended in Larry's tragic death had seemed to take hours. But all accounts, including Joel Allen's, who admitted that, above the volume of his music, he had been aware of the altercation, had agreed that the Fergusons had a history of domestic violence, that Carole, usually the victim, was the only person who could have stabbed her husband, but that it must have happened in self-defense.

Marge, their main witness, had agreed. Now all she wanted was to forget the entire hideous incident and get back to her story, but it kept repeating itself in her mind.

How odd, she thought, remembering that the only first line she had read and neglected to enter into her computer had all but predicted the unpleasantness. She picked up Rice's *Knocked for a Loop* from the reject pile of mysteries and read it again.

"Something unpleasant was going to happen, something incredibly and overwhelmingly unpleasant."

Tired and discouraged, she put it down again and opened another, hoping to tease her concentration away from the actual murder she had witnessed and toward a fictional one. The book was another by Fischer, *Murder in the Raw*, and presented another truth.

"The first time I saw her she was in trouble."

Marge remembered that a Ferguson argument had disturbed her sleep the very first night she had spent in this apartment. Carole had been in trouble all right. So why had she stayed with Larry? If she had only had the sense to leave him, none of this would have happened. Something must have kept her from leaving and there was no sure means of predicting the reactions of battered wives.

"It never pays to resist arrest," Harold Q. Masur informed her next in *Tall, Dark and Deadly*.

Resist was certainly what Carole had done today. Confronting the police officers with bloody hands that matched the red that soaked the front of her dress, she had shouted hysterically that it had been an accident, that Larry had come at her with the knife, but that she hadn't meant to hurt him. It had taken three of them to put handcuffs on her slim wrists and wrestle her into a squad car. Marge had never seen her so overwrought or assertive. Usually she had seemed the victim in disputes with her husband and he the hostile, aggressive one. Perhaps this final battle had pushed her over the line, but Carole's nervous outburst now seemed unreal and out of character to Marge.

She opened another mystery, *If You Can't Be Good* by Ross Thomas, and flipped pages to chapter one.

"It began the way that the end of the world will

begin, with a telephone call that comes at three in the morning," he informed her.

Interesting. Most of the Ferguson fights *had* occurred late at night. This final one had uncharacteristically taken place on a Saturday afternoon, when a large number of witnesses were in the building, home for the weekend, awake and aware. Bad timing—*or not?*

Bothered, unanswered questions nagging from the back of her mind, Marge frowned as she reached for another book, John D. MacDonald's *A Deadly Shade of Gold.*

"A smear of fresh blood has a metallic smell."

Shutting the cover with a startled snap, she sat up straight in her chair, suddenly recalling that, as she had stood looking into the Ferguson apartment at Larry's dead body, there *had* been a smear of blood to her right on the outside of the door frame. Carole must have touched it as she fled the scene.

Closing her eyes, she tried to visualize what she had seen. Had it really been a *right* hand print? That didn't make sense. Carole's left hand would have been closest to that side of the frame, and she had not turned, but had run straight out into Marge, transferring red from her right hand to the left shoulder of her neighbor's gray sweatshirt as she clutched it to regain her balance before rushing on past. *Perhaps I'm remembering it wrong,* Marge thought. Maybe the print had been on the left door frame.

Short story. Dammit, I'm supposed to be writing a story.

"Something funny was going on," read the line Ellen Hart had used to begin *Robber's Wine.*

You've got that right, Marge mentally agreed.

Distracted by her inability to recollect the placement of the bloody print, she momentarily abandoned the story, deciding to find out. Maybe then she would be able to forget it and concentrate on her writing.

Knowing the hall light would not have been replaced, she took a flashlight, and left the front door open for a little more light. She walked quietly down the hall to the door of the Ferguson apartment, now sealed and festooned with yellow tape that warned: POLICE LINE DO NOT CROSS.

It was dark enough to make the flashlight necessary, but, as she had remembered, the handprint was there, slightly smeared, dry and rusty, on the right side of the frame as she faced the door, and it *was* a right handprint—a large handprint. She had not registered the size of it, automatically assuming it to be Carole's.

She remembered the other woman's slender wrists encircled by the handcuffs, and could not imagine how Carole could have made this print that seemed half again as large as her small hands. She could also see that Carole could not have left the mark in her rush from the apartment, for she would have had to turn back toward the door in order to be in the correct position to lay her right hand on the frame.

The print was too large and wrongly positioned. But if it wasn't Carole's, whose was it? Not Larry Ferguson's, surely. She knew he had not exited the apartment following the struggle and the stabbing, though she now suspected that their order was wrong.

As Marge stood examining the print in the beam from the flashlight, she suddenly wondered how she could have seen it at all. The only real light she had been aware of had come out the door of apartment twenty-two, *after* Carole's exit. She could almost see its brilliant, sunny shining from within, in a contrast that had made it impossible to see much of anything in the darkness of the hallway. But Marge knew she had clearly seen and remembered the handprint.

She had also seen the brass numbers, doorknob, and dead bolt. How could she have seen them, when she had fumbled to find the lock on her own door? There must have been another source of light.

Turning, slowly, it became clear that the only possibility could be Joel Allen's door. It had to have come from there. It must have been open at least enough to allow a small amount of light through into the hall and make the brass discernible. But he claimed to have heard little and to have ignored it by turning up the volume of his music—said he had never opened his door until the police came knocking. The sound of the music had not increased, so the door must have already been open a crack as Marge had come along the hall, but not wide enough to cast a strong, noticeable line into the hall.

I was focused on the sounds of the fight in twenty-two, Marge recalled, and knew she hadn't noticed if the door to twenty-three had been open or not with so much going on to distract her.

She stood staring at the number, her mind racing. Lowering the flashlight's beam, she examined the hall carpet. Near the Ferguson's door were several spots of blood that could have fallen from Carole's hands or clothing as she ran out. Very close to Joel's were two more, one only half visible. The other half of it disappeared under his now-closed door, only possible if the door had been open when the drop fell. So—he *had* lied about it. Why?

There had been a lot of blood on Carole's person and around Larry's body. Too much for a stabbing, with the weapon still in the wound like a cork? Even if it had gone clear through, creating an exit wound in his back, if he had been lying on it the bleeding would have been slow, wouldn't it? Wouldn't it have taken longer than the few minutes between the struggle Marge had heard taking place in the Ferguson kitchen and Carole's frantic exit to spread to the pool of blood she had clearly seen around the body?

Another thought crossed her mind. Could Carole have thrust a butcher knife clear through Larry's torso? She was a small woman; it was difficult to imagine the possibility. Wouldn't it have taken someone larger, heavier, stronger? Maybe . . . Joel?

Swiftly, Marge went back to her own apartment and closed and locked the door, decidedly uneasy about remaining in close proximity to Joel Allen's door. Force of habit took her back to the chair in front of her computer, though she was no longer the least bit interested in fiction. Fact and suspicion had replaced deadlines on her priority list.

Absently, she took another mystery from the unexamined pile, as she ran scenarios through her mind regarding Larry Ferguson's death.

"Detective Steve Carella wasn't sure he had heard the man correctly." Ed McBain spoke from the first page of *Sadie When She Died*.

If Joel had lied, as she suspected, the police might have heard him correctly, but he had given an incorrect report. But why would he lie?

The picture of him consoling Carole on the stairs leaped into her mind, and the look on his face—more adoring than friendly. Now she recalled that there had been anger mixed into that look as well, but she had not paid attention, familiar with Joel's sympathetic camaraderie and regard for his fellow tenants. She remembered his hands, one turning Carole's face to the light to examine a bruise along her cheekbone, the other on her waist in a familiar fashion.

"He wasn't a small man, but he walked small."

Paula Gosling was right in *Solo Blues*. Joel was well over six feet tall and strong. As she passed his apartment, Marge had often heard the thud of the weights he lifted daily. But he was puppy-like in his helpful, friendly ways with his neighbors, asking to be liked by everyone—"walking small" could be a way of putting it.

This was all just theory—conjecture, Marge told herself. She could easily be wrong, but somehow she knew she was not. There were unanswered questions, but confronting Joel Allen did not appeal to her, especially when he seemed the most likely person to have murdered Carole's husband. Only women sleuths in fiction or movies were dumb enough to put themselves in harm's way by directly challenging a killer.

"There are no hundred percent heroes," John D. MacDonald assured her. Relieved, she laid *Cinnamon Skin* on the growing pile of mysteries she had already considered and opened Margaret Lawrence's *Hearts and Bones.*

"Whatever they thought when they found her was bound to be wrong."

The police would soon know they were mistaken about Carole Ferguson's role as a victim. She might have deserved better than abuse from her now-dead husband, but killing him was a poor and risky solution to the problem. Marge had watched her overreact for the police and knew that she had been part of the plot she must have hatched with Joel. It didn't matter, really, which one of them had first suggested the murderous solution, clearing the way for their blossoming relationship, but Joel, eager to please, would have encouraged it, gone along willingly.

"There are some men who enter a woman's life and screw it up forever," began Janet Evanovich in *One for the Money.*

Slut, Larry Ferguson had shouted. But now Marge realized the shout had probably been Joel's. The fight must have been staged after Larry was already dead. There had been too much blood for him not to have died earlier. Carole must have dipped her hands in it and wiped it on her dress. The calling out of her neighbor's name in her rush from the apartment would have warned Joel that there was someone, a witness, in the hallway. He would have waited until Marge had returned to her own telephone to call the police, then slipped back to his own apartment to carefully clean his clothes and hands. Marge remembered the quiet sound of a door closing as she had struggled to open her front door.

Apprehended, Joel would have been charged with murder. Making it seem that Carole had killed Larry made more sense and could have saved them both. The support and testimony of all the witnesses who would be at home on a Saturday afternoon, including Marge, would have insured the success of a self-defense plea.

Sad. It was a sad situation. Mixed with her resentment at being made a dupe, she found a thread of sympathy for both Carole and Joel. Not enough, however, to ignore what she had determined to be the truth—not enough to let them get away with it.

She opened one last mystery and read the first line.

"Ryder opened his tired eyelids and reached for the telephone without enthusiasm."

Right, she thought, closing Alistair MacLean's *Goodbye California* and picking up the phone.

A whole day wasted and I still haven't even the beginning of a story, Marge chastised herself, back at her computer the next morning.

Taking another mystery from the few that remained

unopened in front of her, she hesitated, then smiled and laid it back on the desk.

Of course I do, she realized with relief. *All I have to do is write it down.*

"It was a dark and stormy night. . . ."

If there's one thing that's sure to bring bad blood to the surface, it's the reading of a will. Nothing will divide a family faster than the dividing of an estate. While the death of a loved one should bring a family closer together, in this case, it serves as the final spark to an already explosive situation.

The Prodigal

J. A. Jance

"What are you doing here?"

Slowly Bart Majors swung around on the barstool and faced his sister, Kathleen, the sister he hadn't seen for twenty-three years. She looked so much like their mother—like the way he remembered their mother—that for a moment he didn't answer. Couldn't answer. It was as though Madeline Majors Cahill were still alive and Bart had just seen her ghost—a walking, talking ghost.

Unable to answer, Bart turned away. Settling himself more firmly on the stool, he polished off his scotch and water in one long gulp and shoved the empty glass across the bar, signaling the bartender as he did so. The young female bartender was blond and good looking. Bart knew from experience that just because a woman wore a wedding ring didn't necessarily mean she wasn't available.

"Hit me again," he said when he caught her eye. "Make it a double."

"You haven't answered my question," Kathleen persisted from over his shoulder. "What the hell are you doing here?"

"What do you think?" he answered at last. "Mother's dead. I came for the funeral."

"For the funeral!" Kathleen spat back at him. She was trying desperately to maintain control, but her voice vibrated with barely repressed fury. "What was wrong with coming before the funeral?" she demanded. "Why didn't you come when it might have done some good?"

The bartender delivered Bart's drink. "Keep the change," he said, pushing a stack of bills across the bar.

"How about you?" The bartender caught Kathleen's eye. "Can I get you something?" she asked.

"No," Kathleen answered. "Nothing. Thanks."

As the bartender shrugged and moved away, Kathleen hiked her skirt and climbed onto the vacant barstool next to her brother. She had lived in Bisbee, Arizona, all her life. Never before had she set foot inside Brewery Gulch's fabled Blue Moon Saloon and Lounge. She wouldn't have been there now if Norm Higgins from the mortuary hadn't called and told her that someone claiming to be her brother had come into his office demanding a briefing on all the arrangements for Madeline Cahill's services. He had wanted a full accounting of all expenditures and when he left, Norm had watched him as far as the Blue Moon's door.

"How did you find me?" Bart asked. Their eyes met in hazy reflection in the aging, smoke-dimmed mirror behind the bar. "I suppose little Normy Higgins couldn't wait to call and tattle."

"Norm Higgins had every right to notify me," Kathleen returned. "Since I'm Mother's executor, I'm in charge of all arrangements."

"So what else is new?" Bart said. "You always were. Here's to Mother's little helper. Cheers!"

He lifted the newly filled glass to his lips and drained a third of the amber liquid in one gulp.

"What do you want, Bart?" Kathleen asked. "Why are you here?"

"Why do you think? I came to collect my fair share."

"Your share!" Kathleen Brewster's whole body trembled with indignation. "After all this time without a word or a phone call you still have nerve enough to think you get a 'fair share'? Where've you been for the last twenty-five years, Bart, on the moon? Where were you when Mother had open heart surgery? Where were you when she lost her legs to diabetes and ended up being confined to a wheelchair?"

"I never pretended to be Mother Teresa," he returned. "But I'm as much Mother's son as Little Miss Goody Two-Shoes here is her daughter. And if there's anything left—any money, that is—I want my share of it. I have as much right to it as you do."

"The hell you do! Besides, it wasn't Mother's money in the first place. It was his—Dad's."

Bart Majors laughed outright. "See there?" he said. "The man's been dead for ten years, and you're still kissing his ass. My memory must be a little longer than yours is, sister of mine. Or maybe a little clearer. I had a perfectly good father. I wasn't in the market for another one. The last thing I needed was for Bob Cahill to show up on the scene and screw up my life."

"Robert Cahill was good for Mother and he was good for me," Kathleen protested evenly.

"Oh yeah? Well, he wasn't good for me. The son of a bitch threw me out of the house. No, wait. I take that back. He made Mother throw me out of the house. He didn't have balls enough to do it himself."

Kathleen sighed. She had been over that same quarrel so many times during the years, only always before it had been from the other side of the hostilities—from her mother's point of view. "You put Mother in a terrible position," Kathleen said. "An impossible position. You forced her to choose between you and Bob—between her only son and the man she loved. Of course she chose Bob. How could you have expected anything else?"

Bart swung around on the stool and looked his sister square in the face. "I expected her to be smart enough to see through his charade of manipulative bullshit. I can see how you might have fallen for it. You were just a little kid, but Mother was a grown woman."

"You call it manipulation," Kathleen said. "It wasn't manipulation at all. Bob loved Mother, Bart. He was good to her. Nice. He gave her everything she ever wanted."

"Except me."

"He would have given her that, too," Kathleen replied, "if you had ever bothered to apologize. If you had ever called and said you wanted to come back, Dad wouldn't have stopped you. He wouldn't have stood in the way."

"Don't call him that. He's not my father."

"He was my father," Kathleen retorted. "He was more of a father to me than Tom Majors ever was. There's a whole lot more to being a father than being a sperm donor."

"And there's a lot more to being a mother than turning your back on your only son. Real mothers don't abandon their children."

"She wanted what was best for all of us. She wanted security, and Bob Cahill gave her that. From the time she married him until the day she died, Mother never had to worry about money again."

"Whores do it for money," Bart said. He tossed off the remains of his third drink and slammed the empty glass down on the counter. "That makes our mother no better than a common prostitute. I rest my case."

Summoned by the unmistakable rattle of ice in an empty glass, the bartender moved toward them. "Another?" she asked.

"Why not?"

The bartender turned toward Kathleen. "Are you sure I can't get you something?"

Kathleen Brewster felt deflated. All the fight had gone out of her. "Coffee," she said. "With cream and sugar."

Brother and sister sat in brooding silence for some time. Only after Kathleen's coffee had come and she'd taken the time to stir in cream and sugar did she speak again.

"How did you know?" she asked.

"Know what?"

"That Mother was dead."

"Aunt Penny called me."

Penny Holiman was Madeline Majors Cahill's older sister. "Aunt Penny?" Kathleen blurted in amazement. "You mean to tell me you've stayed in touch with her all these years?"

"There's no law against it, is there? I thought you'd be thrilled to know I hadn't severed all family ties."

"Of course you stayed in touch with Aunt Penny!" Kathleen exclaimed. "She hated Bob, too, hated him from the start."

"What can I tell you?" Bart sneered. "Aunt Penny's a great judge of character. She must have seen the man for what he was."

"What Aunt Penny saw was a man she wanted for herself."

Now it was Bart's turn to be stunned. "You're kidding! Aunt Penny and Bob Cahill? Never!"

"I'll bet Aunt Penny never told you that part of the story, did she?" Kathleen continued, pressing her sudden advantage. "I'll bet she never mentioned that she met Bob Cahill first, at work. They had been out for dinner on two separate occasions before she ever introduced him to Mother."

"The two-timing son of a bitch!"

"It wasn't like that at all," Kathleen interrupted. "From the moment he laid eyes on Mother it was love at first sight for both of them. Naturally, Aunt Penny hated him after that, and Mother, too. She never forgave either one of them."

"Are you sure?" Bart asked.

"Sure of what?"

"That Aunt Penny never forgave them? Maybe she did. After all, if it hadn't been for her calling me, I never would have known about Mother—that she was in the hospital. That she was dying."

"If you knew . . . if Aunt Penny called you and told you . . . why didn't you come sooner?" Kathleen asked. "Why didn't you let Mother see you? Why didn't you give her a chance to say good-bye?"

"What was the point? It wouldn't have made any difference."

Once again Kathleen Brewster sat in silence, this time staring into the milky dregs in her coffee mug. She thought about her aunt, Penelope Holiman. She had never felt close to her mother's older sister. She remembered seeing the woman from time to time, at the grocery store or in the post office. They had always been cordial enough in public, stopping and making polite small talk when they ran into one another in town, but the ongoing quarrel between the two sisters—between Penny and Madeline—had always stood between Penny and Kathleen, aunt and niece, as well. It was startling now to realize that the whole time Aunt Penny had held Kathleen and Madeline at arm's length, she had stayed in touch with Bart, the estranged brother and son.

"It might have," Kathleen said at last.

"Might have what?"

"Made a difference," she answered forlornly. "It might have made it easier for Mother to go."

"Like cleaning up one last piece of unfinished business?" Bart asked.

"Something like that."

"Speaking of unfinished business," Bart said, "what about the will? Has anyone taken a look at it yet?"

"No. I'm sure it's still in Phil Dalton's office. Phil was Mother's attorney. I didn't see any reason to rush since . . ."

"Since you're both the executor as well as the sole beneficiary," Bart finished for her.

"Well, yes. I suppose that's true."

"Suppose it isn't true?" Bart asked. "Suppose Mother changed her mind and put me back in the will after all?"

"She wouldn't do that."

"Why not?"

"She wouldn't, that's all. I'm the one who looked after her all these years. I'm the one who took her to the doctor when she needed to go and brought her groceries and made sure the bills got paid."

"In other words, you've earned it and I haven't."

"I loved her," Kathleen said flatly.

"I loved her, too."

"You turned your back on her."

"Only after she sent me away."

Kathleen Brewster took a deep breath. "Look, Bart. We've been over this before. No matter whose fault it was originally, the truth is, you went away and never came back."

"I'm here now."

"After all these years, how could Mother possibly have known that you'd turn back up like this?"

"I want to know what's in the will."

"It'll just give you something else to blame her for, something else to be mad at me about for the next twenty years."

"I want to know if she left me anything," Bart replied. "Maybe at the last minute the woman had a sudden change of heart. Maybe she decided to be fair with me for a change and give me my just due."

"Fair? You'd call that fair?"

"Isn't that what's supposed to happen to the Prodigal Son when he finally bothers to show up? Aren't you supposed to go out and kill the fatted calf?"

"The hell I am!" Kathleen stood up. "You really are a chip off the old block, aren't you! Tom Majors's ne'er-do-well son who still thinks the world owes him a living."

"Doesn't it?"

"No, it doesn't. And I'll tell you something else. You stay away from me and from Mother's funeral as well. You have no business being there."

"I'll come if I want to. You can't stop me."

"Try me!"

Almost falling off her stool in her need to get away, Kathleen Brewster raced across the darkened barroom. Swinging open the door, she stumbled out of the air-conditioned darkness and into the scorching noonday sun. Standing trembling on the sidewalk, she was blinded not only by the light outside but also by the searing glare of outrage that was pulsing inside her head.

How dare he! she thought. Instead of crawling in on his hands and knees, begging forgiveness, Bart was actually arrogant enough to demand—demand!—his fair share.

For years before her death, Madeline Cahill had worried about her son. She had wondered where he was and what he was doing. And all the time, Aunt Penny had known where Bart was. All that time, Aunt Penny had been in touch with him, keeping him up to date on everything that was going on.

Quaking with fury, it was all Kathleen could do to jam the key into the ignition of her Acura. It took three different tries before she finally managed to ease it out of the parking place without banging the two cars in front and behind her.

When she reached the intersection at the bottom of Brewery Gulch, Kathleen signaled to turn left. She intended to go straight home to her house five miles away in Warren. By the time she finished waiting for a lumbering motor home to make its way past her, she had changed her mind. Signaling for a right-hand turn, she drove up Tombstone Canyon to the courthouse. Half a block away, she pulled into the visitor's parking place in front of the small tin-roofed house her mother's attorney, Phil Dalton, had converted into a suite of offices.

The lawyer stood up and greeted Kathleen cordially as his receptionist showed her into his private office. "To what do I owe this pleasure?" he asked.

"I want to know what's in Mother's will," Kathleen answered brusquely.

"But I thought we were going to do that on Friday morning, after the funeral."

"I want to do it now."

Phil Dalton looked uneasy. "Shouldn't your brother be here?" he asked. "And your aunt as well? For the official reading, I mean."

"Bart and Aunt Penny? Why should they be here? What business is it of theirs?"

"Please sit down, Kathleen. And please bear with me. It is their business. I don't know how to tell you this, but there's a new will."

"What do you mean a new will?"

"Just that. Your mother had me come to the hospital and draw it up for her just two weeks ago. It's properly drafted, signed, and witnessed. I can assure you, it's all in order."

Not trusting her legs to support her any longer, Kathleen Brewster dropped into a nearby chair. "Why?" she asked.

"Why? Because I did it properly, of course. Your mother said those were her wishes and—"

"Why did she do it, Phil? Why did she rewrite her will?"

"Because your brother was coming home. He had evidently been in touch with your aunt Penny. He told her he was coming home to bury the hatchet and ask your mother's forgiveness. If Madeline didn't tell you about this, I'm sure it's because she wanted it to be a surprise. I think she thought you'd be pleased when that whole ugly chapter was behind you and your brother was back in the fold."

"It's a lie."

"No. It's isn't a lie. Not at all. I'm sure Madeline thought you'd be thrilled. I had a call from Norm Higgins a few minutes ago, so I know Bart's in town. It's unfortunate that he didn't arrive prior to your mother's death, but—"

"Bart never had any intention of getting here before Mother died," Kathleen interrupted. "He didn't come here to ask her forgiveness. He's here because he thinks there's something in it for him. What's in the will, Phil? What does it say? I need to know."

"I can give you a copy, if you like."

"Please."

With her heart pounding in her chest, Kathleen waited while Phil Dalton disappeared into the outer office. Minutes later, he returned and held out a thin envelope. "I'm sure you'll find it's all in order."

With tears blurring her eyes, Kathleen ripped open the envelope. It was all there. For effecting Madeline's reconciliation with her long-lost son, Penelope Holiman was to receive a lump sum bequest of $10,000.

After that and after the payment of all final expenses,
Madeline Cahill's property was to be liquidated and
the proceeds divided evenly between her two beloved
children, Kathleen Lorraine Brewster and Matthew
Bartholomew Majors. Should any or all of the benefi-
ciaries predecease Madeline, his or her share would revert to the survivors. If both children predeceased
Madeline, the entire estate, excepting the lump sum
going to her sister Penny, would revert to the Bisbee
High School Alumni Scholarship fund.

Kathleen read the document through completely not
once, not twice, but three times before she folded it and
slid it back into the ragged envelope.

Phil Dalton studied her carefully as she shoved the
torn envelope into her purse. "You are all right with
this, aren't you, Kathleen?" he asked solicitously. "I
can see it's something of a shock, especially after
everything you did for your mother, but . . ."

"Oh, no," she responded quickly. "I'm fine. If that's
the way Mother wanted it, that's the way it should be."

Phil Dalton breathed a sigh of relief. "Good girl," he
said. "I knew you'd be sensible. That's what Madeline
always said about you, you know. 'Kathleen has such
a good head on her shoulders.' Your mother loved you
very much. You and poor Bob Cahill were the only two
rays of sunshine in her life. You're the only ones who
didn't break Madeline's heart."

Unsteadily, Kathleen Brewster rose to her feet.
"Thank you for saying that, Phil. It's what I really
needed to hear."

"Are you all right?"

"I'm fine," Kathleen managed. "Never been better."

At ten past ten the next morning, Norm Higgins Junior burst into his father's pristinely neat office. "What is it, Normy?" Norm Senior asked.

"I thought you should know that we're running late on the services for Madeline Cahill."

Norm Senior consulted his watch. "That was supposed to start ten minutes ago. What's the matter? Is that worthless Lenny Cox late again?"

"No. Reverend Cox is here, warmed up and ready to go, and the chapel is pretty well filled. What's missing is the family."

"No one from the family is here yet?"

Junior shook his head.

"Are you sure they knew it was supposed to start at ten? Has anyone called them to check?"

"I tried, but there's no answer. I called Kathleen Brewster's place. I also tried calling Penny Holiman up the canyon. I called the Copper Queen. The desk clerk told me Bart Majors is still registered, but that he went out last night around dinnertime and hasn't been back. He left his room key with the desk clerk and it's still there."

"That's the strangest thing. . . ."

"Phil Dalton is out front," Norm Junior continued. "He's Madeline's attorney. He thinks it's pretty strange, too. He told me we should call the cops. He sounds worried. He said something about a long-term family feud and about Madeline Cahill writing a new will. What do you think, Pop? Should I call or not?"

Norm Higgins leaned back in his worn leather chair

and regarded his son thoughtfully. "If anybody's going to call, I will," he said. "As for the Cahill service, give it another five minutes. If the family members still aren't here, tell Lenny to start without them."

Nodding, Norm Junior started toward the door. "And, Normy," his father added, stopping his son in his tracks, "as soon as you get back from the cemetery, make sure the decks are clear. I want all the loose ends tied up around here. I don't want anything left hanging."

Junior frowned and looked puzzled. "Why?" he asked. "Is something wrong?"

"Nothing's wrong," his father returned, "but I have a funny feeling Higgins Mortuary and Funeral Chapel is going to have a very busy week."

Forty-five minutes later, a call from the Cochise County Sheriff's department confirmed that Norm Higgins was right. With three more funerals to schedule, his mortuary would be extremely busy.

The hobby of collection is a pleasurable pastime enjoyed by many, I'm sure. I haven't had much luck with collecting anything, except maybe trouble. I seem to find much more of that than I require. Our next story concerns a collection of antique chairs, and the clues to solving a murder hidden among them.

Miss Chatfield's Chairs

Stefanie Matteson

The call came in while Charlotte Graham was in Jerry's office. She had stopped by to say hello after having dinner with an old friend from Hollywood at a seafood restaurant that was one of her favorites, as well as one of Jerry's. To say hello, and to tell Jerry about the shad roe at Jed's, food being the second of the shared interests to which the perpetuation of their friendship could be attributed, the first being that of detection. They'd met over a murder at an upstate mineral spa. Jerry had worked there briefly as a trainer after leaving the N.Y.P.D.; she'd been a guest. Later, they'd worked together on another case after he'd become chief of police in the small Hudson River Valley town of Zion Hill. Now it looked as if they were about to team up for a third time.

It quickly became evident from Jerry's side of the conversation that he was talking about a murder. Charlotte didn't need to be a detective to figure that out from questions like, "Are you sure he's dead?" and "Did you find a weapon?" Moreover, judging from Jerry's gentle tone, the caller was a woman.

After advising the caller not to touch anything, Jerry finally hung up. "C'mon," he said. "We've got a corpse. Must be something about your presence that incites citizens in my jurisdiction to homicide, Graham," he teased.

It was true. Charlotte had been in Zion Hill for the last murder, too. In fact, she had an uncanny knack for attracting murder cases. She sometimes felt like the controller of a police target range: she caused the targets to pop up, and somebody shot them.

"That's okay," Jerry said as he buckled on his holster. "As far as I'm concerned, you can keep coming around. You know what the last corpse we had around here was? A deer carcass on the Post Road that turned out to be an old leather jacket."

Charlotte gave him a sympathetic look. Jerry had been one of New York's top homicide detectives before being forced to retire on a disability pension after losing the tip of his trigger finger in a shoot-out. Life hadn't been the same for him since.

"Let's go," he said. He was grinning from dimple to dimple.

•   •   •

They left the station a few minutes later at the head of a string of police cruisers. Charlotte was willing to bet that Zion Hill hadn't seen this much action in a long time. On the way to the scene, Jerry filled her in on what he knew, which was little. The murder had occurred at an old Hudson River villa called Chatwold that had been owned until the previous month by a ninety-seven-year-old spinster named Emily Chatfield. Miss Chatfield had died in her sleep, leaving Chatwold to the Chatwold Preservation Association. The association was a nonprofit trust that had been set up prior to Miss Chatfield's death for the purpose of preserving the house and its contents. The report of the murder had been called in by a woman named Pamela Kelleher, who was chairman of the association and Miss Chatfield's great-niece.

What Jerry knew about the victim was even less: he was a New York antiques dealer by the name of Miles Morey, and he had been Miss Chatfield's great-nephew.

They pulled up in front of the villa ten minutes later. If ever there was a house that looked as if it should have been the site of a murder, it was Chatwold. It stood high above the Hudson: a turreted villa in the Victorian Gothic style with tall, narrow windows and a steep mansard roof decorated with a line of porthole-shaped windows. It had seen better days: the siding looked as though it hadn't been painted in fifty years and great swaths of slate shingles were missing from the roof. The foundation plantings grew up to the ornately bracketed eaves and the grass stood a foot high. The gloomy picture was completed by a rainy mist.

They entered to find a petite blonde standing on a riser of the central staircase with her arms stretched out like a school crossing guard. A cluster of eight or ten men and women stood at her feet, clamoring for her to let them by. "I'm sorry," she was saying, "but you may *not* go upstairs." She was met by a chorus of questions and complaints: "Why not?" "What's going on?" "I have to get to another appointment." Looking up, she saw Jerry and sighed with relief. "This is Chief Jerry D'Angelo of the Zion Hill police," she said. Then she signaled for him to come forward.

Shouldering his way to the front, Jerry announced that a murder had taken place and directed the witnesses to step into the adjacent parlor, where a police officer would take their statements.

"Who *are* these people?" Jerry asked, once the group had been shepherded into the parlor.

"Antiques dealers," the woman replied. "I'm so glad you got here quickly. I was afraid I was going to have a feeding frenzy on my hands." She went on to explain: "The preservation association's goal is to restore the original Louis Comfort Tiffany interior of the first floor, which will take a lot of capital." She looked around her at the ornate staircase, whose every surface seemed to be carved, inlaid, or gilded. "One way to raise this money is to sell the furniture that we don't need. Since we plan to turn the ballroom into offices, we figured the best place to begin was with my great-aunt's chair collection, which is stored there. The dealers were invited here to preview the collection. There's always a lot of excitement when a large collection that's never been on public view comes up for sale. They've been told that none of the chairs is terribly valuable, but they're all hoping that they'll be the one to spot an undiscovered treasure."

"And the victim?" asked Jerry.

"The victim is my cousin, Miles Morey," she said. Her voice caught, and she took a deep breath. "He's also an antiques dealer. Upon my great-aunt's death, the association hired him to inventory the contents of the house and to sell the unneeded furniture. He was chosen to supervise the sale because of his knowledge of antiques, and because, being a relative, we figured he would have the interests of the association at heart. He had set up a series of appointments with antiques dealers to look at the chairs."

Jerry nodded. "Where's the body?" he asked, skipping ahead to the important stuff; for the moment, he was leaving the antiques dealers to his men.

"In the ballroom," she replied. "It's on the third floor. Just go straight on up."

The ballroom occupied the entire third floor of the villa, under the mansard roof, and it was filled with chairs, chairs, and more chairs. They lined the walls of the room, two and three deep. Probably a couple hundred of them.

One would expect to see chairs in a ballroom, of course, but one would have thought they'd be a set of

Louis XV side chairs perhaps, or, on a more modest level, gilt bamboo occasional chairs. But these were not all of a type: they were chairs of every conceivable style and period and for every conceivable purpose. A glance to Charlotte's right took in a Ming garden chair, a bentwood rocker, a Barcelona chair, a Windsor armchair, a Victorian chair inlaid with mother-of-pearl, a cane-backed deck chair, a Duncan Phyfe side chair, and a platform rocker.

But all of these chairs were eclipsed by a chair that stood near the opposite wall. It was the bloodstained Queen Anne wing chair in which the victim was slumped, his head resting against one of the wings. He was middle-aged, with curly black hair going to gray and a large, fleshy face, which, appended as it was to his small, lifeless body, gave him the look of a ventriloquist's doll. Even in death he had the snappy, slightly dandified appearance typical of his profession: a silk bow tie with a pocket handkerchief to match, a double-breasted blazer, hand-sewn Belgian loafers. Snappy, that is, except for the blood that stained his crisply starched shirt and the cuff of the sleeve clothing the arm that still gripped his bloody midriff.

It was apparent that he had been shot, and from the extent of the bloodstains, more than once. It was also apparent that he had not been shot in the wing chair, but had collapsed there after a bloody perambulation around the ballroom. In fact, it looked as if he might have dragged the wing chair away from the wall before he died, since it stood out at an angle from the others. There was no telling where the trail of blood began,

only that the victim appeared to have staggered back
and forth among the chairs that lined the room, as well
as those in the center. The latter were curiously lined
up in three rows facing the porthole-shaped windows.
The rain covering the glass lent the scene a curious,
Jules Vernish atmosphere, as if the chairs had been set
up in anticipation of an audience with Captain Nemo.
The parquet floor was patterned not only with the
pools and spatters of blood that had dripped from the
victim's wounds, but also with his bloody footprints.
Charlotte didn't envy the person who would have to
make sense of it all.

As in the other murder cases Charlotte had worked on,
there was a peacefulness about the fresh murder scene.
It was like a house before the party begins: everything
ready and waiting for the guests who are about to come
knocking on the door. The sound of footsteps on the
stairs signaled that the party was about to begin. In a
few minutes, it was in full swing. Police officers
swarmed over the room, setting up lights, talking on
their walkie-talkies, roping off the crime scene. The
coroner poked and prodded the corpse, the crime scene
unit measured, photographed, and otherwise went
about their business with the efficient, perfunctory air
of those for whom homicide was a routine occurrence.
Other officers, whose function was not readily apparent and who may have been there only out of curiosity,
stood or sat at the fringes of the room, like shy swains
mustering the courage to ask for the next dance.

Leaving the technicians to their gruesome task,

Charlotte and Jerry retreated to a second-floor parlor to interview the witnesses. The parlor was as gloomy as the rest of the house. The silk wall covering hung in filthy tatters and the room was dank with mildew. A police officer sat in an ornately carved Victorian chair next to a table on which a tape recorder had been set up. The matching antique sofa was occupied by the two antiques dealers who had found the body. Their names were Brian Fessler and James MacGillvray, former partners in an antiques shop in the Berkshire Mountains of western Massachusetts. MacGillvray had since opened his own shop, Essex Antiques, in New York, but they remained friends.

It was MacGillvray who answered Jerry's questions. He sat on the edge of the sofa, his large hands clasped between his knees. His burly physique and red, ginger-bearded face contrasted with the effete appearance of his colleague.

"I had the first appointment, but it was Fessler who got here first," he was saying. He spoke in a deep voice, appropriately solemn. "He was just getting out of his car when I pulled up. That was about ten of ten. My appointment was for ten. Morey's car was parked under the porte cochere. I joined Fessler at the front door, which was open. When no one answered the doorbell, we went on up. I had been here earlier in the week, so I knew the chairs were in the ballroom. I thought Morey hadn't answered because he couldn't hear the doorbell. When we got there, we found . . ." His voice trailed off and he looked up. "Well—you saw what it looked like."

Fessler said nothing, but his pale face seemed to grow paler at the memory.

"How far into the room did you get?" Jerry asked.

"Only to the door," said MacGillvray. "That was enough."

"Good. You did the right thing," said Jerry, relieved that they hadn't contaminated the crime scene. "What then?" he prompted.

"We went back downstairs," MacGillvray replied. "We were going to call the police. On the way down, we ran into Pamela Kelleher and told her what had happened. She was very upset, needless to say. She told us that the telephone in the house had been disconnected after her great-aunt's death, but that she had a cellular phone in her car. We went out to her car to call you, and then we came back inside to wait. By that time, the others were starting to arrive, and we agreed not to say anything until you got here."

"You didn't return to the crime scene?"

MacGillvray shook his head.

Jerry asked a few more questions. Neither man reported seeing or hearing anything unusual; neither knew of any reason why someone would want to kill Miles Morey. Then Jerry instructed them to give their addresses to the police officer at the door and dismissed them. It was indicative of the extent to which they had been traumatized by the murder that they didn't seem the least bit curious about Charlotte's presence. As far as they were concerned, there was nothing remarkable about the fact that a movie star known for her New England accent and her four Oscars was assisting Zion Hill's police chief. Charlotte wished she could be this invisible more often.

The same was true of Pamela Kelleher, the next witness, who had now replaced the antiques dealers on the Victorian sofa and sat nervously twisting an embroidered handkerchief. The pink spots in her pale cheeks indicated that she'd been crying, but she now calmly described her relationship with the victim. She was a type, Charlotte thought as the woman spoke. Straight blond hair, bluntly cut; a trim, athletic figure; an expensive, conservatively cut suit; an earnest manner; a little girl voice. Born to the tennis club.

"Miles and I were second cousins," she explained. "Our parents were first cousins and Emily Chatfield was their aunt. We were very close as children." She stifled a sob, then took a breath. "We were the same age," she continued after regaining her composure, "our birthdays are only a few days apart. Aunt Emily would often have all of us here on holidays: there were twenty-six great-nieces and -nephews. She liked having a full house. Miles and I have drifted apart as adults, but we still see one another quite often professionally. We both deal in antiques. Miles has a shop in the city and I'm in the decorative arts department at Sotheby's. Aunt Emily had a love of the decorative arts that she passed on to her great-nieces and -nephews."

She paused to allow Jerry to catch up with his note taking and then added: "Miles had called me several times over the last couple of days. He left messages on my answering machine saying that he had something important to tell me. I left messages in return, but we never caught up with one another." She took a breath and then added quietly, "Until now."

"Do you have any idea what that something important was?" Jerry asked.

"Actually, I think I might," she replied. "But I'd like to see the crime scene first. Do you think that would be possible?"

"Does it depend on seeing the body?" Jerry asked. "Because the body's just been removed." He nodded at the open door. "The EMTs just carried it out."

"No," she said. "In fact, I'm just as glad not to see the body."

"Okay," Jerry said.

As they entered the ballroom, Pamela Kelleher's anxious blue eyes scanned the bloody scene. She seemed to shrink back, and then, as if remembering a parental admonition of the stiff upper lip variety, strode toward the bloodstained chair. She came to a stop at the tape that blocked access to the crime scene. The empty chair was dramatically illuminated by police floodlights, as if it were an important piece in a sale at Pamela's auction house.

"Jim MacGillvray told me that he and Brian Fessler found Miles's body in a wing chair," she said. "I just wanted to make sure he was talking about the same chair that I thought he was."

"What's the significance of the chair?" asked Jerry.

"Maybe nothing," she replied. "It's just a hunch. May I take a closer look?"

"Don't touch anything," Jerry warned as he lifted the tape.

Pamela stepped forward, followed by Jerry and Charlotte. She gazed at the chair for a moment, and then spoke: "My great-aunt started collecting chairs for the utilitarian reason that she needed chairs to furnish the ballroom. But she ended up collecting them for what she called their personalities. She maintained that each of her chairs had a unique personality. She liked to imagine which chairs were friends, which were enemies, what they talked about after everyone had gone to bed." She smiled at the recollection. "And just as she liked eccentric people, she also liked eccentric chairs: too high, too short, an interesting flaw, an unusual wood. That's why she loved this chair. The wings are oversized by comparison with the narrow wings of the reproductions we're used to, and they're set at a shallow angle to the back. She used to say they gave the chair the appearance of an open mouth. She called it her 'chair that laughs.' She used to say that of all her chairs, this one had the best sense of humor."

They looked at the wing chair, whose oversized wings and capacious seat did indeed make it look like a big laughing mouth, although its air of jocularity was considerably diminished by the presence of blood-stains on its seat.

"When Jim told me that he found Miles in a wing chair, I found myself picturing this chair in my mind," she went on. "It's been years since I've really looked at it. I've been up here several times since Aunt Emily's death, of course, but"—her glance swept the room—"there are so many." She continued, "As I said, my great-aunt collected chairs because of their personalities, not because of their value, either monetary or practical. She used to quote Théophile Gautier: 'Nothing is really beautiful except that which is good for nothing.' Most of the chairs in her collection therefore aren't terribly valuable. But remembering this chair's unusual lines, it struck me that it might be quite old, that the oversized wings might have been designed to screen out cold eighteenth-century drafts. And now, seeing it in person, as it were, I'm convinced of that."

Charlotte looked at the chair. It certainly didn't look valuable; it didn't even have a proper slipcover.

"The finest examples of American wing chairs are works of art," Pamela went on. "They're very carefully thought-out constructions of lines, angles, curves, and proportions. The back, for instance, has to slope at the proper angle and it has to be the proper height in proportion to the width: not too tall, not too squat. The wings have to meet the back at the right angle and they can't be too wide or too narrow. They have to flow into the arms in a graceful sweep." Her arm traced a flowing line. "The lines of a good chair are so natural that they give it an anthropomorphic quality. That's why it's not surprising that Aunt Emily thought of this as her chair that laughs."

Jerry was staring in disbelief at the chair. "How could it be valuable? It's not even upholstered right," he said, voicing Charlotte's earlier thought.

"It's not upholstered at all," Pamela said. "This is just a coarse linen undercover, original by the looks of it. But the cover doesn't really matter. It's precisely *because* an uncovered chair looks so unassuming that a masterpiece can be mistaken for an ordinary piece. It's the framework that matters. It has to be original. Of course it would have to be analyzed, but I have a hunch that this chair was made in the Affleck workshop in Philadelphia in the late eighteenth century, which would make it very valuable indeed."

"How valuable is very valuable indeed?" asked Charlotte.

"We sold one like this about five years ago. It came out of a shed on an estate on the coast of Maine. A country antiques dealer bought it for five hundred dollars. It went through several sets of hands before it was recognized for the masterpiece that it was. We ended up selling it to the Met for their American wing for $1.8 million."

Jerry let out a long, low whistle and gazed at the chair with new respect.

Pamela continued, "Obviously Miles lived for some time after he was shot. But he must have known he was going to die. He could have chosen any of these chairs to die in. At last count, there were two hundred and six. Why this one? And why pull it away from the others, as it appears he's done? I think what he wanted to tell me—what he *is* telling me through his choice of chair to die in—is that this chair is very valuable and that it shouldn't be sold for the price of an ordinary antique."

"But if it's so valuable, why did he keep it here where it might be vulnerable to theft?" Jerry asked. "Why not put it in a vault?"

"For the same reason people hide diamonds in the flour canister: because they figure that a thief won't look in the most obvious place."

"Okay," Jerry acceded. "But how do we find out if it's a masterpiece or—as you put it—an ordinary antique?"

"The wood will have to be analyzed, the tack marks, any shreds of the original upholstery fabric. There's no need for you to do it," she told Jerry. "I would be obligated as chairman of the association to do it anyway. I can have the report sent to you."

Their conversation was interrupted by one of the crime scene technicians, who proudly held up a bullet in a rubber-gloved hand. Jerry excused himself, and Charlotte could hear them talking excitedly about trajectories and shell markings.

"Charlotte," said Jerry as he rejoined them a moment later, "I'm hereby turning the furniture angle of this case over to you."

Three days later, Pamela Kelleher called Charlotte with the expert's report on the chair. The chair dated from 1770 and had been commissioned from one of Philadelphia's most prestigious cabinetmakers by a colonial patron of the arts who subsequently became a Revolutionary War hero. The furniture expert had even managed to locate a copy of the original bill, which secured the chair's distinguished pedigree. She estimated its worth at $2 million.

"This is what Miles must have been calling me about," she concluded. "That chair was always one of his favorites, though he liked it for what he called its hairy paws—its carved claw-and-ball feet—rather than its laughing mouth. He would have been delighted that it was a diamond in the rough. It was always one of my favorites, too. But for a different reason: I liked it because it was one of only two Q's. The other was a Quaker side chair. Q's always were a problem, just like in Scrabble."

Charlotte was mystified. "What are you talking about?" she asked.

"I'm sorry," Pamela said. "I guess I should explain. We used to play a spelling game with the chairs. Each chair stood for a letter of the alphabet. We called it 'Chair Scrabble.' One player would arrange the chairs in a line—a word, if you will—and the other players would try to guess the word or words that the chairs spelled."

Was this a clue? Charlotte wondered. Judging from the amount of blood that had leaked from his wounds, Miles Morey had gone through considerable pain and effort to line the chairs up before he died. Now it struck Charlotte that the dying man might have arranged the chairs to convey a message, perhaps even the identity of his killer.

If the case could be compared to a word game, Pamela might have just supplied the missing letter. If Charlotte's hunch was right, the solution now lay right in front of her; it was a simply a matter of arranging the letters on her wooden tile rack.

"Tell me more," she asked eagerly.

"I haven't thought about that game in years,"

Pamela said. There was a pause as she tried to remember. "As I said," she continued after a moment, "Aunt Emily was very interested in the decorative arts and very concerned that her descendants gain a firm educational footing in that area. She used to grill us on styles, using the chairs as examples. The cousins devised the game as a way of remembering. God forbid we should miss a question on one of her pop quizzes. So we would spell our names with the chairs. Miles, for instance, might be Morris, Italian, Louis XV, Empire, Sheraton. Pam might be Pilgrim, Adam, Moroccan.

"When Aunt Emily found out about our game, she was delighted. Under her direction, the game evolved from spelling names or single words to spelling entire sentences. Then she started buying chairs with the game in mind. It gave a focus to her collecting. She always said that a collection without a focus was too arbitrary to be worthy of the name, while a collection with a focus became its own systematic universe. That's how she ended up with the Voltaire chair, the Yorkshire chair, the Zanzibar chair—we needed examples of the less frequently used letters."

"Pamela, do you remember how the chairs were lined up in the center of the ballroom?" Charlotte asked.

She thought for a moment. "I can't say that I do. I guess I was too overwhelmed by the sight of the wing chair in which Miles had died."

Charlotte described the arrangement of the chairs.

"Do you think Miles might have arranged the chairs in such a way as to reveal the identity of his killer?"

"I think it's a possibility, yes. But why something so complicated? Why wouldn't he just have written down the murderer's name? Or used the phone to call someone?"

"Maybe he didn't have paper with him. Or a pen. As a matter of fact," Charlotte remembered, "the police found his briefcase in the downstairs parlor. As for the telephone, didn't you say that it was disconnected after your great-aunt's death?"

"That's right," she said. "I forgot."

"Here's something else to consider," Charlotte went on. "What if someone else recognized the chair for the valuable antique that it is and realized that with Miles out of the way he or she would be able to buy it for a modest price? That person shoots Miles and leaves him for dead. But Miles is still alive and uses his last minutes to arrange the chairs to reveal the identity of his killer."

Pamela thought for a moment. "But how would the murderer have known that Miles knew the chair was valuable?" she asked.

"I don't know," Charlotte said. "But it's a motive—and a strong one. Do you have time for a ride up to Zion Hill?"

They arrived an hour later and found Jerry waiting for them under the porte cochere. Though the weather was better than on their first visit—a beautiful April afternoon, in fact—the house looked no less gloomy. With

Pamela in the lead, they made their way up the dimly lit staircase. This time, Charlotte noticed details she had missed before. The naked lightbulb hanging from a frayed cord, the excrescences flowering in the ceiling plaster, the dark, tooled leather walls, which looked as if they had withstood a major fire and a revolution or two. The Chatwold Preservation Association would need every penny of the chair's $2 million expected price to restore this place, she thought. But she could also see the magic of the eclectic mix of materials and styles: once it was fixed up, the stained glass windows, the iridescent glass bricks, the mosaics and friezes would turn the house into a fantasy stage set: a combination of medieval sanctuary and Moorish palace.

The ballroom was dark. The police floodlights had been removed, and, though the day was bright, the windows admitted little light. After fumbling for the switch, Jerry turned on the chandeliers, illuminating the "laughing" chair and the three rows of chairs in the center whose arrangement now made sense in the same way that the arrangement of letters suddenly makes sense to a child who has learned that they represent words.

"Now tell me again how this game is played," Jerry said as they crossed the room to the chairs in the center.

"Actually, we played it several ways," Pamela replied. "It became more complex as our knowledge became more sophisticated. On the most basic level, which is how it was played among the youngest cousins, the criterion was simple description: color, type of wood, general style, period, function. If you needed a B, for instance, you might choose a bamboo chair, a baroque chair, a black chair, or a bishop's chair."

"What's a bishop's chair?" asked Jerry.

"Anything that looks as if a bishop might sit in it. The rules were pretty loose. We called it 'Free for All.' On the next level of complexity was 'Style,'" she continued. "For 'Style,' the chairs were chosen on the basis of a particular style. In that game, B might be Biedermeier or Belter or Bentwood. Then there was 'Geography,' in which the chairs were chosen according to their place of origin. If your opponent was knowledgeable, 'Geography' could be really tough. For instance, for a Z, you might choose a Zanzibar chair or a Zoarite chair, which is a chair that was made by a nineteenth-century utopian community in Zoar, Ohio."

"And I thought I'd asked a simple question," Jerry commented.

"It was by no means simple," Pamela replied. "I didn't even mention the time element. Actually, I don't remember how that worked except to say that the faster you guessed the words, the more points you earned. On the most sophisticated level was 'Designer.' For instance, for an O, you might choose a chair designed by Jean Oudry, an eighteenth-century French rococo designer. For an M, you might choose a Barcelona chair, which was designed by the Bauhaus designer Mies Van der Rohe. Or, for a Z, you might choose a foam rubber chair designed by Marco Zanuso, a twentieth-century Italian designer."

"She remembers all those Z's," teased Jerry.

"That's hardly surprising," Pamela replied with a smile. "You had to be able to come up with those letters fast. My brother and sister and I were very good, but the cousins were stiff competition, and Miles was the best of the lot."

"Which game would he have played?" asked Charlotte.

"Considering that he was mortally wounded, I should think he would have picked 'Free for All,' which is the simplest. We'll soon see. I used to be pretty good at this," she said as she pulled a notepad out of her pocketbook. "But I'm a little rusty."

"Take your time," said Jerry.

"We used to play that each row of chairs was a word," Pamela said. She had taken a position at the front of the group of chairs.

"Then there are three words," offered Charlotte. "First word, nine letters; second word, six letters; third word, three letters." The first chair in the first row was the Barcelona chair that Pamela had just mentioned.

"I'm going to assume that Miles was playing 'Free for All.' First letter, B for Barcelona or Black; second letter, E for Eastlake; third letter, R for Regency; fourth letter, K for Kent; fifth letter, S for Siège d'amour."

"Siège d'amour?" said Charlotte.

"Seat of love," she translated. "Specially designed for the exclusive use of Great Britain's Prince Albert in

Paris's most luxurious brothels," she added with a smile. "An early form of the recliner."

Charlotte raised an eyebrow in her signature expression as she imagined the corpulent prince coupling with a *putain* in what looked like a plushly upholstered version of a dentist's chair.

Pamela continued, writing down each of the letters as she spoke. "Sixth letter, H for Hitchcock; seventh letter, I for Indian; eighth letter, R for Regency; ninth letter, E for Empire."

"Berkshire," said Jerry, who had also been writing the letters down. "Does that mean anything to you?"

Pamela shook her head. "But it's not gibberish, which means we must be on the right track." She turned her attention to the second row of chairs. "Second word, first letter: V for Voyeuse—it's a chair for card games," she explained to her mystified onlookers. "The padded back rail was for a friend to lean on while watching the game."

"I had no idea there were so many different kinds of chairs," said Jerry.

"And for such unusual purposes," said Charlotte archly, with a sidelong glance at the rose-colored velvet of the siège d'amour.

Pamela continued. "Second letter, A for Adam; third letter, L for Louis XV; fourth letter, L for Ladderback; fifth letter, E for Egyptian; sixth letter, Y for Yorkshire. V-A-L-L-E-Y," she said, looking down at her notebook. She looked up at the chairs. "You know, Miles used to love this game. I'd like to think he had some fun with it during the last moments of his life."

"Whether he was having fun or not," said Charlotte, "he was thinking of you. He was counting on you to solve his puzzle."

Pamela considered this and seemed to take solace from the thought. She went on. "Third word, first letter: A for Art Deco; second letter, N for Napoleonic—that's the Directoire-style chair he's seated on in a famous portrait—third letter, T for Thonet. Then there's the Queen Anne chair," she said looking over at the wing chair, which, it now seemed clear, was intended to be the next letter in the word. "I think Miles must have been dragging it over when he died. A-N-T-Q," she said. "Antiques, I would guess, without the I. I's always were hard to come by."

"Berkshire Valley Antiques," Jerry said. "Congratulations. You win the grand prize of two thousand dollars. The only question is, what does it mean?"

Pamela looked over at Charlotte: "I think you were right," she said.

When Jerry had turned the furniture angle of the case over to Charlotte, he had unwittingly handed her the key to its solution. Leave it to a man to favor a bullet trajectory over an antique. Berkshire Valley Antiques was the antiques shop in western Massachusetts where Jim MacGillvray had worked before opening his shop in New York, Jerry told her the next day. He didn't know why Miles hadn't simply spelled out MacGillvray's name or that of his new shop, though he speculated that perhaps Miles couldn't remember either, a memory lapse that wouldn't have been surprising in light of the amount of blood he had lost.

This prompted a comment from Charlotte about being unable to remember names under ordinary circumstances, much less when riddled with bullets.

In fact, Jerry went on, the coroner had determined the cause of death to be loss of blood, rather than bullet wounds. And though a final surge of adrenaline may have fueled Miles's rearrangement of the chairs, the precipitous drop in his blood pressure meant that he wouldn't necessarily have accomplished this with the clearest of minds.

A few more telephone calls established the circumstances leading up to the murder. After his initial look at the chairs, MacGillvray had consulted with an expert in early American furniture about the wing chair. The expert told MacGillvray that he'd been asked by Miles Morey just the week before to look at a chair fitting the same description. He also told MacGillvray that the chair was authentic and estimated its value at $2 million, thus sealing Morey's fate. Knowing that Morey would be alone at Chatwold—perhaps Morey had even told him as much—MacGillvray arrived early and, taking advantage of the fact that no one was around, committed the murder.

"Has MacGillvray owned up to any of this?" Charlotte asked.

Jerry shook his head. "But we found a revolver in the underbrush downriver. He must have ditched it right after the murder. He knew the police would be called to the scene and he didn't want the weapon to be

found in his car. Then he returned, making it look as if
he had just arrived. Now all we have to do is link the
revolver to him, which shouldn't be too hard. We also
have some footprints that we found in the mud near the
riverbank where he threw the weapon away."

Charlotte was about to take a seat when she noticed
that Jerry's chair was missing from behind his desk,
which may have explained why he was still standing.

"I thought you'd never ask," he said when she in-
quired about it. "It's out here. He led her out to the hall,
where four chairs were lined up against the wall. "This
is a chair quiz," he said. "If you guess correctly, you
get lunch on me. I owe it to you for solving the case.
Here's a tip: don't think too hard. This isn't as sophisticated as 'Designer'; in fact, you could call it brain
dead."

Charlotte eyed the chairs. The first was the leather
chair that usually stood behind Jerry's desk. The second was an old easy chair that lived next to the water
cooler in the kitchen, which was what the men (and
one woman) in the department called the former closet
that held the microwave and the coffeepot; the third
was an old mahogany dining chair from God-only-
knew-where; and the fourth was an ordinary desk
chair.

Taking her time, Charlotte turned the possible letter
combinations over in her head. The only letter that
confused her was the third. At first, she was going to
assign it a P for Duncan Phyfe, which was the style,
but she knew this was far too sophisticated for Jerry.
Besides, even if he'd known the name of the style, he

probably would have spelled Phyfe with an F. Spelling wasn't his strong suit.

"C'mon," said Jerry. His arms were folded, his foot tapping impatiently.

"I'm taking my time," she replied firmly. "It's important that I get this right. After all, there's a meal at stake." Then she had it. Brain dead was right. It was the simplest possible solution: D for Dining chair.

"Time's up," Jerry said, making a buzzing noise.

"Okay," she said. "First letter, J for Jerry's; second letter, E for Easy; third letter, D for Dining; and fourth letter, S for Swivel." Then she spelled the word: "J-E-D-S. Jed's," she added triumphantly, naming their favorite restaurant. "Have I got it?" she teased, as if the answer weren't patently obvious.

"You're on," he said. "Let's go."

*We journey to an exotic land for our next story, in this case
the island of Bora Bora. While I'm not all that fond of
tropical climates, I'm obviously in the minority, as there
are thousands of people who flock to the sandy white
beaches and dazzling waters. However, sometimes it's not
all sun and fun, as the detective in this story discovers.*

Honeymoon for One

Sharan Newman

The island of Bora Bora rose from the South Pacific,
green, lush and provocative. I pressed my face
against the tiny airplane window. Below me lay the lagoon, a volcanic crater now filled in with water a shade
of blue-green that I hadn't known nature could pro-
duce.

The plane landed, not on the main island but on one
of the motus, the thin strips of islets that protect the lagoon from the ocean. I clutched my reservation confir-
mation and took a deep breath. The travel agent had
said that the hotel would send a launch for arriving
guests. Now that the moment had arrived, I wasn't sure
I could go through with this.

I let the other passengers get off first. Almost all of them were in pairs, couples on vacation, a few families with children, and honeymooners. Lots of honeymooners. The newlyweds made up the greatest part of the travelers. It was unmistakeable; they had that look about them that said they couldn't imagine anything bad ever happening to them again.

Watching them made my stomach twist in knots but they were impossible to avoid. As I gathered up my carry-on bags, I knew that my family and friends had all been right. It was a terrible mistake to come here. How could I enjoy paradise alone?

I clenched my teeth. Damn it, I said to myself, I'm not going to give up my honeymoon just because the groom decided to run off with a brilliant, beautiful biochemist three days before our wedding. Most men wait thirty years for a trophy wife; George had just decided to skip the preliminaries.

Anyway, taking the trip alone was my second choice. The first was to track George down and eviscerate him. When I explained that to my mother, she agreed that two weeks in the tropics was a fine idea.

So, here I was and not at all sure about this. Maybe I should have cashed in the tickets and gone somewhere less romantic. Chernobyl, perhaps. As we crossed the lagoon to the hotel, the hormone level around me was enough to make my eyes cross. This boat was a veritable ark, a dozen nationalities, and all of them in twos.

Except for one person. A little woman, in her early sixties, I guessed, with that incredible sense of style that could only be French. Even in the hundred-degree heat, she looked cool and aloof. How did she manage it? I fixated on her to keep my mind off the rampant sex steaming from the others.

She must have felt my gaze, for she looked across at me and smiled. It was a welcoming smile, including me in her special club, where the two of us knew more about life than anyone else. I smiled back with less sophistication, vowing to practice in the mirror until I mastered that confident air. She patted the empty seat beside her and I moved to take it, tripping over several suitcases in the process.

"You are American," she said. It wasn't a question. I nodded.

"And traveling alone!" Again I had no need to answer. She shook her head in amazement. "You American girls, so brave and silly. You go everywhere alone. You don't think of danger."

"At a four-star resort?" I tried not to laugh. "It's not as if I were going up the Amazon in a canoe."

She shrugged. Oh, how I yearned to be able to shrug like that! The gesture said more than any words exactly what she thought of my credulity.

"Evil," she said, looking straight into my eyes, "is not stopped by gates or guards . . . or money."

I tried to make a polite and banal reply to this, all the while moving away from her, but something in her voice made me shiver, a movement far less graceful than hers had been.

"But, madame," I said lightly. "You're here alone. Aren't you afraid?"

"Ah, there you are mistaken," she answered. "I'm here with my son and his wife; they are sitting over there."

I looked. The couple was nice looking, perhaps in their midthirties. The man was of middle height, with brown hair. He wore a thick pair of prescription sunglasses. His wife was a bit shorter and in coloring very like her husband. Neither had the air of sophistication of the woman next to me.

"My goodness!" I said without thinking. "Imagine taking a honeymoon with your mother!"

She laughed. "Actually, it's their anniversary. The tenth. I offered to stay home and play grandmother but they insisted that I join them. They knew how much I wanted to see the South Pacific again."

"Again?" I was going to ask her when she'd been here before but the boat had docked and we were being greeted with leis and sunhats by the hotel staff. My name was called and I was handed into the care of one of the most beautiful women I'd ever seen. She was wearing a light cotton dress and a pair of black pearl earrings set in rich gold that accented the gold-brown of her skin. Even in the high humidity, she was perfect, not a wrinkle in the dress or a hair out of place. I knew by feeling that my hair had escaped from the scrunchy and was frizzing around my face, on which I was sure there were streaks of mascara. My clothes were sweaty and rumpled from the long trip.

"My name is Françoise," the hostess said with a light accent. "Allow me to show you to your room and help you get settled."

As I watched her glide before me to my bungalow, I had the distinct feeling that our positions should be reversed, except that, looking as I did now, no one would have hired me to work in such an upscale place.

The hotel was made up of a number of frame bungalows with palm leaf roofs. Inside there was a sitting room, a wet bar, a bedroom and bath. Fresh flowers had been placed in all the rooms. A fruit and cheese plate and a bottle of chilled champagne were on the bar. I picked up the card propped up on the ice bucket.

The management welcomes Mr. & Mrs. Prescott and wishes you a long and happy life together.

I dropped the card. Françoise saw me and rushed over to snatch the card and tear it into bits.

"I'm so sorry!" she exclaimed. "The kitchen must not have received the message after you changed the reservation."

"It's all right," I said, although it wasn't. "Does that mean I have to send back the champagne?"

"Of course not!" she answered. "It means I'll see that they send you another bottle tomorrow, as well. Now let me show you the rest of the bungalow."

There wasn't much to it. The hotel was far too refined for affectations like air conditioning. There were ceiling fans instead. However, Françoise pointed out that I was right on the lagoon. If it got too hot, I could just walk right into the water, not six feet from the door.

I thanked Françoise, not sure if I should tip her. Perhaps a discreet envelope at the end of the two weeks? I'd have to call my mother for advice.

As soon as she left, I took off my traveling clothes and hurried into the shower. The first thing I discovered was that there was no need to turn on the hot water. The cold was warm enough. The second thing was that I wasn't alone. The shower was built as a tropical atrium and among the plants little salamanders skittered. I decided not to scream. I wasn't dressed for company and they seemed harmless.

"Just no snakes," I said. "One snake and I'm outta here."

There were no snakes. I dressed in the lightest outfit I had brought and went out to open the champagne.

"Here's to me!" I raised the glass. "All alone in paradise. Eat your heart out, George!"

I finished the bottle, ate all the fruit and cheese and went to bed.

The next morning I was wakened by a strange skritching sound from the beach. Still concerned about snakes, I peeked through the shutters. Three men were raking the sand, removing any detritus that the lagoon might have deposited during the night. No tourist would cut their bare foot on a broken shell today.

It was barely dawn. The sky was the shade of an opal, shot through with the red of the approaching sun. What was anyone doing awake so early, much less working? What about the easygoing island life I'd heard so much about?

I reminded myself that I was on vacation and tried to go back to sleep. It didn't work. After a few minutes

I got up, dressed and went up to the main building in search of breakfast.

There was a young man at the desk. *"Ia ora na!"* he greeted me. *"Bonjour,* good morning, *guten tag!"*

"Good morning," I answered to give him a clue as to what language to continue in. "I suppose it's way too early for breakfast?"

He looked at his watch. "We usually don't get many people this early," he admitted. "I don't think the kitchen could manage more than coffee, fresh mango and *pain au chocolat.*"

Mouth watering, I said that would be fine and he led me to a small table. He came back in a moment with a fax copy of a summary of yesterday's *Wall Street Journal* and the crossword from the *New York Times*. Well, I suppose one can't get completely away from the real world if one wants to afford this sort of escape. At least it gave me something to do while I waited for the food.

There was nothing in the paper about George being hit by a truck or his new wife choking to death on fumes from her laboratory, so I turned to the crossword. I was puzzling over five across when I sensed someone standing next to me. I looked up. It was the woman from the launch.

"May I join you?" she asked. "I don't wish to make the staff set two tables."

"Of course." I put the puzzle down and held out my hand. "We didn't introduce ourselves. I'm Clarissa Hoar." I saw her look. "It's not what you think; different spelling."

"Ah." She seemed satisfied. "I am Mireille Dumont. How do you do?"

She seated herself and I tried to think of some small talk that wouldn't sound like prying. Mme. Dumont seemed to feel no need to speak at all. She waited until the coffee had arrived, took a sip and pronounced it good before addressing me.

"Michel and Delphine have decided that we shall take the tour of the inner island this morning," she said. "What are your plans for the day?"

I hadn't thought. Getting here was as far as I could manage. I admitted that I had no plans. "What is there to see?"

"I don't know," she answered. "That's why I've decided to go."

It sounded as good a reason as any. "If there is space, perhaps I'll do that, as well."

There was space so, at nine o'clock, I stood in the lobby with six other people waiting for the tour bus to pick us up.

Three of the people were Mme. Dumont, Michel and Delphine. She introduced me to them and they nodded with polite disinterest. The other couple was from Australia, an executive and his wife taking a second honeymoon. The last person was a man. I couldn't tell his nationality from his accent, and he didn't give his name. He was in his early forties, I guessed. There was a touch of gray in his hair and fine lines at the corners of his eyes. He gave the impression of being an international spy or gigolo. His smile was dazzling. Thank goodness I was at the moment impervious to male charm.

We were all chatting aimlessly about the weather when the bus pulled up and the driver got out. Mme. Dumont took one look, gasped and turned away.

"*Maman!*" Michel rushed to her. "Are you all right?"

She answered rapidly in French. He nodded solicitously and guided her back toward her bungalow. When he returned, he apologized.

"My mother didn't realize that we would be traveling in an open truck instead of a bus," he explained. "She has had a terror of such things since she was a child during the war."

We all expressed our sympathy. Once more I had a glimpse into Mme. Dumont's past. It seemed exotic and mysterious and only increased my fascination for the woman.

The driver looked the epitome of the castaway sailor: leathery skin, worn blue shirt and jeans and a fringe of white hair underneath a ragged skipper's hat. He wasn't Polynesian, obviously. I wondered what storm had thrown him up here.

At the moment he was talking to Françoise, now on duty. They were speaking a sort of French-Tahitian patois and I could understand none of it, but their voices were rising and it was clear that an argument was going on. Finally she cut him off with the comment, "*Non! C'est aita maita'i! Tu es tout à fait taravana! Va! Je suis fiu!*"

They were suddenly aware of our curiosity.

Françoise collected herself at once, nodded to us and returned to the desk. The driver grinned and shrugged as he approached us.

"Women!" he said. "Now, are all of you for the island tour? Everyone understand English?"

We all admitted to both and he piled us into the back of the truck.

"I'm Henri!" he said as we started down the road. "No, I'm not a native, but I've lived here thirty years and more and there's nothing about the island that I don't know."

"He comes well recommended," the Australian man told us. "The hotel won't contract to just anyone."

Thus reassured, we settled back to enjoy the tour.

Actually, the settling lasted only as long as we were on the main road circling the shore. Henri dutifully pointed out the pearl shops, restaurants and condos owned by movie stars and princes, none of whom were in residence at the moment. Then we turned into what I thought was a parking place. But Henri kept driving and we passed through a curtain of vines to find ourselves on a rutted road, barely as wide as the truck, that seemed to go straight up. The jungle was all around us and my nervousness about snakes returned. But I soon was enraptured by the sense of being in the middle of a tropical bouquet of hibiscus, jasmine and orchids. Henri encouraged us all to pick a flower to put behind our ears, the left if one is taken, the right for availability. I noticed that the mysterious stranger with the great teeth put the flower behind the right ear. I held mine in my lap, unsure about declaring my solitary state so obviously. The man saw my indecision, reached over, took the blossom and tucked it firmly behind my right ear.

"It is my greatest hope," he whispered.

In Boston I'd have called the cops. In Bora Bora, I just blushed from the hairline down and tried to look blasé, as if handsome men murmured such things to me every day.

Soon we broke through the jungle to a clear area, where there was a white house and a manicured lawn. Beside the house was a field of pineapples. Henri leapt from the truck, taking out a huge bolo knife from a sheath behind his seat. He told us all to follow as he loped through the field as if stalking a rogue fruit. He stopped at last and slashed two pineapples from their plants. With amazing delicacy, he peeled them and handed the pieces around on the knife blade. I had never tasted anything so good in my life.

"It's not native to the islands, you know," the Australian said, juice dripping down his chin. "Pineapple was brought here by the missionaries, British Protestant missionaries."

Was I supposed to cheer their generosity? I had no idea so I just continued licking my fingers.

We piled back into the truck and, a little way down the road, Henri stopped again and had us pick some leaves. I assumed it was to wipe our hands but a moment later he stopped again and told us to throw the leaves into a dry ditch on our right.

I did so and then waited for the truck to start again. When I heard the startled cries of the others, I looked back. Little crabs, about as big as my hand, had appeared from nowhere, it seemed, and were making short work of the leaves.

"Land crabs." Henri chuckled. "They eat anything. Island garbage collectors."

Everyone but me laughed. I didn't like the way those little claws ripped the leaves to shreds and stuffed the pieces into tiny mouths.

We saw the rest of the island, bumping up and down the ruts. The roads, Henri said, were courtesy of the Americans stationed here in World War II. They must have all gone home to work on the back roads of Massachusetts. The potholes felt familiar. We looked at the leftover cannon and bunkers and marveled at the view of the lagoon from the slopes of Mt. Pahia.

By the time we got back, all I wanted was to put on my swimsuit and soak off the film of dust and sweat in that lagoon. I had been assured that the daily shark feeding was far from my bungalow. I thanked Henri and gave him a tip. Everyone but my mysterious stranger went back toward their rooms or the bar. He stayed to chat with Henri. He must be French, too. That's what they seemed to be speaking. I caught the phrase *vieux chameau,* which made the stranger laugh. He had a nice laugh.

I spent the rest of the afternoon snorkling. Fish make no emotional demands.

The next day Mme. Dumont and I met at breakfast again and agreed to go shopping in the main town of Vaitape. My mother had told me to get her monoi oil, made from coconut oil and gardenias. She had heard that it retarded wrinkles better than any of the new things on the market. I lusted after a black pearl necklace. Every woman I had seen since I got here had been wearing pearls in one form or another. How expensive could they be?

Very.

After much soul-searching, I bought a pendant. Just one beautiful, teardrop-shaped pearl. Mme. Dumont, however, delighted the sales woman by getting two necklaces, one for her daughter-in-law, with bracelets and earrings to match. I tried not to let my jaw drop at the size of the final bill.

My companion laughed. "This voyage is my special treat. I would be foolish to waste it on caution."

When I had recovered, we explored the rest of the town, getting some shell bracelets for her granddaughters and my nieces. I found the oil for Mother. I looked at my watch. It wasn't even ten o'clock yet.

"I don't understand it," I said. "What about the slow pace of island life? Everyone here seems to be working their . . . uh . . . to be working very hard."

"It wasn't always like this," Mme. Dumont said. "But many of these people have children in college in Hawaii or France. Others want to retire comfortably. I sometimes wonder if the idea of lazy days in the tropics was a wishful myth put about by visitors."

"How do you know these things?" I asked.

"Oh, I listen," she said quickly. "They all learn French as soon as they start school, you see. I talk with people. We share stories about our lives, our children."

She must have been much more sociable than I, to learn so much in two days.

"There is a house in the center of the island, where they make amazing batiks," Mme. Dumont said, changing the subject. "I was thinking of hiring a closed car and going there this afternoon. Would you like to come with me?"

I agreed readily. It was already clear to me that I owned nothing light enough for this climate. Most of the other women at the hotel were wearing skirts and blouses of local fabrics. The price for those was quite reasonable. Mme. Dumont seemed pleased and told me she would meet me in the lobby after lunch.

I had my lunch in the open-air bar as I enjoyed the breeze from a short but refreshing rainfall. The Australians were eating a local specialty of raw fish but I decided on a hamburger. To keep from seeming too gauche, I washed it down with fresh coconut milk, right from the shell. I had always wanted to try that and it was actually better than I expected. I ordered another.

"They're better with rum," said a sultry voice at my elbow.

I must have started, for, when I turned to him, the man from the tour was regarding me with an amused smile. I gathered up my dignity.

"Perhaps I'll try it this evening," I said.

His smile grew. "I hope you'll allow me to buy you your first one."

My God, how could the man make that sound like an offer of seduction? I finished my coconut and slid off the stool, trying not to look nervous. I'm sure I failed. This man was well aware of his looks and charm and enjoyed making me feel like a teenager at her first dance. I didn't look back as I went up to meet Mme. Dumont.

She drove the little car up the bumpy road with great skill, most of the time in first gear. We found the house and spent an hour trying on various loose outfits in beautiful patterns based on island flowers and fish. Finally we made our purchases and started down the mountain.

It hadn't occurred to me that getting down would be so much trickier than getting up. The ruts in the road kept trying to lead the car into the jungle and Mme. Dumont's lips were tight as she fought to keep us going slowly downward.

All at once the tires skidded through a patch of mud and we went sliding sideways into a tangle of vines. The car was left half on the road and half in the foliage that kept us from plunging the rest of the way to the ocean.

"Mon Dieu!" Mme. Dumont exclaimed. "I apologize! Are you harmed?"

"No," I said. "Just shaken a bit."

It took us a bit of time to ease out, me first, since my door was still on the road. Then I helped Mme. Dumont.

"Well," I said, "at least there's no danger of our getting lost. We'll just hike down to the hotel and have them send someone to get the car. Can you walk?"

She nodded and we set off. Neither of us were wearing shoes that were intended for a dirt road just after a rain and soon we were both spattered with mud. She wore it better than I did.

We were almost to the bottom; we could hear the noise of scooters on the main road when Mme. Dumont stopped.

"What is that awful smell?" she exclaimed.

I sniffed and looked around. There was a cloud of flies not far from us rising from a ditch. I walked toward it.

"Someone must have been dumping garbage here," I said as I peered down. The flies lifted and I saw what was underneath.

"Oh, my god!" I shrieked. "The crabs really do eat anything!"

I backed away from what was left of Henri. Then I threw up.

"Don't look!" I gasped between retches. "It's a man. The driver from yesterday, I think. It's awful!"

Mme. Dumont paid me no attention. She went over and looked down to where the flies had settled again.

"Ah, non!" she wailed. "Henri! Mon pauvre fou! Pourquoi?"

Then, still crying, she ripped a long frond from a nearby bush and began swishing it wildly, chasing the flies away, all the while screaming at them. Then she fell to her knees and reached down to touch the body.

Her actions startled me out of my nausea.

"Madame!" I cried, rushing over to her. "What are you doing? I told you not to look. Please, we have to go for the police. Look, you've cut yourself. It's no use. The flies will only come back."

"No, no!" she cried. "He doesn't deserve this! Oh, my poor Henri!"

"You knew him?" I asked. It didn't seem possible.

"Of course, you silly child!" She wiped her nose with her wrist. "He was my husband!"

The chief of police for the island seemed as stunned by the death as I had been. He was a man about my age, not long out of college, I guessed. There was a diploma from the University of Lille on the wall behind him. His name was René Tefatu. Chief Tefatu kept shaking his head.

"A murder!" he repeated. "In my whole life we've never had a real murder here. And now, in my first month as police chief. What will the office in Papeete say?"

"Are you sure it was murder?" I asked. From what I had seen, there was barely enough left to identify, much less tell the cause.

"His bolo was found not far from the body and his throat had been slashed," Chief Tefatu answered. "Even I had to assume he was murdered."

I didn't know why he was being so defensive. After all, I'd never found a body before. I would have preferred Henri to have been the victim of a heart attack or something.

I stood up. "I've told you all I can, monsieur," I said coldly. "Now I'd like to go back to my room and wash."

"You may go now, madame," he answered after a

quick glance at the mark where my engagement ring had been. "But you haven't told me everything you know. You spent most of yesterday with M. Dumont and I shall have to question you again."

"You make it sound as if we'd had a date," I retorted. "He was the island guide. We didn't exchange confidences."

Then I remembered Henri's argument with Françoise and the little tête-a-tête with the other man afterwards. Really, those weren't worth mentioning. Or were they? Right now I just wanted to be clean and cool again. I left the office with a sigh of relief.

That evening in the bar, I found myself the center of attention. Mme. Dumont and her family were in seclusion and everyone else wanted to know all about the death and her astounding revelation.

"She *must* have come here to kill him!" a breathless American voice rose above the others. "It can't possibly be a coincidence."

"Mme. Dumont is obviously grief-stricken," I defended her. I took another sip of my Southern Cross, a fruit and rum concoction that I needed to soothe my nerves.

"Nonsense, everyone knows what a great actress she is." This speaker was French.

I looked up. "Actress?"

The woman regarded me with scorn. "You've never heard of Mireille Dumont?" she asked. "One of the most famous actresses in France. She could certainly pretend to feel anything she wanted."

My goodness! I had been shopping with a famous actress! Mother would be very impressed.

From his seat at a nearby table, the mysterious stranger gave me one of his amused smiles. I must seem such a provincial dolt to him!

I clung to my original impression.

"She wasn't acting when we found him," I insisted. "I'm sure she had nothing to do with his death."

"Maybe not. Old Henri was a real bastard, by all accounts." The well-informed Australian was speaking now. "He cheated the tourists and the locals. He beat his native wife until she went back to her family. Nasty piece of work."

"How do you know that?" I asked.

He tapped his nose. "I have a good rapport with these island people, you know. I pick up information."

I took another sip of the Southern Cross. It was making me sleepy. I decided I'd better go back to my bungalow before I fell over.

The bungalow was at the end of a long path, almost to the edge of the hotel enclosure. As I went back, I was sure that I heard the crunch of steps on the sand behind me. I went faster and the steps did, too. I was almost running when he overtook me. When his hand touched my shoulder, I screamed.

"No, no! Please, Mme. Hoar. I have no wish to harm you!" It was the police chief.

"Good grief!" I said. "You scared me to death! You might have called out."

"I apologize. I didn't want to disturb the other guests," he said. "My assistant, Tapé, called from the

bar to say you had just left. I wanted to speak with you
again, as long as I was here. Also, Mme. Dumont has
asked if you would stop by to see her. She's worried
about you."

"About me? Whatever for?"

He shrugged. "You will have to ask her. Shall we return to her room?"

I couldn't think of a reason to refuse. And I must
admit I was rather relishing being involved in a murder
with a celebrity, even if I'd never heard of her.

When we entered, she was on the sofa in the sitting
room. She opened her arms to me.

"Ma mignonne!" she exclaimed. "Are you recovered? What a horrible thing to happen to you!"

Timidly, I hugged her. "Much worse for you. I
barely knew the man."

"Ah, yes, but I have seen ugly death before; you
hadn't." She kissed my forehead and released me. "I
have been telling this nice man that I didn't know until
yesterday that my husband was on Bora Bora, although
I always believed he was still alive. Henri would never
have drowned within sight of land. He was a strong
swimmer and I was very much aware of his love for
the Polynesian way of life. It was in Tahiti that we
met."

Chief Tefatu interrupted. "I have always admired
you, madam, for never denying your island heritage."

"There was no reason to," she answered. "But when
I came to France, I put it behind me. I had only one
grandmother from Tahiti and she died when I was
small. My children only knew it as the place where

their father had been lost. But now I have returned to find my husband alive and you think I fought with him and murdered him with his own knife in revenge. Is that correct?"

"It seems unlikely to me," the chief answered. "But you were seen last night with Henri at Ben's Place and no one saw him afterward."

"Yes, I've already told you." She sighed. "I met him. It was like seeing a stranger who resembled someone I had once known. I had hated him for a time, but long ago. My dear"—she turned to me—"it is ridiculous to hate someone for not loving you anymore. It's not something anyone can help. I thought he should have left more to care for the children, but he wasn't like that, and I suppose I knew it when we married. Anyway, my anger couldn't touch him, so what was the point? I created a better life without him."

She smiled at Chief Tefatu. "If you will excuse my saying so, it is the people here who suffered most. They had to live with him these past thirty years."

"Yes," he answered.

I stared at him. There was more anger in that one word than in all of Mme. Dumont's story. He said nothing more but asked if he could use the sitting room to finish his questioning while Mme. Dumont prepared for bed in the other room.

When she had left, he turned to me.

"I want you to try to remember everything that happened when Henri took you out yesterday."

"Very well." I tried to stay calm and objective but I didn't want to mention that I had seen Henri arguing with Françoise. Unfortunately, the others who had been there had already told him.

"I didn't understand what it was about," I said. "They weren't speaking English. All I remember is the last thing she said: *'Je suis fiu.'* What does that mean?"

"Disgusted, fed up," he answered. "Which is a feeling I'm getting from a lot of the people who dealt with Henri."

He was more interested in the interchange I had witnessed between Henri and the mysterious stranger.

"I'm sure they knew each other," I said. "He's the one you should question."

"I already have," Chief Tefatu told me. "He's a police detective from Papeete. He says Henri has been helping him in an investigation involving the illegal export of pearls."

What? My mysterious stranger was a cop?

"Even police detectives can have cause to murder." I stuck to my theory. Anything to keep Mme. Dumont and Françoise from being suspected.

The chief's face hardened. "That's true," he said sadly. "I assure you I am terribly aware of that."

He let me go then. I didn't understand what he meant until much later that night. I was lying on the lounge chair on my deck, hoping for a cool breeze so I could sleep. I heard voices coming from the public beach, just beyond mine. Nervous, I sat up and looked. There in the light of the tiki torch were Françoise and Chief Tefatu. She was crying and he was holding her. His expression did not show professional detachment.

• • •

I spent the rest of the night sitting awake on the deck chair, watching the real Southern Cross rise and then be blotted out by the approach of dawn. I had no idea what to do. Obviously René Tefatu was even less fit to solve the murder of Henri Dumont than was the detective from Papeete. Should I confront him with the fact that I had seen him embracing a suspect? That didn't seem wise. Should I ignore it? After all, this wasn't my country or my problem. That didn't seem right. That left me with one alternative and I hated it.

He was taking a morning stroll along the beach. I had seen him there before. Very well. I combed my hair and put on one of the island outfits that had been salvaged from the rental car. I took a deep breath.

"Monsieur!" I called softly. No sense in attracting attention. Damn it, I wish I'd thought to ask his name.

He stopped, saw me, smiled and waved. I came down the steps to join him.

"Good morning," I said. "I understand that you're a policeman."

I didn't want him to think I had any personal reason for accosting him.

"Yes," he answered. "But I specialize in smuggling, not homicide. They'll be sending someone else to deal with that."

"You mean that Chief Tefatu isn't in charge?"

"For now he is, but he could hardly investigate honestly, since he's engaged to the victim's daughter."

Dominos began to cascade inside my brain. "Françoise is Henri's daughter?"

"Amazing, isn't it?" he answered. "Her mother was

half German, I understand. A beautiful woman. Of course Henri disapproved of the match."

"Whatever for?"

He stopped and stared at me. "You're American; you should know these things."

I was honestly in the dark and told him so.

"René is pure Tahitian. He looks like an islander."

I thought about this. The chief was tall and dark. His features were broader and flatter than those of the people I had met working at the hotel. He looked more like the people Gauguin had painted.

"Exactly," the detective said. "Henri wanted her to marry a European. He complained to me about it. Of course, he was right. Her children would look like natives. All the good office jobs and hotel positions go to people with European features. Hadn't you noticed?"

I hadn't. But he was right. The only people I had seen who appeared to be true Polynesian were the men who swept the beach before anyone would normally be awake.

"Are you trying to tell me that Chief Tefatu murdered Henri because of Françoise?"

"No, not at all." He smiled at me again. He did have amazing teeth. I wondered if they were capped. "Françoise is of age. She didn't need Henri's permission. But it looks bad for René to head the investigation."

"So who do you think killed Henri?" I asked.

He shrugged. God, had everyone but me mastered that Gallic shoulder twitch?

"I don't know," he admitted. "Why don't we go up and have breakfast while we consider the problem?"

I was hungry. It would have been rude to refuse. So we went.

The dining room was almost empty. A few tables down from us sat Mme. Dumont's son and his wife. Mme. Dumont must still be in her room.

The detective got his croissant and sat down across from me. The waitress poured the coffee. When the ceremony was complete, I leaned toward him.

"Don't you have any clues, any ideas, outside of Mme. Dumont and Chief Tefatu?" I asked.

He looked at me a moment, seeming to consider my trustworthiness. Finally he nodded.

"The only thing we found at the scene that seemed out of place was a piece of broken glass. Just a sliver, the color of a wine bottle—Bordeaux. We sent it to Papeete on yesterday's flight. It's probably nothing."

I thought for a moment. Something was rattling in my head. The dominos were forming a pattern.

"Mme. Dumont cut her hand on something," I said slowly. "She reached in to touch the body and cut her hand."

"I noticed the bandage," he said. "She told me it was from a branch she had grabbed to chase the flies away."

I tried to remember clearly. "No, she cut herself when she reached into the ditch. Was there blood on the glass?"

"Not that I could see," he told me. "We'll have to wait for the lab report."

I sipped my coffee and added more sugar and cream. I waved politely at the younger Dumonts. He looked different, but I couldn't think why. Then I knew.

"The glasses," I cried, spilling the coffee. I lowered my voice. "Michel Dumont is wearing regular glasses."

The detective turned around to look. "So he is. What of it?"

"He's had on thick prescription sunglasses all the time we've been here," I said. "The sun is terribly bright and shining right in the windows. Why isn't he wearing them now?"

The detective considered this.

"What color were they?" he asked.

"Dark green," I said. "The color of a wine bottle, Napa Cabernet."

"Excuse me." He got up. "I need to make a phone call."

The police arrived an hour later and took Michel away, sobbing. He had confessed as soon as he was asked about the broken lens in his sunglasses. Mme. Dumont was devastated, even more than Delphine, who seemed impervious to emotion.

"It was so long ago!" She wept. "We were better off without him. I thought Michel understood. But all this time he's been eating himself with hatred, wanting to find his father and punish him for running away. Oh, my poor son!"

"We'll get him the best *avocat* in France," Delphine

assured her. "It was a crime of passion. The court will understand."

"Perhaps. I hope so," Mme. Dumont sniffed. "But I never will."

Soon everyone was gone, the hotel staff back to their jobs and the honeymooners back to their beds. Somehow I found myself standing alone with my mysterious stranger, now just a French cop.

"Before you go, I would appreciate knowing your name," I said pettishly.

He gave me the full smile.

"Philippe," he answered. "Philippe LeBeau. But I'm not leaving just yet. I've booked a boat tour of the lagoon with lunch on a motu. It would be nice to have some company. And, of course, I'll be all alone for dinner afterwards. If you would care to help me look less conspicuous . . . ?"

"Well." I smiled back. "I suppose I could do that."

The rest of the vacation went better than I had ever dreamed.

"Darling!" My mother's high heels clattered across the airport tiles. "My precious. How are you? You didn't get much of a tan. Oh, my dear, I knew you shouldn't have gone on that stupid trip. You stayed in your room the whole time, didn't you? All my friends told me it would be like that, you all alone with nothing to do but mope about George."

I hugged her, trying to take in the flow of words. So much had happened to me, so much that she could never understand. Certainly nothing I could explain in the middle of Logan Airport. Only one thing penetrated.

"George?" I said. "George who?"

It hit me like a cold towel. *That* George! The one I had gone to Bora Bora to spite. When I left, I had thought my life was ruined. In two weeks I had forgotten all about him.

"*Merci,* Mme. Dumont," I whispered. "You were right. In everything, you were right."

One of the best things about writing is the ability to ex-
plore other worlds and times. The late medieval world of
Japan comes alive in this next piece about love, betrayal,
and murder at a Kabuki theater in Tokyo. All is not what
it seems behind the scenes of what begins as a simple play,
and our woman sleuth must uncover a wicked plot while
hampered by the social conventions of the times. How she
accomplishes this is a delight, as you'll soon see.

Onnagata

Laura Joh Rowland

Edo, Genroku Period
Year 4, Month 2
(Tokyo, March 1691)

Sunshine filtered through the skylight of the Nakamura-za Kabuki Theater, upon the beautiful young
woman onstage. Dressed in a red brocade kimono,
with black hair cascading to her knees, she glided
through a forest of painted artificial trees, while musi-

cians played a sad tune on samisen, flute, and wooden clappers. She sang in a sweet, heart-rending voice:

> *"Alas! My love has rejected me,*
> *I cannot bear the agony."*

The vast building echoed with the cheers of the crowd seated on the floor. This was divided into compartments that each held ten people. Hundreds of heads protruded above the dividers—low, sturdy walkways along which the audience could enter and exit the theater, and refreshment vendors carried food and drink during performances. From a compartment along the wall near the front, Lady Reiko, the twenty-one-year-old wife of the shogun's Most Honorable Investigator of Events, Situations, and People, watched the play.

Reiko, the only child of a magistrate, had enjoyed an unusual girlhood. Her father had given her the education customarily reserved for sons. She'd developed an interest in crime while listening to trials in his court. During discussions of cases, she'd impressed him with her insight, and he'd valued her advice. After her marriage, Reiko had begun helping her husband investigate crimes. Often she found witnesses and evidence in places where male detectives couldn't go, and gathered facts from a special communication network composed of women associated with powerful samurai clans. However, the spring season had brought a dearth of crimes. Restless for excitement, Reiko had joined a group of other ladies from Edo Castle on a trip to see "Love Suicides at Oiso," based on the true story of a prostitute named Hanako. Now, dressed in jade silk,

with an upswept coiffure framing her delicate oval
face, Reiko anticipated the climax of the play.

Onstage, Hanako sang:

> *"I shall end my misery,*
>   *Farewell to this sad, cruel world!"*

She drew a dagger from her sleeve. Beside Reiko,
the shogun's elderly mother, Lady Keisho-in, sighed
happily. "Isn't Kantaro magnificent? He's my favorite
actor."

By law, all Kabuki actors were male. The famous
Kantaro was an *onnagata*—a specialist in female roles.
A purple kerchief covered his shaved crown, the mark
of his true sex. Now starring in the role of Hanako the
prostitute, he gazed into the audience and sang his last
verse:

> *"We were secret lovers,*
>   *Until I broke the instrument of my spite,*
>   *Now my purpose is served, and your love defiled."*

While Reiko couldn't see what these strange words
had to do with the story, Lady Keisho-in said, "How
clever of Kantaro to invent extra lines to prolong his
performance!"

Kantaro pretended to plunge the dagger into his
throat. Reiko applauded with the rest of the audience
as Kantaro collapsed in an agony of death-throes. His
performance was utterly convincing.

A nearby commotion distracted Reiko. Murmuring

apologies, a man climbed out of a compartment and strode along the walkway toward the stage. Reiko noted his proud bearing and handsome profile. Then he leapt off the walkway and disappeared.

At last Kantaro lay still in feigned death. Stagehands moved trees in front of his body, hiding it from the audience. The musicians played a mournful dirge. Then their clappers beat in accelerating rhythm. Anticipation stirred the audience.

Down the gangway that extended from the back of the theater to the stage strutted the actor playing the dead prostitute's beloved: a dandyish samurai in wide maroon trousers and broad-shouldered surcoat, his two swords at his waist and a sake jug in his hand. He swaggered through the forest, singing:

> *"Tonight I've drunk my fill of liquor,*
> *And enjoyed the favors of all the town beauties.*
> *Tomorrow I shall do the same!"*

Stagehands removed the trees, and the samurai tripped on Kantaro's body. "What's this?" he cried. Then he looked down, and horror blanched his face. Kneeling, he gathered the limp Kantaro in his arms. "My dearest, are you all right? Speak to me!" He began shouting, "Help! Somebody, help!"

"That's not how the story goes," Lady Keisho-in complained. "He's supposed to perform a speech about how he realizes he loved her after all. That fool actor must have forgotten his lines."

A terrible premonition chilled Reiko. That looked

like blood on the samurai's hands and Kantaro's face, although the *onnagata* hadn't really cut himself. "No, something's wrong," Reiko said.

"She's dead!" Bursting into tears, the samurai laid down Kantaro while the audience murmured uneasily. He snatched up the dagger that lay nearby. With an ear-splitting scream, he stabbed himself in the chest.

"But he shouldn't commit suicide yet," Lady Keisho-in said. "First he has to sing about how he hopes to be reunited with her in paradise."

The audience booed. Theater officials rushed onto the stage. They wrested the dagger away from the samurai, hauled him offstage, and moved a tree in front of Kantaro's body. The theater manager, a dignified man in a black kimono, announced, "I regret to say that the rest of the performance is canceled. Kantaro has been murdered."

Exclamations of surprise, then hysterical weeping arose from the audience. Reiko stood, curious to see what was happening onstage, where the officials conferred anxiously. The killer must have struck during the interval between Kantaro's suicide scene and the samurai's entrance, while Kantaro lay hidden from view. Who had dared to commit murder in the presence of hundreds of people? And why?

In Reiko's compartment, the ladies prepared to leave. But Lady Keisho-in grabbed Reiko's hand and hurried her along the walkway toward the stage. Their male guards followed, battling the tide of the departing audience.

"Since you are a detective," Lady Keisho-in said to Reiko, "I want you to find out who killed Kantaro!"

Reiko had never expected to fulfill her dream of solving a mystery of her own, because she had no authority to investigate crimes and had always been limited to working behind the scenes as her husband's assistant. But Lady Keisho-in, as mother of Japan's supreme military dictator, now invoked his power. She ordered the theater folk to cooperate with Reiko, and assigned guards to enforce her command.

"Perhaps it would be better if my husband investigated the murder," Reiko said. Her spirit rose to the challenge, but she foresaw the disadvantages of a woman doing a man's work.

Typically oblivious to everything except her own whims, Lady Keisho-in waved away the suggestion. "I have perfect faith in you, my dear."

Then she went home, while Reiko searched the stage for clues. But she found none. The dagger was a harmless wooden prop that couldn't have cut the fatal slash across Kantaro's throat; the real murder weapon was nowhere in sight. Reiko interviewed actors, stagehands, officials, and servants. Cowed by the guards, they hid their scorn of a female detective, but they hadn't been backstage at the time of Kantaro's death. All had witnesses to confirm their whereabouts—except the actor Itaguchi, who had played Kantaro's beloved.

In his dressing room, Itaguchi sat weeping. He still wore his bloodstained costume, open to reveal a cloth bandage covering the minor wound he'd inflicted upon himself. Standing in the doorway, Reiko said, "I'm sorry to disturb you, but I must ask you some questions."

Itaguchi glared at her. Tear-smudged stage makeup turned his youthful face into a grotesque mask. "I know why you're here," he said. "You think I killed Kantaro."

"Did you?" Reiko said, anxious to succeed at her first case. If she did, she would win Lady Keisho-in's favor and prove her worth as a detective. If she failed, she would disgrace herself and damage her husband's standing with the shogun.

Instead of answering, Itaguchi gave an incredulous laugh. "What if I did kill Kantaro? Are you going to arrest me and haul me off to jail?" His defiant gaze mocked her femininity.

Anger flared in Reiko; she wasn't used to blatant disrespect from commoners. "Answer my question," she ordered.

"I'm not telling you anything."

After Itaguchi responded with hostile silence to her continued attempts to question him, Reiko reluctantly decided that she couldn't let pride stand between her and the facts she needed. She called her guards. In their presence, Itaguchi cooperated.

"I was nowhere near the stage when Kantaro died," he said. "During the suicide scene, I changed my costume here, then went directly to the back of the theater to make my entrance. Besides, I could never have hurt Kantaro. I was in love with her. And now that she's gone, I can't bear to live any longer." Itaguchi mourned, "They should have let me kill myself!"

"But Kantaro was a man," Reiko said, puzzled by his choice of pronoun.

"Kantaro always dressed like a woman, acted like a woman, and lived like a woman. To me, he was a woman."

Reiko knew that the best *onnagata* maintained their female personae offstage—a practice that supposedly improved their performance—and attracted admirers of both sexes. Yet although Itaguchi's grief seemed real, he could have sneaked backstage without being observed, killed Kantaro, then made his entrance down the gangway. The blood on his dark garments wouldn't have been visible to the audience, and he could claim that it came from touching Kantaro after the murder.

"Did Kantaro share your feelings?" Reiko asked.

"Yes." False bravado tainted Itaguchi's declaration; he sighed, hung his head, and said, "Oh, well. If I don't tell you, someone else will. Kantaro encouraged my affection because it flattered her vanity, but she didn't really care for me. She had . . . masculine needs that I couldn't satisfy. She preferred that woman Akane." Itaguchi spat the name with bitter hatred.

"Who is Akane?" Reiko asked.

"The wife of the man who owns the theater." Cunning shone in Itaguchi's eyes. "She and Kantaro were lovers until they quarreled recently. I saw her here before the play. You should talk to her about the murder."

"I will," Reiko said, bidding the actor farewell.

Though she knew that murder suspects often tried to shield themselves by incriminating other people, Akane merited an interview. But first, Reiko had business to finish at the theater.

"This is Kantaro's dressing room," said the theater manager, ushering Reiko into a chamber where cabinets lined the walls. Colorful costumes hung on racks; a low table held a mirror and jars of makeup. "I'll be in my office if you need anything else."

Examining her surroundings, Reiko noticed a table under the window. It was piled with flower bouquets, boxes wrapped in pretty paper, and scrolls tied with silk cords—tributes from Kantaro's fans, Reiko guessed. Opening a box, she found expensive sweets inside. She unrolled a few scrolls and read letters praising the *onnagata*. But one contained a different message:

> *In vain have I tried to win your love. But you have cruelly spurned me. Now I shall take my revenge in the way that will hurt you the most.*

The letter bore no date, salutation, or signature. Reiko had no time to wonder about the source of what appeared to be a threat against Kantaro's life, because she experienced the sudden, disturbing awareness that she wasn't alone. She tucked the letter under her sash, then reached for the dagger she wore under her flowing sleeve for protection. Before she could draw the weapon, a cabinet door burst open. A burly, dark figure jumped out and bolted toward the door.

"Stop!" Reiko blocked the man's path and snatched at him, but he shoved her aside and ran from the room. Cursing the disadvantage of her small size, she called, "Help! Catch him!"

She hurried into the corridor and saw her guards seize the man. They stripped off his two swords and twisted his arms behind him. He was a samurai in his thirties, with a long, homely face.

"Let me go!" he yelled, struggling against the guards.

The theater manager appeared. When he saw the captive, he grimaced in disgust. "Not you again!"

"Who is he?" Reiko said.

"Hatomi Murashige, a masterless samurai," said the manager. "He's been pestering Kantaro, spying on him, trespassing in the theater, and brawling with other fans. I've had enough of his trouble. I'm calling the police."

As the manager stalked away, Reiko turned to Hatomi. "Why were you hiding in Kantaro's dressing room?"

Kicking and thrashing, Hatomi gave her an insolent stare. "I don't answer to women. Who are you, anyway?"

Reiko introduced herself, then said, "I'm investigating Kantaro's murder."

Shock widened Hatomi's eyes and drained the resistance from him. "Kantaro is dead?"

"Then you didn't know?" Reiko said.

Dazed, he shook his head. "For two years, all I've thought about is Kantaro. I've attended his every performance. My passion for him rules my life. All I wanted was to be close to him, in the hope that he would come to love me in return."

This admirer had no illusions about the *onnagata*'s sex, Reiko noted; apparently, he desired Kantaro as an object of manly love, in the tradition practiced by not a few samurai.

"Kantaro refused to see me, so I hid in the cabinet and waited for him," Hatomi continued. "I fell asleep. I had no idea. . . ." Then rage darkened his expression. "How did it happen? Who did it?" After Reiko explained the circumstances of the *onnagata*'s death, Hatomi fought to free himself. "I'll kill the evil person who destroyed Kantaro!"

His story sounded plausible, and his reaction seemed genuine, but Reiko had only Hatomi's word on his whereabouts at the time of the murder. Maybe he'd stabbed Kantaro, then hidden, intending to escape once everyone had left the theater. Reiko saw no blood on Hatomi, but perhaps he'd avoided getting any on himself, or washed afterward. Obsessive, unrequited love gave him motive for murder, and his behavior branded him a sly, violent, vengeful man.

Showing Hatomi the letter, Reiko said, "Did you send this to Kantaro?"

He read it and snorted. "No."

The manager returned with two samurai police officers. He pointed at Hatomi, declaring, "There's the man who has been disturbing the peace in this theater."

As the police led away the protesting Hatomi, the manager said, "I wouldn't be surprised if it was he who killed Kantaro."

Nor would Reiko, but she had another possible suspect to interview before drawing conclusions.

The owner of the Nakamura-za Theater lived nearby in a large house with half-timbered walls and a tile roof, on a narrow street lined with similar dwellings. As a mauve sunset immersed the city in cold twilight, bearers set down Reiko's palanquin outside the gate. A servant conveyed to master and mistress the news of her arrival and Lady Keisho-in's orders to cooperate with her investigation, then escorted Reiko into the lamplit parlor. Screens decorated with paintings of scenes from Kabuki plays brightened the room. Nakamura and his wife, Akane, welcomed her with the tea usually offered to guests. After the way Itaguchi and Hatomi had treated Reiko, she found the couple's courtesy a relief that inclined her to favor them, even while her instincts distrusted their motives.

Nakamura was a strikingly attractive man in his early forties. Clad in a brown kimono, he had thick black hair knotted at his nape and somber, aristocratic features. Akane, some twenty years his junior, was a dainty beauty with large, frightened eyes. She wore a pale yellow dressing gown, and her silky, disheveled hair loose. The couple knelt opposite Reiko, shoulders touching.

"Perhaps you would prefer not to have your husband

present during this conversation," Reiko suggested to Akane.

Alarm leapt in the beautiful eyes: obviously, Akane didn't want to face the interview alone. Then she murmured, "It doesn't matter. My husband knows about my affair with Kantaro. I confessed this evening, after we received news of his death." Tears spilled down Akane's face. Turning to Nakamura, she cried, "I'm so ashamed. Can you ever forgive me for betraying you?"

Nakamura embraced her. "Of course I forgive you. You made a mistake, and you've repented." Tenderness hushed his voice. "We shall put this behind us."

Although embarrassed by this private exchange, Reiko observed that Akane had verified Itaguchi's story about her affair with Kantaro. But had she only just learned of the murder? Why was she so afraid? "I have just a few more questions," Reiko said, "then I won't disturb you any longer."

The couple disengaged; Akane fidgeted nervously, while Nakamura watched her with grave concern.

"How and when did you and Kantaro become lovers?" Reiko asked Akane. Discussing such a personal matter with complete strangers made her blush under her white face powder.

"Last summer, after I married Nakamura-*san,* he introduced me to his actors. Soon Kantaro began courting me." Akane's voice was strained. "We started meeting at an inn."

"Were you happy together?"

"For a while, yes. But later . . ." Akane's gaze wavered; she spoke in a rush: "I felt so guilty that I told Kantaro I couldn't see him anymore."

Reiko had the impression that Akane had almost said something else, then changed her mind. "Did you and Kantaro quarrel about your decision?" Reiko asked, recalling what Itaguchi had told her.

"No," Akane said. "Kantaro didn't care if I left him. I think he'd grown tired of me."

The quaver in her tone made Reiko wonder whether the lovers had parted with acrimony, or whether it had been Kantaro who had ended the affair. Reiko passed the letter to Akane. "I found this in Kantaro's dressing room. Did you write it?"

Reading silently, Akane frowned, shaking her head. Nakamura read over her shoulder, then said, "My wife didn't send this."

He handed the letter back to Reiko, who had gotten a similar reaction upon showing the letter to Itaguchi. Now she observed Nakamura's defensive gaze and Akane's haunted look.

"Where were you this afternoon?" Reiko asked Akane.

"I was here." Akane toyed with her hair. "I was sick. I didn't go out all day."

"Was anyone with you?" Reiko said.

"The servants will confirm her whereabouts," Nakamura said, adding, "My wife is suffering from severe distress and ill health. If you need any more information from her, perhaps you would be good enough to come back tomorrow."

"Of course." Reiko bowed and rose. She distrusted

alibis from servants, who owed loyalty to their employers. However, she had only the word of Itaguchi—who'd hated Akane as rival for Kantaro's favor—to place the woman at the scene of the crime. And Reiko had already decided to question Akane again when her husband wasn't around to shield her.

"I'll see you out," Nakamura said.

When he stood and turned toward the door, lamplight illuminated his profile. Recognition startled Reiko.

Nakamura was the man she'd seen leaving his compartment just before Kantaro's murder.

"Yes, I was in the audience this afternoon," Nakamura admitted.

He and Reiko stood in his front garden, where she'd confronted him with her knowledge. Lights glowed behind the house's paper windowpanes; a full moon rose in the cobalt sky above the pine trees. The sound of voices drifted in from the streets. Nakamura continued, "I often watch plays from a compartment. When I left, I went out a side door that leads directly to the alley and came straight here. I was worried about my wife's health, so I decided to go home early."

"Can you name anyone who saw you along the way?" Reiko asked.

"No. So I have no alibi." Nakamura's sad smile enhanced his good looks. Reiko guessed that many women found him as attractive as she did, but maybe he was less likable than he seemed. That nobody had observed Nakamura at the crime scene didn't mean he hadn't been there, or prove his innocence.

"Did you and Kantaro get along well?" Reiko asked.

"As well as could be expected. Kantaro was a difficult person. He constantly argued with the cast and musicians. He complained about his costumes, the roles assigned him, the size of his dressing room." Nakamura shrugged. "A theater owner grows accustomed to temperamental actors."

Although Nakamura claimed an absence of professional animosity toward the victim, circumstances gave him a personal reason for wishing harm upon Kantaro. "Was this really the first you'd heard of Kantaro's relationship with your wife?" Reiko asked.

Nakamura nodded unhappily. "I love my wife more than anything in the world, and I've always been faithful to her. I believed she felt and behaved the same toward me. I know I must seem a fool, but I never even suspected."

His plight evoked sympathy in Reiko. Still, she found it hard to believe that the affair had remained a secret from anyone in the small world of the theater. "Itaguchi found out," she said. "Surely other people knew, too. But no one told you?"

"No."

"If Kantaro was unpopular, wouldn't his enemies have welcomed the chance to get him in trouble?"

"Kantaro was largely responsible for the success of the theater," Nakamura explained. "Everyone there understood that. They also knew I wouldn't tolerate the presence of a man who'd seduced my wife, even to preserve my livelihood. Had I discovered the affair, everyone would have expected me to dismiss Kantaro. My business would have been ruined, and my employees put out of their jobs. Their fortunes depended upon Kantaro remaining in my good graces. They wouldn't have told me about the affair."

An outsider might have, Reiko speculated; perhaps a rival theater owner seeking to eliminate competition. However, if Nakamura hadn't known, then Kantaro had been worth more to him alive than dead. Contemplating Nakamura's story, Reiko saw him watching her with thoughtful interest. Her heartbeat quickened as she sensed that under different circumstances, she and this man could have been friends—or more. Then a shadow veiled Nakamura's eyes; he spoke in a voice tense with hatred:

"If I'd known what Kantaro had done, I wouldn't have just dismissed him. I would have killed him. But I didn't know. Now I can only rejoice in his death."

The next morning found Reiko back at the theater, where performances had been canceled in respect for Kantaro's memory. Accompanied by her guards, she interviewed the employees a second time. She found no one who'd seen—or admitted seeing—Itaguchi, Hatomi, Akane, or Nakamura near the stage around the time of the murder. Kantaro's affair with Akane had been an open secret, but no one had informed Nakamura, for the reasons he'd stated. Yet Reiko didn't give up hope of solving her first case. She still had another source of information: the victim's family.

Now she sat alone in the parlor of the modest home where Kantaro had lived with his mother and father. A maid had served her tea, then departed, presumably to fetch the parents. Reiko studied the room with curiosity. At one end, incense and candles burned on a funeral altar, before a portrait of Kantaro in theatrical costume and offerings of rice, fruit, and sake. More altars held portraits of his ancestors, all *onnagata*. As time passed and no one came, Reiko grew restless. She tiptoed down the corridor and heard low voices coming from an open doorway. She peered inside.

There, a gray-haired couple knelt side by side, their backs to the door. On the man's left Reiko could see the naked legs of a body lying on a low table beyond them. The woman rinsed a cloth in a water bucket and handed it to the man. They chanted prayers as he bathed the body; incense smoke hazed the air. Embarrassment filled Reiko. Kantaro's parents were preparing his remains for the funeral, and Reiko had almost interrupted their private rites. She started to back away, but then the mother hobbled toward the side of the room, exposing a view of Kantaro's head and torso. The *onnagata*'s hair was cropped short; without makeup, his features were barely recognizable. The fatal wound was a raw, red gash across his throat. But it was the sight of his body that held Reiko transfixed. Where she would have expected flat chest muscles, round breasts peaked. A smooth mound of black hair covered the crotch.

The *onnagata* was a woman.

Reiko gasped in shock. The old couple turned and

saw her; their expressions changed from surprise to horror. Then Kantaro's father recovered his manners. "I'm sorry, we didn't know we had a guest," he said, ushering Reiko back to the parlor. After they were seated and introductions exchanged, he said, "What can I do for you?"

Flustered by her discovery, Reiko explained that Lady Keisho-in had ordered her to investigate the *onnagata*'s murder, adding, "I came to find out whether you know anything that might help me determine who killed Kantaro."

"And instead, you learned our family secret." Guilty shame colored the father's voice.

"How did Kantaro fool everyone?" Reiko blurted. "And why?"

With stoic resignation, the father said, "Before Kantaro was born, I was an *onnagata* myself—and, it seemed, the last of my line, because I was already advanced in years, and fortune hadn't favored me with an heir. Then my wife gave birth to a child, but alas! It was female. Because of our concern for the future of our clan, we decided to raise the child as a boy, teaching him the art of acting and telling no one his true sex. Our family heritage could continue for another generation." Pride shone in the father's eyes. "The plan worked. Kantaro became a brilliant actor."

He'd been even more brilliant than the public had ever guessed, Reiko thought, to have mastered the challenging role of a woman playing a man who played women.

"To prevent a scandal, we planned to cremate Kantaro's body before anyone could discover our deception," the father said. Bowing, he humbly entreated Reiko, "I beg you not to reveal what you saw."

Although Reiko pitied the man, she couldn't promise. "I'm sorry, but a murder investigation respects no secrets," she said regretfully. "This particular one may be an important factor in Kantaro's death—perhaps the real reason behind it."

Reiko found the actor Itaguchi assuaging his grief with sake in a teahouse, an open storefront in the theater district. A maid carried decanters and cups to peasants refreshing themselves between plays, while crowds thronged the street. Itaguchi looked up sullenly from his table beside the window. "What do you want?"

Kneeling opposite him, Reiko said without preamble, "You were right. Kantaro was a woman."

"What?" Itaguchi gaped in drunken shock. As Reiko explained, his round, boyish face went blank. He began laughing hysterically, then laid his head on the table and sobbed.

Reiko waited as the other customers eyed them curiously. At last Itaguchi subsided into gasps and hiccups. "Then you never guessed?" Reiko asked.

He lifted a teary, red face. "I had no reason to believe that Kantaro was female, even though I felt it in my heart. I never touched her. I never saw her naked body."

Itaguchi's desire to maintain his illusion of the *onnagata* as a woman might have helped Kantaro hide her true sex, but Reiko wondered if the actor's shock was a performance for her benefit. Had Itaguchi accidentally seen Kantaro undressing and learned the secret?

"If only I had known!" Itaguchi lamented. "We could have been lovers." He began weeping again. "But now she's gone, and it's too late!"

If Itaguchi was telling the truth, then he wouldn't have killed Kantaro for tricking him. Still, Reiko knew of at least one suspect who might have.

Edo Jail was a bleak compound of stone walls, watchtowers, barracks, and dilapidated dungeons in a poor section of town. Reiko stood with her guards at the small barred window of a prison cell, one of many that lined a filthy corridor that stank of urine. Hatomi glared through the window at her, his face contorted with rage.

"You're lying!" he shouted. Wails arose from other prisoners. "Kantaro was no woman!"

When Reiko tried to reason with him, Hatomi pounded the door. "Evil witch! How dare you claim that the great Kantaro was a weak, foolish, disgusting female? I'll kill you for slandering his memory!"

"Maybe you killed Kantaro because you found out his secret and couldn't bear it." Unnerved by Hatomi's ranting and the jail's squalid atmosphere, Reiko fought to maintain her composure. "While you were spying on Kantaro, did you see her unclothed? Were you upset and angry? Did you punish her deceit by stabbing her?"

"Liar! I'll kill you!"

The other prisoners began screaming and hammering on doors. Had the news provoked Hatomi's anger, Reiko wondered, or was it an echo of the feelings he'd experienced upon previously discovering that the target of his obsession had made a mockery of his manly love? With his violent temper and samurai expertise with weapons, he made a better suspect than the pathetic Itaguchi.

Jailers interrupted Reiko's attempts to extract a confession from Hatomi. "Quiet!" they ordered him. "You're disturbing the peace!"

Rushing into the cell, they bound and gagged Hatomi. Shaken, Reiko departed with her guards for another visit to the suspect who should have known about Kantaro.

A maid at the Nakamura house showed Reiko into the garden. Wrapped in quilts, Akane sat forlornly in a small pavilion amid beds of irises. When Reiko joined her in the pavilion, she said in a timid voice, "I've nothing more to tell you."

"It is I who have something to tell you," Reiko said quietly, then described what she'd seen at Kantaro's house.

Shock melted into disbelief, then horror within Akane's wide-eyed gaze. Her complexion turned white, and she crumpled in a dead faint.

Alarmed, Reiko patted Akane's face, trying to revive her, calling, "Help!"

Then Akane stirred; her eyes opened. Sitting up, she whimpered, "When we were together . . . Kantaro would take off my clothes and . . . pleasure me with his hands and mouth. . . . But he never let me touch him or see him undressed. He said it was because he cared more about my enjoyment than his own. . . . And I believed him!"

Anguished sincerity pervaded her words, yet Reiko couldn't believe that Akane had never thought Kantaro's behavior odd, never questioned his explanation. And perhaps she was as good at acting as the *onnagata* had been.

"Were you in the theater yesterday?" Reiko said.

As if too weak to resist, Akane sighed and conceded, "Yes. I went to see Kantaro. It had been eight days since he'd told me he didn't want me anymore and ended our affair. But I still loved him. I missed him so much! I slipped backstage and waited behind some scenery. I was going to beg Kantaro to take me back. But after the suicide scene"—Akane gulped—"I saw the shadow of someone tiptoeing past me toward the stage. Kantaro was lying there, pretending to be dead. I could see the back of his head and neck. Then—"

Shuddering, Akane whispered, "I saw a hand slash a knife across Kantaro's throat. He made a horrible gurgling sound. I screamed, but the music was so loud, no one could have heard. The killer ran away. Somehow I managed to stumble out of the theater and get home."

If Akane was telling the truth, she was no longer a suspect, but a witness. "Did you see the killer?" Reiko asked.

"No. Just his shadow, and his hand." Akane closed her eyes and wept silently.

Yet she'd lied yesterday about her breakup with Kantaro and her whereabouts during the murder, Reiko remembered. Was Akane now trying to hide her guilt by pinning the crime on a shadow?

Nakamura came hurrying across the garden. He entered the pavilion, knelt, and gathered Akane in his arms. To Reiko, he said, "What's going on here?"

As Reiko explained and Akane sobbed, Nakamura's handsome face went completely expressionless, as if the news had stunned him. Then he shook his head slowly. "A woman performing as an *onnagata,* and no one the wiser. This is unprecedented."

"Then you didn't know that the star of your theater—and your wife's lover—was a female?" Reiko said.

"I did not." Irritation edged Nakamura's voice. "I fail to see why you bother us with this revelation. Whether or not we knew about Kantaro, neither of us killed him. We were nowhere near him when he died."

"Your wife has just confessed that she was backstage during the murder," Reiko said.

Nakamura looked down at Akane, his features sharp with consternation. Clinging to him, Akane repeated her story, then cried, "I saw the murder, but I didn't kill Kantaro. Please, you must believe me!"

"I believe you, my dearest." Nakamura caressed her hair.

Reiko said to Akane, "When you got home yesterday, was your husband here?"

Confusion puckered Akane's brow. "No. He came a little while later."

Reiko constructed scenarios around this assertion and the premise that Akane had indeed witnessed the murder and left the scene after the killer did. If Nakamura had stabbed Kantaro, then gone directly home, then he should have arrived before his wife. The same held true if he'd gone straight home after leaving the audience, because he would have had a head start on Akane, who was backstage at that time. But if he wasn't the culprit and he'd dawdled along the way, Akane could have killed Kantaro and still managed to get home first.

Or maybe both husband and wife were lying about what they'd been doing at the time of Kantaro's death.

Reiko's face must have betrayed her thoughts, because Nakamura said coldly, "You had best be on your way, because we have nothing more to say to you."

Later, Reiko sat with her husband, Sano, on silk cushions in the private chamber of their mansion in the Edo Castle official quarter. Lanterns and charcoal braziers dispelled the chill darkness of night; forest landscape murals created the illusion of a secluded paradise. They often spent evenings talking about Sano's cases; now they mulled over Reiko's, in the hope of discovering a solution together.

As they drank heated sake, Reiko said, "Things in this investigation keep turning out to be the opposite of what they first appeared. In the play, Kantaro was a woman suffering from unrequited love. But in real life, he was a man with admirers who suffered from unrequited love for him—or so I thought, until I found out he really was a woman." Reiko shook her head in worried frustration. "There are plenty of suspects with various possible motives for the murder and no alibis. But I have no evidence to prove who killed Kantaro. If I can't solve this mystery, Lady Keisho-in will be disappointed, and the shogun may punish you for my failure."

"Perhaps other elements of the case aren't what they seem, either," Sano said, his strong, intelligent face thoughtful. A former masterless samurai, scholar, and martial arts instructor, he'd achieved wealth and prominence by solving many baffling mysteries. Reiko admired his creative spirit, his dedication to serving justice. "If you turn all the clues around, perhaps they'll reveal the truth."

The idea lit a flame of inspiration in Reiko's mind. She pondered the letter, which she'd interpreted as an obvious threat against Kantaro and evidence of the killer's motive. What if it hadn't been written by any of the suspects, or intended for the murder victim? Reiko considered Kantaro, an object of desire whose own desires remained unknown, and the question of who had loved whom. She thought about which of the suspects were most or least likely to have learned Kantaro's secret, and who would or wouldn't have told. Then she reversed the assumptions she'd made. Suddenly the case shifted focus, and the relationships between the characters changed, as when a troupe of actors begins performing a different drama with a new plot. Now Reiko smiled. She believed she knew the identity of the murderer.

She could tell from Sano's enlightened expression that he'd guessed, too, but his smile was tinged with concern. "If we're right, then this killer has already destroyed one woman because of the trouble she caused," he said. "Promise you'll be careful."

Without actors, musicians, or audience, the theater was a gloomy, silent cavern; performances wouldn't resume until tomorrow. Earlier this morning, Reiko had shown the letter to Kantaro's parents and questioned theater attendants about it, gaining evidence to support her theory. She'd already sent her guards to arrest the killer. Lady Keisho-in, eager to witness the excitement, had accompanied them, but Reiko needed to subject her theory to one final test.

She located a particular seating compartment near the stage and moved along the walkway from it, following the route she'd noted during the play. A narrow aisle separated the audience area from the stage. Reiko clambered down into this and saw a door in the wall to her left. Crouching so that the raised walkway hid her from view of an imaginary audience, she went over and opened the door. Outside, an alley ran between the theater and the adjacent building. Reiko looked to her right and found what she'd expected: another door to the theater, some thirty paces down the alley.

This door led her up a flight of stairs, into the musty-smelling area backstage. Sun from the skylights barely penetrated the dimness. Cautiously Reiko moved among stacked crates and wooden scenery, onto the stage, toward the artificial tree that had concealed Kantaro's murder from the audience. She halted at the dark bloodstain on the floor.

"So now you know."

At the sound of Nakamura's voice, Reiko started, crying out in surprise. She turned and saw the theater owner watching her from the top of the stairs. A current of fear shot through her. Yes, she knew how and why Nakamura had killed Kantaro. Now she was alone with him.

"I didn't think anyone was here," Reiko said with false gaiety. "I was just looking things over again."

Nakamura walked toward her, his face set in hard, hostile lines. Reiko backed away. Together they emerged into the brightness of the stage. Abandoning pretense, Reiko said, "What are you doing here? My guards were supposed to arrest you."

"How fortunate for me that I left my house before they arrived," Nakamura said. "I saw you tracing the path from my compartment to the murder scene. How did you guess?"

"From the letter," Reiko said, trying to stay calm. "It was written *by* Kantaro, not *to* her. Her parents have identified her writing. One of your attendants recalled Kantaro asking him to take the letter to you. When he delivered it, you read it, frowned, and sent it back. He put the letter in Kantaro's dressing room, with those from admirers."

Reiko finished the story she'd pieced together by turning clues around: "Itaguchi, Hatomi, and Akane loved Kantaro, but Kantaro loved you. She confessed her secret to you and tried to win your love. But the only woman you want is your wife. When you rejected Kantaro, she took revenge in the way that would hurt you the most."

"She seduced Akane. She stole my wife's innocent heart." Nakamura's voice trembled with anger. "Ever since she came to my theater, she'd flirted with me. I thought it was just an *onnagata*'s act, but one day, Kantaro came to my house. She told me she loved me, then opened her robes to show me that she was female. She tried to entice me into bed.

"I was horrified. If the authorities found out that I'd allowed a woman on my stage, they would have shut down the theater. I told Kantaro that I wasn't interested in her; I was in love with Akane, and unless she wanted a scandal that would ruin us both, we must forget what had just happened, go about our business, and keep our relationship strictly professional."

Nakamura's mouth twisted. "Kantaro pleaded, wept, raged, and finally stormed out of my house. A few days later, I received her letter. I decided it was an idle threat, because Kantaro didn't bother me again, and I assumed she'd gotten over her disappointment. But during the play yesterday, she looked straight at me and added a verse to her last song. It told me that she and Akane had been lovers. She'd used Akane and cruelly discarded her, just to get even with me!"

Belatedly, Reiko understood that Kantaro's final lines, which had seemed irrelevant to the play, had been a secret message to Nakamura. Reiko considered running away or calling for help. The fact that Nakamura was willing to tell her this story could only mean one thing. Yet although her heart thudded with fear of this man she'd once found attractive, she needed his confession.

"I was stunned," Nakamura continued. "I thought of Akane at home, sick from a broken heart. I watched Kantaro perform, and I hated her for hurting Akane and trying to ruin our marriage. A mad fury came over me. I left the theater, walked down the alley, and reentered through the stage door.

"Kantaro was lying behind the tree. She didn't hear me come in. I was too angry to think of the danger or to wait until later to punish her. I took out the knife I carry for protection, and I slashed her throat. Blood spurted all over me. I hurried to my office, where I washed myself and changed into a spare kimono. Then I went home. I threw my bloody clothes on a heap of burning trash along the way."

His detour explained why Akane had beaten Nakamura home although she'd left the scene after him, Reiko realized.

"I didn't know Akane was there," Nakamura said. "She doesn't know I killed Kantaro. But you do." From under his sash he drew a knife. Its short, pointed blade gleamed as he advanced on Reiko.

"Don't come any closer!" Reiko reached under her sleeve and unsheathed the dagger from the scabbard strapped to her arm.

Surprise flared in Nakamura's eyes; he stepped back. He'd thought she would be an easy victim, hadn't expected her to be armed. With irony, Reiko realized that she, too, was not what she seemed. She wasn't a helpless woman, but a trained fighter ready to defend herself.

With a furious yell, Nakamura charged, lashing out wildly at Reiko. She leapt aside, but he whirled and sliced at her. His knife cut her kimono; her longer blade slashed his arm. Their cries echoed in the empty theater. Then Reiko's two guards stormed into the building, followed by Lady Keisho-in. They obviously had traced Nakamura here.

"Surrender!" the guards ordered Nakamura.

They leapt onto the stage. Lady Keisho-in stood below it, exclaiming, "A battle! How exciting!"

Nakamura fought with increasing frenzy, his eyes crazed. As Reiko dodged and returned cuts, the guards rushed at Nakamura, swords drawn. A small figure hurried onto the stage, long hair and pale pink robes flying.

"Honorable husband!" Akane cried. "Stop!"

She darted over and grabbed Nakamura's arm, just as the guards attacked him. A sword blade aimed at Nakamura sliced deeply into her back. Crying out in pain, she sank to the floor.

Alarm cleared the madness from Nakamura's expression. "Akane!" Kneeling, he cradled his wife.

She gasped, moaning, "I'm sorry, my dearest. If you can forgive me, I gladly forgive you." Then her eyes closed and she lay still.

"No!" Nakamura's weeping filled the theater.

The guards looked to Reiko for orders. Horror rendered her speechless. Love had destroyed not only the vindictive Kantaro and the jealous Nakamura, but the innocent pawn Akane. Reiko had identified the killer, but might things have turned out better if not for her? If she were a man, perhaps Nakamura wouldn't have fought; or perhaps she could have defeated him before the guard slew Akane. Sex was at the heart of this case, and she would never know the extent to which her own sex had determined its outcome.

"Congratulations on solving the mystery!" Lady Keisho-in hoisted herself onto the stage and hurried over to hug Reiko. "The shogun will be so impressed. What an honor for you and your husband!"

Although I'm more a tea person myself, there are those who can't get enough of gourmet coffee. Luckily the coffee shop explosion hasn't really hit Cabot Cove yet. Our local cafés do just fine, thank you. Our next story features a detective who initially begins sleuthing to clear her name and get her old job back, but by the time she's finished, she may have launched a whole new career for herself.

Moonlighting

Janice Steinberg

The one thing I hate about this job? I hate all the people who ask me what I am, "really." You know, like I must "really" be a student or an artist. Or maybe I'm an actress and then they can ask if I'm in a play and write it in their Day-Timers like they'd actually go and see some play I was in. How come a person can't "really" be a server at a coffee bar? They think it's so easy, have any of them ever made a perfect low-fat decaf latte? I don't mean just throwing some decaf espresso and low-fat milk together, I mean getting the proportions exactly right and creating a cohesive froth of milk at the top? And never, never blowing it and giving a person caffeinated coffee when they asked for decaf since a "real" coffee server knows her product and is fully aware that for some people, people with certain medical conditions for instance, caffeine can be—

But I'm getting ahead of myself.

It's not just the customers who keep bugging me about this "real job" thing. Jeff and Linda are the worst of all. The first year I worked here, they were totally cool about it. I mean it. They didn't just act cool when deep down they felt uncomfortable, they *were* cool. How do I know? Because the second year it changed. "How's the job?" one of them would say within moments of calling. They call together, using a speaker phone. It makes them sound like they're talking to me from Venus. When I told them that, they thought it was hilarious. Now they start every call by pretending they're transmitting from somewhere in outer space. It cracks them up. I have to sit there and listen to these fifty-year-old people giggling and using funny "alien" voices for a full minute before we can start to talk.

Anyway, at first "what I did for a living" would just sort of fall into the conversation somewhere between world peace, my love life (the less said about that the better, okay?), Jeff's latest nutritional discovery, and the house remodeling project that was taking a year and a half. Maybe the problem was that the house finally got finished, and they needed something else to worry about. But why worry about what, one time when I pushed them to the wall, they had the nerve to call my "lack of ambition"? Even if Jeff and Linda did

leave the commune when they hit their thirties and
rapidly blasted into the middle class, complete with a
house in the suburbs and straight jobs; even so, they
claim they still basically believe in the ideals that got
them to drop out in the first place. If they were trying
to be utterly normal, they tell me, wouldn't they have
insisted I start calling them Mom and Dad? Yeah, well,
I wouldn't have done it, I say. It was hard enough to
switch from calling them Rainbow and Pippin. (Rainbow was Linda. Pippin was Jeff.)

I, a psychedelic diaper baby, didn't have a normal
name to go back to. I was stuck with the name they
gave me on the commune. Moon. That's right, like
Frank Zappa's daughter. Only without her conspicuous
career success. (Can the ambitious Moon Zappa make
a perfect decaf latte? I bet she can't come close.)

I, as you may have figured out by this time, *can*
make a perfect decaf latte. This is how I do it. How I
invariably, always do it, as I emphasized to the
cops . . . and therefore why would I have done anything differently when I made what turned out to be the
last latte of Bill Jacobson's life?

"I start by—"

"Let's take it from the time Mr. Jacobson came up to
the counter," the older cop, a balding white guy who
looked kind of like Jacobson, said. "Did he specify that
he wanted decaf?"

I stood with the milk pitcher in my hand. "He didn't
have to. He's come here every morning for at least two
years, which is how long I've been working here. He
always gets a decaf latte. And I know, because he

makes sure to tell any new employee, that it absolutely has to be decaf because he has a heart condition and caffeine could kill him."

You always see in books where someone talks about a person in the present tense and then realizes, duh, the person's dead. Well, sure enough, that was what I did. Maybe that was why the other cop, the African-American, got a funny look on her face.

"I'd never get his order wrong! I never get any orders wrong!" It was stupid to yell. But it had been a bitch of a morning, and I'd had lots of caffeine myself. My usual double espresso when I came in to work at five-thirty, a latte around seven, and then whatever someone handed me after the ambulance came and took Bill away. That was before the manager decided we shouldn't drink any of our own product until the beans, grinders, and espresso machines were all tested.

"When he came up to the counter," the balding cop said, "did he say anything to you?"

He made his voice calm, the way you do when you're talking to a street person who just might decide that you personally are the Antichrist. But I would have calmed down, anyway. I never get upset for long. Even after Jeff and Linda moved to the burbs, we all spent half an hour every day sitting in a half-lotus, doing alternate-nostril breathing.

"He said, 'Hey, Moon.' And I said, 'Hey, Bill. How about a blueberry muffin today?' Because they're low-fat, and he had to watch his cholesterol. He got different things to eat, y'know, but his coffee order was always the same. A low-fat decaf latte."

"Did he get the muffin?" the male cop asked.

"Yeah," I said. Now there was an idea, that the muffin, which we got from an outside vendor, was poisoned. The second before Bill fell over dead, he'd clutched at his chest and said, "The coffee"—but how would he really know?

"Walk us through what you did when you made his latte," the woman cop said.

"His low-fat decaf latte," I corrected, just in case she'd set a trap for me.

Step by step, I showed them how I filled the metal pitcher with low-fat milk, up to the hip of the pitcher, and then steamed the milk.

"You have to let it slurp till it foams," I explained. I was doing a beautiful job, not one wasted movement, but they didn't look like they noticed. "We have two grinders sitting on the counter, see?" I went on. "The smaller one is filled with decaf beans and the big one with regular. For a single decaf latte, like Bill ordered, I do two pulls on the decaf grinder, like this. For a double, you do three. The ground beans fall into this filter basket, and I stick it on the espresso machine."

"What about when the beans get put in the grinder?" the man said. "How often do you fill it?"

"Wait a sec, let me finish." I was just pouring the milk over the espresso, and you have to pay attention to the foam. "We might need to fill up the regular grinder twice on a busy morning. Usually with the decaf, we fill it once and it lasts all morning," I said as I put the coffee on the counter. Neither of them looked like they were even going to try it.

"Gets busy here, a lot of customers, seems like someone could go for the caff instead of the decaf," the woman said.

"I wouldn't, especially not with Bill. What about the guy who was sitting with him? He got a regular latte, a double. That's a lot of caffeine. What if their cups got switched?" What had happened to Bill's friend's cup? I looked over to the table where they'd been sitting, but the view was blocked by cops.

They weren't listening to me. I don't even know why they bothered to make me show them what I did, since their minds were already made up.

A few days later, Marianne, our manager, called me into her office. Marianne is a good manager, even if she talks about her boyfriend so much it makes you want to become a lesbian, and first she explained about the results of lab tests the Company had paid to have done. Both Bill's and his buddy's cups had contained double regular lattes, so there went my cup-switching theory.

Then, after she'd explained, Marianne said, "Moon, I'm sorry, we've got to let you go."

"Just like that?" I said. "People complained it was too gross to look at Debbie's pierced tongue, which it is, and she didn't get fired. Roger spilled on two customers in one week, and he's still got his job. I've been a good employee for two years."

"I know, Moon. It's a mistake anyone can make, but it's a sign of our good faith if we let go of the employee who gave him the wrong kind of coffee."

"What if somebody put the wrong beans in the decaf

dispenser?" I said. None of the customers that morning had complained about being "caffeined," but it doesn't always hit right away. "Or what if the stuff we got from the Company was marked decaf when it was really caff?"

The Company, by the way, is this sort of monolith of coffee that I wouldn't dare name in these litigious times. What if they were sacrificing me to cover up someone else's mistake? It happens.

"We had the beans in the grinders tested," Marianne said. "The caff was caff, and the decaf was decaf."

She said something about my final paycheck. I couldn't even hear her. I might have looked normal, but my head was spinning like Linda Blair's in *The Exorcist*. Why was everyone so willing to believe that I, Moon Harris, had personally screwed up and given a man with a heart condition a double caffeinated latte?

There was another possibility. It took an hour of walking on the beach to clear my head enough to even think of it. If I didn't "accidentally" get the order wrong; if Bill and his friend didn't switch cups "by accident"; if the Company didn't "accidentally" mislabel the sacks of coffee—then maybe somebody gave that double caffeinated latte to Bill Jacobson on purpose. Somebody who knew exactly what it would do to him.

A murderer.

No one had listened to me so far. Not the police. Not Marianne. Definitely not Jeff and Linda, who took this opportunity to encourage me to go to college and find a safe profession where I couldn't kill anyone. (Okay, they didn't say the part about not killing anyone, but with Jeff and Linda, I have years of reading between the lines.)

I knew if I wanted to clear my reputation, I'd have to do it myself. What the hell, I'd just been fired. I could start looking for another job, or I could live off the eight hundred forty-three dollars and thirty-six cents in my savings account and try to get back my "real" job.

I started by writing down everything I could think of about my dead customer. You see someone nearly every weekday morning for two years, you get to know things. For instance, you know he was fifty-nine years old because he mentioned it when he came in on his birthday. (We gave him a birthday latte free.) You know he worked as a stockbroker downtown, someplace with one of those names like six different companies merged and everyone wanted to keep their name in the title. You know he took a lot of ribbing as a Dodger fan in a Padre town, and you figure he was married from the wedding ring. You realize the poor guy never took a vacation—really, never? Yeah, you can't remember him being away more than a couple days in two years, and you think, now that he's dead, he must wish he'd done that trip to wherever instead of putting in another week at the office. This makes you think about your own savings, which you are about to live off of instead of using them to go to Turkey. But hey, this isn't just about money, it's about redeeming your reputation.

After twenty minutes of this, I reached a terrible conclusion. Even though I'd talked to Bill Jacobson for hours, if you added it all up, I knew almost nothing important about him. A pitiful commentary on modern life, huh? And a rotten start for my detecting.

I could have tried to get more information at the library, maybe looked for newspaper articles about the firm he worked for or pictures of him and his wife at some charity event, but I was getting bored just sitting. Plus, I was thinking of this awesome disguise I wanted to try.

I started with the wig—short, kind of kooky blond hair, like Dharma in *Dharma and Greg* on TV. (There's a name that makes me grateful my parents' creative child-naming only went as far as celestial bodies and not to any religion that believes you can be reborn as a gnat.) It was a little tricky getting my long black hair tucked under the wig, but once I'd done it I was already halfway to looking like another person. Like Dharma, in fact. See, I definitely don't share Dharma's interest in dressing like her hippie parents used to; I'm sure she wouldn't either, if she got to pick her own wardrobe. I always wear black. Skinny black jeans, black turtlenecks, a black sweater when it's cold. Put me in a gypsy skirt and a loose Mexican top (which I just happen to own, thanks to my mom), and voilà! The sixties live. All it took to complete the look was to leave off my usual heavy eyeliner, mascara, and brown lipstick, and go to a department store to put on some pink blusher and lipstick. I would have gone for nail polish, too, but the woman at the makeup counter was getting uptight about my using all their stuff and not buying anything.

It was time to road-test my disguise.

•　•　•

"Carl! Carl!" I whispered, standing off to the side of the deck, half hidden by a potted plant.

He looked up from his seat outside the coffee bar, the place where he planted his butt for three hours every day while he nursed a plain coffee, read newspapers other customers left behind, and mostly just sat and watched the world go by.

"You talking to me?" he said.

My pink-lipsticked mouth spread into a grin. He had no idea who I was.

"Carl, it's me. Moon."

"Moon, what are you doing here?" He was whispering, too. Not that Marianne had warned me off or anything like that. But you don't expect an employee who's been fired for killing a customer, accidentally or not, to come around and visit the old job.

I sat at his table. I even turned so people inside could get a good look at me. If I could fool Carl, none of my former workmates was going to recognize me. Carl could be a little unfocused, but every time I'd decide he was a dim bulb, he'd come out with something that made me wonder if sitting and observing the way he did was some kind of advanced spiritual discipline. He noticed everything.

"Remember the morning Bill Jacobson died?" I asked.

"Sure. In fact, you look like—"

"Dharma. I know."

"Who's Dharma? I meant, you look like a woman

who was here that morning. Man, she was gorgeous. Blond hair like that, and this incredible skin."

Neither the woman's presence nor the Dharma look was real surprising. It's a busy place in the morning; somebody new probably comes in every two minutes. And the hairstyle is hot these days. But who would've thought Dharma was Carl's type?

"Remember, Bill was here with another man?" I said, nudging him back to the subject.

"Right, Donald Raglan," Carl said. Like I said, just when you thought the guy was a dim bulb, he'd put out two hundred watts. "Of Raglan Oak Bowers Fenn," he said, as if that explained anything.

"Huh?"

"The venture capital firm. He's always in the paper." He tapped the *Wall Street Journal* he'd been reading. Carl was especially happy when he scavenged a *Wall Street Journal* someone had left behind.

"Is he from San Diego?"

"He got started in L.A., but now he lives in North County. Rancho Santa Fe."

Carl must have gotten his hands on a lot of *Wall Street Journals*. And read every word. He told me Donald Raglan was almost as big as that other Donald, the guy with the casino and the trophy wives. And lately there'd been rumors that Raglan's financial empire had hit hard times.

"Bill was a stockbroker," I said. "Was Raglan discussing business with him?"

Carl always sat on the deck and Bill inside, but Carl moseyed in regularly for refills and free newspapers.

And I happened to know he eavesdropped, thanks to a humiliating little incident involving my last boyfriend.

Carl shrugged. "Maybe family business," he said. "Bill was married to Raglan's sister."

I started to tingle, and it wasn't from drinking any of the Company's coffee; going to the counter and ordering was farther than I wanted to risk my disguise. "Bill's friend," I'd called Raglan in my mind, I guess because he hadn't seemed like a business aquaintance. But every time I'd thought it, I felt funny. Now I understood why. Because he hadn't seemed like a friend, either.

I was so excited I took off right away. Too bad, because there was one more thing Carl could have told me that might have gotten my job back sooner, and maybe it would have prevented . . . Or maybe it wouldn't. Jeff and Linda always talk about karma. What happened next might have been necessary for my karma. Or maybe I was simply an agent for Bill's karma. Or Raglan's. Or Syl's, although I hope that wasn't true.

Anyway, at that moment it was totally obvious what had happened. Raglan was in financial trouble and his brother-in-law's death helped him in some way. Maybe he'd get his hands on money that Bill had willed to Raglan's sister. Maybe Bill knew about some shady dealings and was threatening to blow the whistle. Whatever the reason, Raglan needed Bill dead. I didn't know how he'd done it. But I knew exactly what I had to do next.

• • • •

You're thinking, I'm probably going to get on my computer and find out everything I can about Raglan's business. This may come as a brutal shock, but some people in America do not own computers! Even if their parents promise to buy them a computer if they'll enroll in college. Some people also do not own cars, trucks, or even motorcycles, making it impossible for them to stake out Raglan's house.

I had a better plan, anyway. My friend Stacy works for the phone company, and she gave me Raglan's unlisted home phone number. Now that I didn't have to get to work at five-thirty A.M., I could stay up late. I started to call Raglan in the middle of the night.

The first time, he picked up the phone himself.

"Donald?" I said.

"What do you want?" he said.

I hadn't planned what I was going to say. Hearing him sound alert, as if he'd been lying awake, I said, "Confession is the best sleeping pill."

He didn't ask who I was or what I was talking about. He didn't get mad at me for calling him at two A.M.

He just laughed and hung up the phone.

"Donald, you killed him," I said the next night, from a phone booth in Hillcrest, a couple of miles from the booth on India Street I'd used the night before. At one or two A.M., I could borrow my roommate's car, so I could drive to a different phone booth every time. "Why don't you tell the police," I said, "before I have to tell them?"

This time I hung up first.

I liked the late-night drives. I'd fuel myself with a double espresso. Then I'd get in the car and go. I don't do much driving, and I almost never drive alone. I loved the feel of the night air whipping through my hair as I zipped down the freeway at seventy-five.

And the calls. I never planned them. They were improvised, like jazz riffs, me on vocals and Donald—he didn't say anything. After the second night he didn't even speak when he picked up the phone. He'd just breathe. Still I had the sense of a duet, one that wouldn't have been the same with any other partner. I didn't remember him well from the day Bill died, just a vague mental picture of a tall, stringy man who looked like he worked out. I found a photograph of him in a newspaper that I cut out and put on my wall. I thought of sending him a photo of me. Just kidding.

"How did you do it?" I asked the third night, from La Jolla. "Did you drop some NoDoz in Bill's coffee?" Like I said, it was improv. Unexpected twists and sudden inspirations. I didn't think of the NoDoz until that very second, but it was just the kind of thing the police should have thought of, if they hadn't been so obsessed with making it my fault. Caffeine was caffeine. Could a lab tell if it came from a pill or from the Company's premium beans? Could I ask Marianne about this? And hadn't Bill left the table shortly after he got his coffee? I sort of remembered him going to the back of the store, I suppose to use the bathroom or the phone. Donald could have dropped in the NoDoz then. I decided to hold off on all this exhausting research until I'd called Donald a few more times.

He wasn't into it as much as I was, though. The fifth night, he'd changed his phone number. It took me a couple of days to get the new number from Stacy. And this time when I called, he talked.

"Do you want money?" he said.

I hung up. I hadn't thought about money. I wanted . . . See, that's what bugs Jeff and Linda, my lack of goal orientation. I could see the parental point in this case. What *did* I want from Donald Raglan? It had felt right to call, to have intimate contact with this man who'd deprived my customer of his life and me of my livelihood. But ultimately, what did I hope to get from it?

Justice. I wanted justice, of course. I could agree to meet with him, and the police could fit me with a wire . . . Right, and since when would the police pay attention to the word of a coffee server versus a captain of industry? Okay, so if justice was unlikely, would it be really awful if I asked him to finance my trip? A long trip, and not just to Turkey. What if I asked for enough to travel around the world for a year? At least, in some way, he'd be paying for what he did.

But people like Donald don't get rich by giving money away. If he said he'd pay me, I'd have to tell him a way to get the money to me. And if he knew how to reach me . . . well, he'd already murdered once.

This soul-searching did have an effect. I decided I had to stop playing telephone at night and watching soaps all afternoon. I had to take some action. I set the

alarm for eight in the morning. I couldn't think of a
way to show up at Donald's door. But I had a great excuse to visit his sister. Plus, if I'd found the right Jacobson in the phone book, she lived in Point Loma,
easy to get to by bus from my apartment in Ocean
Beach.

I wore my regular clothes—an all-black wardrobe is
so practical. The house was uphill from the main
street where the bus dropped me off. Up a steep hill,
where the houses got fancier and fancier with every
step I took. Jacobson's was near the top. In my new
spirit of being goal oriented, I'd rehearsed exactly
what I was going to say to Mrs. Jacobson. *I wanted to
tell you how sorry I am about your husband. I knew
him from the coffee bar.* I wouldn't tell her about me
being the one who'd allegedly botched her husband's
coffee order, at least not right away. I'd try to get inside first, get her talking.

Turned out I didn't have to work at getting her to
talk.

"You were supposed to be here fifteen minutes
ago!" she said when she answered the door. "I was
about to call the agency and complain."

"Sorry," I said—and then added, getting into it, "the
bus was late."

"Well, I want you to start downstairs. The cleaning
supplies are in here," she said, leading me into the
kitchen. She wasn't young, but from the back she
looked about thirty, with a firm butt and long, slim
legs under little blue culottes. "I have to go, I'm late
for a golf date. I'll be back at two."

See? Why even try to be goal oriented when things like this always happen? Would *you* have stuck with your original script? And passed up the chance to spend the entire day snooping? If nothing else, I could find out what cream she used on her face—in spite of some wrinkles, she had the softest, most glowing skin I'd ever seen. If I snuck a little face cream for myself, would she miss it?

I started to clean downstairs, in case she came back for something she'd forgotten. Or to check on me. It was some house. Living room bigger than my entire apartment, kitchen with shining pots and pans hanging on the walls and every appliance known to man. (There was an expensive coffeemaker, but of course Bill preferred my lattes.) After about ten minutes, a woman showed up who said she was from the agency; I told her she wasn't needed.

I figured I could take a break then. First, I went looking for family pictures, just to make sure I was in the right house. I found a photo of Bill in the master bedroom. That seemed like a good place to start my search. I pulled out drawers, things like that. Read some boring mail. Mrs. Jacobson—her name was Pam, I found out from the mail I read—had some great clothes, and I tried a couple of things on. A sparkly cocktail dress. A great sort of forties-style suit in red gabardine. They were great on me but I had to admit, they'd look every bit as good on her. She even had a few old hippie things in her closet, just like my mom. From love beads to the golf course. And their generation worries about the lack of moral values in mine. I checked out her bathroom and put on some of her moisturizer. It made my skin glow, too.

Since I had no idea what I was looking for, I figured it would be smart to keep cleaning the house and give myself a chance to come back. She'd told me to start downstairs, so I decided to do the kitchen next.

Wasn't there some famous guy who was sitting in a bath and said, "Eureka! I found it!" Well, that was how I felt when I plunged my hand into that plastic tub of cleaning supplies and came out with . . . I took a long look at what I had found and thought about what it meant. Then I put it back in the tub, and I cleaned Pam Jacobson's house until it shone. I didn't want to make her suspicious. Not when I was right on the verge of proving my innocence. And her and her brother's guilt.

I don't know how he tracked me down. Maybe he had investigators sitting by every phone booth in San Diego County, waiting for a woman to make a call at one or two A.M. He'd signal that he'd gotten the call. Then all the investigator had to do was take my license number. My roommate Jeannie's license number, that is. It didn't matter, since both Jeannie and I breathed the gas from the sabotaged wall heater. And it would have killed both of us, if it hadn't been for Syl.

You know the idea of taking a canary into a coal mine, because canaries are more susceptible to bad air and will die before humans are affected? Well, I had a canary. Named Sylvester, a play on the cartoons with

Sylvester the cat who always chases the canary
Tweety. I don't know what Syl did, if he gave a thun-
derous warning chirp before he dropped or a final, agitated flutter of his pretty yellow wings. Whatever
woke me in the middle of the night, it came from Syl.
Because I was already across the room, uncovering his
cage, before I even noticed the smell of gas. I grabbed
the cage then and screamed for Jeannie to wake up,
and we ran outside in our pajamas. A neighbor called
the fire department. I gave Syl artificial respiration.
But it was too late.

I wished I had listened to Carl. He was trying to tell
me exactly what I needed to know.

In the morning, full of grief and anger, I put on the
Dharma disguise, went to my former place of employment, and sat at Carl's table.

"Moon? Is that you?" he asked.

See, I'd put on some of Pam Jacobson's magic
moisturizer.

"It's me," I answered. "Tell me about the woman
who looked like this. The one you saw the morning
Bill Jacobson died."

"Well, it was a little funny. When she got out of her
car, she already had coffee, in one of these cups." He
picked up his cardboard cup, printed with the Company name.

"An empty cup? To reuse?" All of Pam Jacobson's
cleaning supplies were environmentally friendly, and
maybe she was trying to save a tree.

"It had a lid and there was steam coming out of the

top. And she held it the way you hold a full cup of hot coffee."

Pam went inside for less than a minute and came out still carrying her coffee cup. Except I was sure it wasn't the same cup she'd carried in. I'd bet she went first to another Company location and bought a double regular latte. She and Donald had to time it perfectly—cell phones, Carl suggested—so she'd arrive just after her husband got his decaf. Donald figured out a way to make Bill go to the back of the store, and she snuck in and switched the lattes.

And just in case Bill got a glimpse of her, she wore a disguise. The hippie-style clothes I'd seen in her closet. And a ratty Dharma wig like mine. Like I'd found, converted to a rag, in her tub of cleaning supplies.

I knew where a lot of the Company coffee places were, and Carl offered to drive. Everyone had an unusually good memory of the morning the Company brew had killed a customer. A server at the location a few miles away remembered a woman who'd looked like me. Like Dharma, that is. She couldn't remember what the woman ordered, but with the three of us going to the police, it was enough to convince them to investigate Pam Jacobson and Donald Raglan. They were charged with Bill's murder.

The Company was generous. They didn't just give me my job back, I got back pay and a bonus. I went out and bought myself a Teach-Yourself-Turkish cassette tape.

Jeff and Linda, true to form, did not share my happiness when I went back to work. At least they stopped nagging about college. Now they send brochures about private detective courses and even, although I'm sure it's tough for two former radicals, info about the police academy. They say I have a gift.

A gift. They're right about that, I think, as I make a perfect latte.

While it's been written that pride is one of the seven deadly sins, for some people, it's all they've got. Our murder victim in this story, however, has a lot more than just pride to hold on to. In fact, she has more than enough to kill for.

The Family Jewels

Kathy Hogan Trocheck

Loudene Jenkins clacked her dentures with the tip of her outsized pink tongue and thrust a handful of glittering glass under my nose.

"Them's my mama's diamonds," she said, nodding for emphasis. "Bet you never seen nothing like that before, have you, Miss Julia Callahan Garrity?"

"No, ma'am," I said truthfully. "I never have, Miss Loudene."

She dumped the jewelry on the battered Formica kitchen table. "Go ahead and look, girl," she insisted. "Real. Sure are."

The kitchen was dark and airless. It was early October, and still hot in Atlanta, but Miss Loudene kept the windows locked tight, with yellowed shades pulled out against the sunlight and "thievin' neighbors."

I went to the window and pulled up the shade. Miss Loudene glared but kept her seat.

I picked up a choker with a diamond and sapphire brooch shaped like a peacock's feather. It was a period piece, from the 1920s, probably, the kind of thing a flapper might have worn. There were earrings to match and a bracelet too. The jewelry bespoke the high life; an era of bathtub gin and ostrich feathers and sleek cars. How had such stuff ended up here in Atlanta, Georgia, in a weather-beaten mill village shack owned by seventy-year-old Loudene Jenkins, who owned neither a car nor a telephone nor a washing machine?

Miss Loudene pointed to a delicate lady's watch. It had a platinum mesh band and an octagonal face rimmed with diamonds. "My granddaddy give Mama that for her eighteenth birthday. See that stone on the watch stem? That there is a yellow diamond. Granddaddy bought that at Tiffany's Jewelry Store up there in New York City. You ever seen the like?"

"No, ma'am."

There were eight pieces in all; besides the peacock set and the watch, a long string of pearls, two rings, each set with circlets of half-carat diamonds, and a gold brooch in the shape of a snarling tiger, with emeralds for eyes and a string of diamonds outlining its curving tail. I'm not a jeweler, only a former cop and a sometime private investigator, but even my untrained eye knew this was the goods.

"This stuff must be worth a lot of money, Miss Loudene," I said. "Are you sure you don't want to put it in a safe deposit box at the bank?"

She shrugged, and the moth-eaten brown sweater slipped from her bony shoulder. "Banks cost money. Anyway, Mama always kept the family jewels in a lard can in the pantry. Reckon that's good enough for me."

"How did your mama come to have such fine jewelry?" I asked. Edna would have scolded me for nosiness, although she'd been wondering aloud on that very subject, ever since she'd discovered Loudene's loot.

"Mama came from money," Miss Loudene said grandly. "Lived in a fine big house up there in Cincinnati, Ohio. My granddaddy was the Chevrolet dealer up there. Mama, she went off to college over there in Michigan, and that's how she come to meet up with trouble. This particular trouble went by the name of Louis D. Jenkins."

She saw the look of surprise in my eyes. "Yes. My daddy. Trouble looking for a place to light. The mill had done sent him up there to Michigan to crate up some big looms they was buying for this here Glenndale Mill. They met on a Saturday and by Monday, Mama had packed up all her stuff and followed Louis D. Jenkins down here to Glenndale, Georgia."

Miss Loudene fingered the diamond watch. "Granddaddy tried to take her back home, but Mama, she wouldn't go for nothin'. And when she told Granddaddy they had done got married in the Baptist church, that was the end for him. All Mama's kin was Methodist."

She scooped the jewelry up and slid the pieces into a faded pink flannel bag. Tying the drawstring, she inserted the bag into a rusted Sno-White lard can, which she then placed on the top shelf of the tiny closet otherwise occupied by a mop, a broom and two shelves of potted meat, roach spray and stewed tomatoes.

Edna had warned me it might go this way. My mother had been treated to exactly the same exhibit only two nights earlier, after Miss Loudene, flush from winning a sixteen-dollar jackpot at the VFW bingo hall, had invited her into her home for a toasted cheese sandwich and a warm Nehi orange soda.

Bingo was the bond my mother shared with Miss Loudene. They were both regulars at the Tuesday night Decatur VFW game, and had become fast friends over their united hate for a woman named Odie, who drove a MARTA bus and took up a whole table with the thirty-two cards she played for each game. Somehow, Edna had gotten snookered into taxiing her new friend to the VFW and the Stone Mountain Elks Lodge, for their Thursday night bingo, and to the bank to help Miss Loudene cash her Social Security check.

Only two nights earlier, she'd tucked her winnings into the lard can, and, after only the briefest hesitation, proudly shown Edna her inherited finery.

Edna, of course, had put me on immediate alert.

"That old lady is gonna get herself killed over that jewelry, Callahan. Living over there in Glenndale, who knows what kind of people in and out of those old mill houses. Why, a strong wind could knock that front door slap off its hinges. I said, 'Loudene, my daughter Callahan is a former police detective. She's a private investigator. She knows about such stuff.' And

Loudene, that impressed her. I want you to go over there and talk her into locking that stuff up in the bank. Or better yet, she ought to go ahead and sell it, move into a decent apartment."

Edna had been right about the neighborhood. The old mill village had seen better days. The cotton mill, closed for a dozen years, had recently been razed. There was talk of a new apartment complex, of a shopping center, and fine new stores. So far, it was just talk. Glenndale's oldest residents, the men and women who'd moved to Atlanta from the Appalachians, worked the mill and taken pride in their tiny wooden "shotgun" houses, were dying off and moving away. The neighborhood had gone transient. There were raucous parties, open-air drug deals, streets lined with empty beer bottles and discarded fast food wrappers.

Miss Loudene's was the only house on her street without at least two cars jammed into the driveway. Hers was the only one with flowers and a neat little green lawn and a mailbox painted bright red. She was seventy, a shrunken gnome who weighed less than most of the dogs I'd seen chained to nearby porches. She lived alone, without a phone or a car. And she had a lard can stuffed with diamonds.

"Your mama sent you over here to make me lock up my jewels, ain't that right?" Miss Loudene said, jutting her chin stubbornly. "But there's a lot Edna Mae Garrity don't know about me."

She went to the window, pulled the window shade down again. She put a liver-spotted hand to my ear and whispered, "I'm fixin' to sell some of Mama's jewelry.

My sister nor none of her kin know that. And it ain't none of their business."

I looked up in surprise. Miss Loudene's colorless lips stretched into a conspiratorial grin. "Mama left it all to me. Got somebody coming over here tomorrow. Knows all about jewelry. Says I can get me enough from that peacock set to buy me a fine setup over there at the senior high rise in Decatur. Get me a stacking washer-dryer and cable television. What you think about that?"

"That's fine, Miss Loudene," I said, patting her hand, relieved to be off the hook. "This person, is it a jeweler, something like that?"

"It's a fine Christian-type individual," Miss Loudene said. "Gonna take me shopping for my washer-dryer soon as we get the money for my jewelry." She stood up, clearly done with our conversation. "Tell your mama Thursday night, pick me up early, we'll eat some supper at the Piccadilly Cafeteria. My treat."

Edna's face was ashen. "She's gone, Callahan. Something bad happened in that house. I just know it."

My mother had left the house at five o'clock Thursday, to take Miss Loudene to supper and the VFW bingo. Thirty minutes later, she was back, alone, shaking like a leaf.

Edna held a wad of envelopes in her trembling hand. "Her mail. It's got her Social Security check. Loudene knew to the minute when that check was coming. She'd had her checks stolen twice, so she always waited for the mailman at the first of the month. Met him at the door."

I took the packet of mail from my mother, tried to calm her down.

"Was the house broken into?"

"It was locked up tight."

"How do you know she wasn't in there—taking a nap maybe? Or sick?"

"I have a key," Edna said. "When she didn't answer, I thought she could have fallen or something. But the house was empty. Bed made up, coffee cup rinsed out in the dish drainer. But the mail was in the mailbox. And that's when I knew."

I thought of that hot, airless house. Of the yellow shades at the kitchen windows. Of the roach spray and the potted meat. And the lard can full of jewelry.

Edna's eyes met mine. "I checked. The can was there. Empty."

The police were skeptical, but Edna kept insisting her friend was dead. I could have told them. My mother is never wrong about these kinds of things. Three days later a backhoe operator found the body in a pile of brush and construction rubble near the old mill's foundations, a block away from Miss Loudene's tidy yellow frame house. The back of her head had been bashed in, and she was fully dressed, but missing one shoe.

The detective in charge of the case was an acquaintance from my days on the Atlanta Police Department.

He gave me a courtesy call when they found Miss Loudene, and I met him over at the old mill site.

Miss Loudene's body was just being wheeled away on a gurney when I arrived. The wind swept through the red clay field and I pulled up the collar of my jacket against the sudden, unexpected chill.

The detective's name was Bayles. Larry Bayles. "No sign of that jewelry your mother told us about," he said, reading over his notes. "No ID found on the body at all. But we did find a pocketbook." He pointed a few yards away, toward a pile of brush and broken bricks. He picked up a large plastic bag containing a cheap brown leather purse. "You recognize this?"

"Not really," I admitted.

"She didn't have much. A handkerchief. A little change purse with three bucks. Some Bible tracts. Oh yeah, and a lottery ticket. Be something if the old girl hit, wouldn't it?"

I gave him a sour look, but I don't think it registered. "Anybody around here see anything?"

"Girl lives across the street, says maybe she saw a car in the driveway the day the victim disappeared."

"A car? That's all? No description of a driver?"

It was Bayles's turn to look sour. "A white man. Apparently, they're on the endangered species list around here."

I repeated what Miss Loudene told me about selling her jewelry, about the "fine Christian individual" who was going to get her set up in her new apartment.

"They set her up all right," Bayles said. "Set her up for a dirt sandwich."

I took a sketch out of my pocket and handed it to him. I'm a lousy artist, but I'd made a rough drawing of the peacock brooch and the tiger pin. "Maybe whoever killed her will try to sell the jewelry," I suggested. "She said the watch was from Tiffany. Yellow diamond. If it was worth killing over, it must be worth selling."

Bayles folded the drawing and tucked it into his notebook. "If it was me, I'd just pry the diamonds, sell the loose stones."

"The antique settings are at least as valuable as the stones," I pointed out. "Let's hope the killer knows that."

The funeral notice said Loudene Jenkins was survived by her sister, Nell Witherspoon, and a nephew. I showed the notice to Edna. "Did you know she had family?"

Edna nodded. "She used to talk about a sister. I gathered they weren't close. She said her sister was uppity, sort of a religious fanatic—'full of God-talk.' I gather the sister didn't approve of gambling."

On the second Wednesday night of October, Edna and I drove over to the F. J. Moody Memory Chapel in Glenndale. The regulars from the Moose Lodge and the VFW bingo were thankful that Miss Loudene was being buried on an "off" night. Even the odious Odie had agreed to sacrifice a shot at the ten-thousand-dollar jackpot at the Lithonia Moose Lodge, in order to give Miss Loudene a proper send-off.

Edna pointed out the regulars, her "bingo babes," in a loud, raspy whisper. "That's Miz Mumbles. Nobody sits at her table because she mumbles to herself. And that's Bernie. She wears that safari hat for good luck. She knew Loudene from back before the American Legion burned down. And right there, that lady with the walker? That's Hey-Hey."

"Hey-Hey?"

"She gets so excited when she thinks she might hit a bingo, she stutters. 'Hey, hey. Hey, hey. B-b-b-bingo!' "

"Who's the man?" He had greasy shoulder-length hair and tinted eyeglasses. He sat with the bingo babes, wearing a MARTA uniform, his hands folded soberly in his lap, not young, not old.

"Odie's son, D'Andre," Edna said. "He comes to all the bingo halls. Doesn't play, just helps Odie keep track of her cards."

Bayles was there too, wearing a sober coat and tie. There was only one other man among the dozen or so mourners. He was young, neatly barbered, with a blue suit, a wispy blond mustache and red-rimmed, pale blue eyes. He sat beside a lumpy old lady in a flowery dress, the two of them slightly apart from the others, over near a large flower arrangement in the shape of a horseshoe. GOOD LUCK, LOUDENE read a gold-scripted banner draped across the carnations and chrysanthemums.

I nodded in his direction. Definitely not a bingo babe. "Who's he?"

Edna pursed her lips and gave it some thought. "Never seen him before."

When the pastor started to speak, he nodded toward the couple sitting near the flower arrangements, extending his sympathy to Miss Loudene's sister, Nell Witherspoon, and her son, James.

"Her family," Edna whispered, loud enough for the rest of the bingo babes to hear. "She's got some nerve coming here."

"Shh," I said, swatting Edna's hand. "Everybody can hear you."

"Good," Edna said. "I want 'em to hear me."

After the service was over, while Edna and the others were admiring Miss Loudene's flowers, I drifted over toward Nell Witherspoon and introduced myself.

I held out a hand to her. "I'm Callahan Garrity. My mother and your sister were good friends. I'm sorry for your loss."

Nell Witherspoon gave my hand a hearty shake. I turned to the son. He merely nodded. "I'm James. I'm sure Aunt Loudene would be glad your mother and her friends came tonight."

"You notice there's none of that mill trash," Mrs. Witherspoon said. "Thank heavens for that."

"The mill's been closed a long time," I offered.

"Not long enough," Nell Witherspoon said. "You know, the day I married Mr. James Witherspoon I promised myself I'd never step foot in Glenndale again. And I didn't. We had Mama buried at my church, Tucker Baptist. But Loudene always insisted she wanted to be buried from Moody's. And we have to respect the wishes of the dead."

James nodded in silent agreement.

"I begged Loudene to move away from here," Mrs. Witherspoon said. "But she wouldn't do it. She said it was good enough for Mama and it was good enough for her." Nell Witherspoon's lips pursed, as though she were tasting sour milk. "Some people, they don't want anything better in life. That was Loudene. But not me. Not Nell Witherspoon. I was always a striver."

She patted her son's blue-suited shoulder. "Jamie here, he's like me that way. Striving. He's a talented musician, you know."

Jamie smiled. "Mother, please. This isn't the place."

She forged ahead. "He's going to London. Next week. To audition for the symphony there."

"How exciting," I said. I looked around the dimly lit parlour, with its cheap blond paneling and threadbare gray carpet. London was a long way from Glenndale, Georgia.

Jamie put a long, slender hand over his mother's short, liver-spotted one. "Mother, we should go. It's late. And you know how it is over here after dark."

"Oh," Nell said. Her face reddened and she blinked back tears. "It's not safe over here. These animals. They killed my sister. The police said one of them bashed her head in with a brick."

She stood up, clutching her son's arm. She was tall and bulky, not at all similar to the late, spindly Miss Loudene.

"Poor old Loudene," Nell said, sniffing. "Why would anybody do my sister that way? Why?"

"The jewelry," I blurted. "Didn't the police tell you her jewelry was missing?"

Mrs. Witherspoon looked blank. "What on earth?"

"Your mother's jewels," I said, babbling now. "The

peacock pin and earrings. The pearls, and the tiger pin and the watch from Tiffany's. I saw them. Miss Loudene showed them to me two days before she was killed."

"Mamaw's things," Jamie said softly. "I told Aunt Loudene she should lock those things up in a safe."

"Whatever for?" Nell Witherspoon demanded. "That old junk? Dime store stuff?"

"No," I said, interrupting. "She said your grandfather gave those jewels to your mother. That yellow diamond, it was at least a carat. I saw it, Mrs. Witherspoon."

Nell Witherspoon's round powdery face lost its mask of gentility. She laughed hoarsely. "Jewels? Don't make me laugh. We didn't even have indoor plumbing in that shack of ours until I was eighteen. My daddy drank and gambled and caroused his whole life. Mama's family had money, or so she said, but none of us ever saw any of it. And if we had, Daddy would have run through it right quick, you can bet on that."

"But she saved Mamaw's jewelry," Jamie said. "She showed it to me too, one time, Mother. She kept it in a lard can." He looked up at me. "And now it's gone?"

Nell Witherspoon coughed loudly. "Well, if somebody killed her for that mess of rhinestones, they'll get what they deserve. Nothing." She pulled at her son's arm. "Let's go, Jamie."

I followed them out onto the concrete porch of the Moody Memory Chapel. A ginkgo tree shaded the cracked concrete driveway in front of the home, and already fat golden leaves were sifting through the cool night air. Acorns crunched under Nell Witherspoon's sturdy black shoes. Her son opened her door and helped her into his car. Neither of them looked back as they drove away from Glenndale.

It was Edna's idea to take the bingo babes to the Knights of Columbus Lodge over in Chamblee. "It's sauerkraut and Polish sausage night," she told the others, herding them into the back of my pink van. She gave me a meaningful look. "Quarter beer, too."

Odie and her son, D'Andre, watched me loading up the babes. Edna saw them. "You can come too," she said gracelessly. "Although the jackpot's only five thousand dollars. Not up to your usual standards, I'm sure."

The Knights of Columbus hall was thick with cigarette smoke and the smells of cooked cabbage and Old Spice. Edna and the others elbowed their way through the buffet line and found a table at the far end of the room. She sent me to get her cards, sixteen—eight for her and eight in the memory of Miss Loudene. They left a tiny patch of space at the corner of the table for Odie and D'Andre—only enough room for two paper plates of steaming sausage and kraut, and four bingo cards. Odie squatted there and glowered at the others, especially Edna.

"Saw you talking to that Nell Witherspoon woman," Edna commented, lining her bingo markers up in front of her. "What did she have to say for her sorry self?"

"Not much," I said, nibbling at a piece of kielbasa. "I don't think she and Miss Loudene had a lot in common. Her son is some kind of musician. He's going to

London to audition for the symphony. And"—I paused for effect—"Mrs. Witherspoon says all that jewelry was nothing but five-and-dime junk."

Edna shushed me then, as the caller seated himself at a table at the front of the room. The room got deadly quiet, heads swinging first from the electronic board displaying the numbers called, then back down to the cards arrayed on the tabletops. After eight numbers, we heard a stir from our end of the table. "Hey, hey! B-b-bingo!"

My mother slapped the table with the palm of her hand. "Looky there. Hey-Hey won! Loudene's looking down on us tonight."

It appeared she was. Bernie won the next jackpot, for twenty-five dollars and a gift certificate to a steak house. Miss Mumbles won a toaster oven and one hundred dollars, Edna hit for twenty-five dollars, and I even eked out a ten-dollar round-the-world bingo. The only ones who didn't win were the two glowering presences at the end of our table: Odie and D'Andre.

The last card of the night, two numbers were called. On the second number, Odie cursed. She took her felt-tip markers, swept them into her tote bag and stood up. "These cards are junk," she announced. "Let's go." She and D'Andre lumbered toward the door.

It took Edna maybe fifteen seconds to recover her calm. She scooted over to Odie's chair, commandeered her remaining cards, and in a flash, dealt them out to the rest of the bingo babes. The game was four corners. The caller seemed to enjoy dragging out the night. I'd crossed off nearly a dozen numbers on my card when

Edna began breathing loudly through her nose, a sure sign that she was excited. "O-62," she was chanting. "Come on, O-62." I glanced over at her cards. Sure enough, her marker was poised over a card with all but one corner scratched off.

The babes were watching. "Come on, Edna," they called to her. "Hit it, girlfriend."

Two more numbers. And she hit. O-62. The jackpot was five thousand dollars.

"P-p-praise the Lord!" Hey-Hey shouted.

Edna beamed. She held up her winning card. "Know whose card this was?" she asked. "This is one of them junk cards Odie gave up on. Goes to show, don't it? Junk is in the eye of the beholder."

It got me thinking. I thought about it all the way home, and after I dropped the bingo babes back at F. J. Moody's Memory Chapel, I did some more thinking, about the perceived value of junk. I got out my criss-cross directory for the city of Atlanta and DeKalb County, and did some research.

The next morning, I borrowed Edna's Buick and parked outside the neat brick ranch house in Tucker by eight A.M. The car backed out of the driveway at ten A.M. It was easy to follow, a rusted blue Oldsmobile. The driver headed for the rarified atmosphere of Buckhead, and I followed. The driver made three brief stops, none of them taking longer than ten minutes apiece. Each time he emerged from one of the chic shops, his shoulders seemed more permanently slumped, his footsteps more dogged.

At his fourth stop, things seemed to be looking up.

He parked the Olds at the edge of a parking lot full of shiny new sports cars and Mercedeses and sport utility vehicles. The sign over the curved, black and white–striped awning said the shop was called Nouveau Riches. It certainly looked rich all right. On either side of the awning, display windows contained just one glittery bauble each, displayed on a black velvet-draped mannequin.

After forty-five minutes, he finally emerged from the shop. He had a spring in his step and a smile on his face.

Inside, a severe-faced woman with a white chignon was arranging pieces on a velvet-lined tray. A bell tinkled discreetly as I stepped inside and she looked up expectantly.

"Yes?"

I'd dressed the part, just in case. My best black wool pantsuit, makeup, hair combed, the works. Maybe I didn't look authentic Buckhead, but I wasn't trailer trash either.

"Do you buy vintage jewelry?" I asked.

"Of course." She went on arranging the items on the tray in front of her. The pieces were all vintage earrings, bracelets, necklaces and brooches, exquisitely wrought of gold and silver, inlaid with colored stones and enamel and any manner of wonderful finishes. The tiger with the jewelled tail appeared ready to pounce from the tray.

I pointed at it. "How much is something like that?"

She smiled serenely. "Something like it, or this piece exactly?"

"Is there a difference?"

"Oh yes. This piece is a signed Coco Chanel. There are knock-offs available, but this is the real thing."

"So the diamonds are real?"

Again the laugh. She was getting on my nerves. "Good God, no. It's costume. But the very best of the best. The Duchess of Windsor had the original of this pin, but of course, those were yellow diamonds, onyx and emerald chips."

"Worth?"

She was wearing tortoise-rim bifocals and looked down her nose at me through them now. "I just got this in today. Haven't had time to price it yet. But conservatively? I have a collector over on Tuxedo Road who buys signed Chanel. She bought a jaguar pin from this same series six months ago. I got $3,600 for it, and some of the small pavé rhinestones were missing. This piece is in perfect condition. I doubt if it has ever been worn."

Not bad for junk.

I bit my lip. "I saw some other pieces like this one recently, at an antique show. It was a set—necklace, bracelet and earrings."

"A parure," she said silkily.

"Whatever. It had peacocks, silver with blue and green stones. Very flashy, sort of uh, twenties, I guess."

She stood away from the counter and narrowed her eyes. "What's this about?"

"Bingo," I said, reaching for the cell phone in my purse.

Larry Bayles caught up with Jamie Witherspoon at

the airport, one-way ticket to London in his hand. Bayles had let me come along for the ride, as a courtesy, you might say.

Witherspoon blanched when he saw Bayles's badge, but he didn't try to run. Guess he wasn't as much of a striver as his mother thought. Back at the station, Bayles counted out the bills he extracted from the money belt he'd found wrapped around Jamie Witherspoon's midriff.

"Twelve thousand dollars," he said, placing the last of the hundred-dollar bills on his desktop. "You killed your aunt for twelve thousand dollars. Not much of a take, Junior."

"She wasn't much of a person," Witherspoon said bitterly. "All those years, she talked about Mamaw's jewels, but she'd never let me see them. Then, a month ago, she calls me up, swears me to secrecy. Says she's decided to get rid of the stuff. Do you believe it? None of it had ever been worn. All that money, lying around in a stinking lard can, in that filthy firetrap of a shack. I told her I'd help her sell it, help her buy a new washer-dryer, get her set up in a condo. She was going to give me money, for helping her."

"But you wanted more," I suggested.

"She would have died in a couple years anyway," Witherspoon said. "And what about me? My whole life was ahead of me. London, the symphony, everything. But it's so expensive. So obscenely expensive. Why shouldn't Mamaw's jewels go to me?"

"And you never had any idea they were only costume?" I said.

He sank his head down into his hands. "Never. My God. Do you think I would have risked everything for a lousy twelve thousand dollars?"

The sleeve of his dress shirt rode up a little, exposing his wrist. Clasped around it was the watch. The Tiffany watch Loudene's mother had been given for her eighteenth birthday. I pointed it out to Bayles.

"Not too smart," Bayles said as he removed the watch and prepared to replace it with a pair of standard-issue handcuffs. He placed the wristwatch in an evidence bag, along with the rest of the jewelry he'd recovered from Nouveau Riches.

"I couldn't sell Mamaw's watch," Jamie said sadly. "I was her only grandchild. The last of the line. She used to call me her family jewel."

Bayles laughed harshly. "Junk jewelry, more like."

About the Contributors

BANNISTER, Jo. "The Fall Guy." Bannister, a former journalist, is well known for her Castlemere police procedurals, as well as *The Lazarus Hotel* (a twist on Agatha Christie's *Ten Little Indians*) and *The Primrose Convention*, featuring a caustic advice columnist and a reluctant psychic gardner. Bannister resides in Northern Ireland.

BECK, K. K. "Hollywood Homicide." Equally proficient at historical mysteries, modern-day thrillers, suspense novels, and whatever else she turns her pen to, K. K. Beck returns to smart, sensible flapper sleuth Iris Cooper with "Hollywood Homicide." Iris is featured in *Death in a Deck Chair*, *Murder in a Mummy Case*, and *Peril Under the Palms*. Beck's most recent books are the Sax Rohmer spoof *The Revenge of Kali-Ra* and *We Interrupt This Broadcast*. Beck lives in Seattle.

CHRISTMAS, Joyce. "Social Death." The author of thirteen mysteries published by Fawcett Gold Medal,

Christmas's one series features an expatriate Brit in Manhattan, Lady Margaret Priam, who solves crimes in a society setting and has appeared in nine books. The most recent title is *Going Out in Style*. Her second series stars retired office manager and senior sleuth Betty Trenka. The fourth in the series, *Mood to Murder*, was published in June 1999. Christmas's Web site address is www.writerswrite.com/authors/joycechristmas

COEL, Margaret. "The Man in Her Dream." Margaret Coel lives in Colorado and is an award-winning author on the American West. Her series featuring attorney Vicky Holden (who appears in "The Man in Her Dream") and Father John O'Malley is set among the Arapahos on Wyoming's Wind River Reservation. Her most recent book is *The Lost Bird*.

DREYER, Eileen. "The Most Beautiful Place on Earth." For her story in this volume, Dreyer draws on her Irish roots—and her distinctive sense of humor—both of which play major roles in her nursing mysteries, *A Man to Die For*, *Nothing Personal*, *Bad Medicine*, and the most recent, *Brain Dead*. Dreyer lives in St. Louis.

EMERSON, Kathy Lynn. "Lady Appleton and the London Man." Susanna, Lady Appleton, who appears in this volume, is a sixteenth-century gentlewoman sleuth and herbalist featured in Kathy Lynn Emerson's novels, which include *Face Down in the Marrow-Bone*

Pie, *Face Down Upon an Herbal*, and *Face Down Among the Winchester Geese*. Emerson resides in Jessica Fletcher's native Maine.

GALLISON, Kate. "The Workshop." Set in her native New Jersey, Kate Gallison's mysteries feature Mother Lavinia (Vinnie) Grey, an Episcopalian priest. Her most recent book is *Grave Misgivings*.

HENRY, Sue. "Murder She Wrote." A former president of Sisters in Crime, Sue Henry lives and writes in Anchorage, Alaska. Her mysteries feature Alaskan state trooper Alex Jensen and include *Deadfall* and *Death Takes Passage*.

JANCE, J. A. "The Prodigal." J. A. Jance lives in Washington and is the author of two mystery series, one featuring Seattle homicide detective J. P. Beaumont and the other Arizona sheriff Joanna Brady. Her many novels include *Breach of Duty* and *Outlaw Mountain*.

MATTESON, Stefanie. "Miss Chatfield's Chairs." Actress Charlotte Graham makes an appearance in this collection and also plays a starring role in Stefanie Matteson's novels, including *Murder on High* and *Murder Under the Palms*. Matteson lives with her husband and children in New Jersey.

NEWMAN, Sharan. "Honeymoon for One." An Oregon native, Sharan Newman is a writer and medieval historian, two things that normally guarantee unemployment. However, she manages to survive through the kindness of readers of her medieval mystery series, the first of which, *Death Comes as Epiphany,* won the Macavity Award. She is a three-time nominee for the Agatha Award. *Cursed in the Blood* is the fifth in her series and the sixth, *The Difficult Saint,* will be published in October 1999. She also is the author of three fantasies on the life of Guinevere, published by Tor Books, and, with Miriam Grace Monfredo, coeditor of the history/mystery anthologies *Crime Through Time* and *Crime Through Time II* (Berkley).

ROWLAND, Laura Joh. "Onnagata." Laura Joh Rowland's mysteries feature samurai detective Sano Ichirō and include *Shinjū, Bundori, The Way of the Traitor,* and *The Concubine's Tattoo.* Rowland lives in New Orleans.

STEINBERG, Janice. "Moonlighting." Janice Steinberg deeply regrets that she can't drink coffee—one decaf in the morning keeps her awake at night—but she loves to fantasize about it, as she does in "Moonlighting." Steinberg is the author of the Margo Simon mysteries, featuring a public radio reporter. The first four books are set in San Diego. The latest, *Death in a City of Mystics*, takes Margo to Israel.

TROCHECK, Kathy Hogan. "The Family Jewels." Kathy Hogan Trocheck, a former journalist, now